DATE DUE

Jul 30 '65			
Oct 17 66			
Nov 23 '66			
Sep 29 '67			
Oct 13 '67			
Nov 27 '67			
Oct 10 68			
Feb 17 '69			
Mar 6 '69			
Mar 20 '69			
Apr 8 '69			
Nov 2 '7			
GAYLORD			PRINTED IN U.S.A

ELECTIVE AFFINITIES

by

Johann Wolfgang von Goethe

---

translated by
Elizabeth Mayer
and
Louise Bogan

introduction by
Victor Lange

HENRY REGNERY COMPANY
Chicago • 1963

INTRODUCTION

1.

WE SHOULD not be surprised that Goethe, by all standards one of the most impressive minds of the Western tradition, is not at the moment much in fashion. The revolution of ideas and manners which he witnessed and recorded at the end of the eighteenth century in an astonishingly varied body of poetical and scientific writings seems to us little more than a first indication of the immense changes which we ourselves are experiencing. And Goethe's faith in the moral and intellectual resources with which the individual human being could and should confront the challenges of an increasingly technical and collective age is bound in our time to seem a noble romantic delusion.

But there are few men of letters who have given a more intelligent and a more articulate account of that great crisis of values from which we have not yet emerged. If Goethe was an incomparably distinguished poet, he owed his greatness, beyond all talent and skill, to a remarkably clear understanding of the complex character of modern life. Although he was deeply indebted to the European Enlightenment, the same humanism that drew him as a young man to the ancients and to the world of classical precepts also persuaded him to question, with Voltaire and Rousseau, the absolute claims of that tradition in a changing world. His extensive and careful scientific studies, his participation in political affairs, his travels and his association with an extraordinary number of European writers led him again and again to reflect upon the character of his time. It was for him not a reassuring view. In spite of his aversion to any theoretical scheme of values or to an ideological view of history, he recognized the ever widening gulf between the forms of his own homogeneous culture and the arbitrary claims of speculation and feeling by which the young European romantics tended to justify their life.

Through his scientific inquiries in several fields, Goethe had developed tentative notions of order and purpose which he was ready to extend beyond the sphere of nature to that of individual and social conduct; but he knew that neither the empirical ways of science nor the code of morality could be defined in rigidly rational terms: neither one nor the other seemed to him immune against the unsettling play of elusive and intractable elements. This conviction of a precarious balance between "natural" phenomena and of "cultural" challenges provides the theme of many of Goethe's works. Of these, *Elective Affinities* is one of the most curious and one of the most moving; when it was completed in 1809, Goethe, sixty years old, had passed through a number of deeply disturbing experiences; some personal, others more related to the changes in the intellectual climate at the turn of the century.

Schiller's death in 1805 had ended the closest and most productive friendship of his mature life; the Napoleonic invasion of the German states seemed to him not so much an attack upon his own world as an historic defense of Western values against the barbarism of the East, by a man he admired immensely. His audience with Napoleon had lost him the sympathy of many of the younger patriots. He had in any case little enthusiasm for the war of liberation and turned more and more to his private studies in optics and morphology. The first part of *Faust* had appeared in 1808, and when this was followed a year later by *Elective Affinities,* it became clear that whatever his political convictions, he had in his aesthetic views modified his previous classicism and moved closer to the sensibilities of the Romantic poets. The novel at once aroused the liveliest interest among the younger writers and, to Goethe's great satisfaction, especially of some of the contemporary scientists.

In its form and its theme, it proved a surprise and a puzzle to his readers. He had for some time past planned a continuation of *Wilhelm Meister* and for this project had written a series of short stories that were to be fitted into the plot of the new novel. *Elective Affinities* was to be one of these, but as he wrote, it outgrew its original limits.

2.

In many respects the novel seems to have much in common with the European tales of manners and romance of the late eighteenth century: its aristocratic society, the alternation of monotonous daily duties and dramatic interludes, the planning of delightful surprises, meticulous landscaping and civilized conversation, sentimental involvements and surreptitious meeting of lovers—all these are the familiar ingredients of romantic fiction. But as we read along we become aware of an extraordinary extension of these cultivated perspectives: the figures of the tale assume a strange luminosity, and the human relationships become ramified and disturbing to the point of incalculable complexity. All assumptions of order are questioned and are threatened by forces which spring from depths of experience that lie beyond rational calculation.

Elective Affinities is, clearly, a book of far greater intricacy and of more meanings than is at first sight apparent. Its theme is difficult to state in a sentence or two, and it is not enough if we say that its chief topics are marriage and divorce, loyalty and betrayal, guilt and redemption, free will and necessity. Nor is it quite sufficient to point to the fateful consequences of the "affinities" that draw two couples together as though they were not responsible human beings but mere agents in a chemical reaction. The concept to which the strange title of the novel refers is familiar to modern chemistry; Goethe borrowed it from a study—*De attractionibus electivis*—which the Swedish chemist Torben Bergman had published in 1775. But the inter-relationship of choice and compulsion, the Kantian dichotomy so familiar from Schiller's philosophical essays and Goethe's earlier narratives, will hardly account for the supernatural shadows of ominous coincidence and error. *Elective Affinities* is in some degree, as the eighteenth and nineteenth century understood the term, a social novel; but the social issue is to such an extent immersed in metaphysical issues, that we cannot focus upon it alone. Nor is it, in the conventional sense, a psychological account of any one of the central characters, to whom the intelligence of the narrator and the sympathy of the reader might satisfactorily relate the theme of the whole.

Goethe himself spoke of *Elective Affinities* in the gravest terms, always with a sense of awe and humility before a spectacle that surpasses human understanding. There is not a single line in it, he said, that he had not himself experienced—but none exactly as he had experienced it. It was the only one of his major productions, his secretary Eckermann recorded in 1827, which he had deliberately worked out according to an "idea". But, unless the term "idea" here refers to the aesthetic discipline which Goethe imposed upon himself, we shall find it difficult to detect and agree on any single unifying philosophical concept.

We must relate the novel not, immediately, to Goethe's social or anthropological thinking but to his philosophy of nature. Ten years earlier he had thought of presenting his views on nature to a large and nonscientific public in a long philosophical poem after the manner of Lucretius. But he realized the danger of artificiality and mere didacticism in such a project and, instead, treated a single aspect of nature in the poem *The Metamorphosis of Plants*. He was about to do the same for magnetic phenomena when he came across Schelling's *Philosophy of Nature*. There he found confirmation of his belief that the entire realm of nature, organic as well as inorganic, was subject to certain uniform and unifying principles. Indeed, two of these, "polarity" and "intensification", he had for long regarded as the key terms of his own philosophy of life. *Elective Affinities* was to represent some of these ideas and, perhaps, even extend their validity to metaphysics. Goethe's announcement of the novel points discreetly to the scope of the book: "It may be that the author was led to the adoption of this curious title by his long-continued studies in physics. He knew that the natural scientists quite frequently use ethical analogies in order to illuminate phenomena that are not immediately within human experience; he wished, in this case of a moral issue, to reduce a chemical analogy to its essential spiritual meaning. This has seemed all the more proper, as nature is one everywhere and as even the clear realm of rational choice is inevitably shot through with those traces of the confusing compulsion of passion which only a higher power—possibly not in this life—can remove completely."

Goethe was at all times averse to any abstract definition of the spiritual reality; ever since the early days of his study of Spinoza he had found comfort not in speculation but only in the reality of concrete experience. He described himself often enough as a friend of the "tangible world," and as late as 1831 he confessed that "the direct contemplation of things" was everything to him; "words," he added, "mean less to me than ever before." He could not have been more to the point about *Elective Affinities*. It is his most symbolic work in the sense that the insights which his contemplation, his *Anschauung*, of the phenomena of nature offered him, are here stated in images which refer to what appears inexpressible in discursive speech. All life, he said on another occasion, is symbolic; and where it is fully represented, "indem es vollkommen sich selbst dastellt," it reveals its unity. Even as he was at work on *Elective Affinities* he insisted that the highest operation in nature as well as in art was the attainment of significant form—"dass die höchste und einzige Operation der Natur und Kunst die Gestaltung sei."

3.

The design of the novel is exceedingly meticulous and most appropiate to Goethe's intention. Almost all the principle ideas of the ensuing action are hinted at in the first two or three pages; each of the eighteen chapters in the first part is related in a precisely complementary rhythm to the corresponding chapter in the second. Within the clearly accentuated framework of the passing seasons, projects mature slowly and expectations and decisions are fulfilled, that came about half in awareness of their consequences and half compelled by the moods or arguments of the moment. As a novelist, Goethe was an artist in indirection: he preferred the oblique view to a straightforward and realistic manner, and, much in the spirit of the eighteenth century, he developed his more important scenes in carefully composed, almost operatic, tableaux. He was not afraid of appearing melodramatic, and all occasions for rejoicing or mourning, birthdays, christenings or funerals, processions and gatherings of one sort or another, he exploited as the very turning points of the narrative action. As the elements of plot are marshalled and the sharply observed details, the controlled gestures, are assembled, they tell the story; when they are reintroduced with slight modifications at a later point, they correlate, as only poetic symbols can, the imperceptible but profound accretion of changing meanings. No important turn occurs without a few carefully set reminders of the double face of time, its steady and productive pace as well as its corroding effects upon all human plans. Eduard's habits as he reads, his dabbling in gardening and music, the drinking glass with the letters E and O, the haunting appearance of the beggar, the asters, the lake—all these leitmotifs, as they are repeated in a transposed context, heighten the intensity of the action. What may sometimes seem mere repetition is actually a variation, on a different plane of experience. This subtle process of poetic dialectic and not a mere accumulation of incidents produces an overwhelming sense of dramatic, of tragic, inevitability.

4.

If Goethe offers us in *Elective Affinities* a number of unusual figures, he delineates them with what we may feel to be the conventional technique of the English or French society painters of the time; they are generalized vehicles of possible human alternatives rather than realistically differentiated individuals. By this deliberate emphasis upon the typical, Goethe evokes a world of manners and conventions that was familiar enough to his readers. This world must now prove its strength under the impact of extraordinary emotional and moral pressures. How, he seems to ask, will this ostentatiously self-possessed society behave when the circumstances of their lives bring them face to face with forces beyond their comprehension? The decorum which all mature members of this landed gentry maintain is seldom forgotten or suspended: Eduard, the most hectic figure in the book, preserves to the end the bearing of a well-to-do and well-bred country squire; Charlotte is considerate and patient almost beyond endurance; and Ottilie, though in a sense an outsider to the society which she so deeply disturbs, chooses, as she becomes aware of her own fateful role, a form of life so self-denying that she seems in the end less a person than a performer of a severe ritual. This extreme formality in the behavior of the characters is, of course, a deliberate artistic projection of Goethe's desire to provide, with the irony of a superb storyteller, a peculiarly appropriate setting for the fatal play of elemental forces. Love in all its forms is of these powers the most confounding; indeed, every relationship that is developed in the novel—not only that between the four chief characters—demonstrates in one way or another the ambivalent nature of love.

Goethe here expounds the theme of a single minded romantic obsession with which in his own day Stendhal and Balzac dealt on a still more impressive scale. But the passion which so suddenly threatens and overwhelms the characters in *Elective Affinities* does not drive them into a disavowal of the social order than seems to paralyze them. If Eduard, as Goethe later suggested, was to be understood as a "heightened Werther", it was not because he acted as a still more uncompromising lover, but on the contrary, because he learned to accept, beyond the mere social decorum, the conviction to which Goethe himself firmly held: that in the face of all our natural instincts, the demands and the satisfactions of culture are necessarily formal and ritualistic.

In each character, in each group, Goethe reminds us of the inescapable dependence of man upon nature; he places each of the couples in a situation in which natural and supernatural elements together produce a reaction which in turn serves to illustrate the human condition. But at the same time he offers a chance to the human being to incorporate his experience of it in a meaningful philosophy of life, instead of denying or circumventing the power of nature. The term he uses here and elsewhere to describe the attitude which enables man to respect the total compass of reality, and to recognize it as most revealing where it appears in symbolic forms, is *reverence (Ehrfurcht);* it is one of the ultimate elements of Goethe's wisdom. Another, equally important for the understanding of *Elective Affinities,* is that of *acceptance (Entsagung)*—perhaps, in Goethe's view, the highest expression of man's capacity to acknowledge the inescapable condition of his life as well as the compelling obligation to choose his mode of salvation.

These two states of mind, reverence and acceptance, are Ottilie's achievement at the end of a life that is at all times ambiguous and frightening to her but that assumes, by her sensitiveness and fortitude, something of legendary character: this, we may be sure, is the reason for Goethe's use, when they offer themselves so readily, of Christian symbols. As a character in the novel she is extraordinarily frail and rarefied. She learns slowly and instead of the quick speech that is Eduard's, she communicates most appropriately in gestures. She is the suffering vehicle of all the natural forces that pass through her into the relationships of the group; she is dependent and forever at the mercy of others. Yet, while

Ottilie appears weak, she is ultimately the strongest of all; her pathological sensitivity gives her power; she obeys, and still, at the end, through her death, she alone achieves complete spiritual freedom.

No greater contrast to her could have been invented than the volatile Eduard, imaginative to excess, wavering between extremes of stubbornness and uncertainty, between a passionate but melodramatic will to conquer and the paralysis of his own weakness. Everything he does is spurious; not even his name is genuine. He lives in a world of sham action as part of a society which is itself palpably insecure and whose every activity, its charades and "Pre-Raphaelite" art forms, betray its insubstantiality. From the first moments of his pointless puttering in the garden to the pose of his desire to emulate Ottilie's martyrdom, he can only deceive himself. "How unhappy I am that all my efforts should be nothing but imitation."

Yet, however weak, however powerless, these two main characters may be, the other pair, Charlotte and the Captain, fail, no less remarkably, to fulfill their lives. With all their strength, their resolute and sensible practicality, and their capacity for hope—so different, incidentally, from the spiritual, the seraphic, "hope" held out at the end for Eduard and Ottilie—they under-rate the elemental forces which are about to destroy the group: as the tragedy draws to its end, they must witness the futility of their faith in mere reason and good will.

In one way or another all the minor figures—Luciane, the Baron and the Countess, the architect, and the tutor—are related to the lives and experiences of the four protagonists; by the ambivalence of their own being, they reflect the range of feeling from the devoutly religious sentiment to the absurdly erratic that possesses Ottilie as well as Eduard.

5.

All these characters reveal themselves, we must note, more by what they do than by what they say. The insufficiency of speech, one of the major themes of modern European literature, is in this novel demonstrated again and again: misunderstanding, whether thoughtless or deliberate, and miscalculation or an unjustified trust in the efficacy of the reasonable argument lead to confusion and disaster; the gesture, Goethe reminds us repeatedly, carries more meaning than the word, and when ordinary language ceases to convey meanings and feelings, it is not romantic effusion but silence and ritual that supersede it. Of such ultimate situations and experiences Goethe himself spoke only with the greatest reluctance; in *Elective Affinities* it is the barely perceptible voice of the narrator that makes these "ineffable and unspeakable" happenings intelligible. With an urbanity that is often ironic, and in language that is sententious rather than impulsive or sentimental he mediates between a world of incalculable tensions and our own; he must not admit his own barely defensible sympathy for Eduard and seldom fails to speak with affection of Ottilie.

He cannot, in all seriousness, have much patience with that meddling busybody Mittler, yet he, (or Goethe) leaves no doubt in our minds that the peculiar ambivalence which is at the heart of the theme of *Elective Affinities* appears most dramatically in the person of Mittler. The discrepancy between what man is and what he says is nowhere in the book more frighteningly demonstrated; only the most naive reader will fail to see that the sensible advice he is forever ready to give springs less from substantial insight and ma-

turity than from his skill in manipulating the clichés of reasonableness. It may be that his model was Jeremy Bentham
for whom Goethe had no little respect. What Mittler says
is right; he too is a man of good will. But he is obtuse and
restless, and, if his zeal and his perpetual protestations of
common sense did not have such shocking effects, he would
be a grotesquely comic figure. He lacks the respect for the
supernatural and therefore remains subject to the elemental
forces which he assumes "unflinching reason" and moral intelligence can banish.

Although Mittler is most volubly concerned with the institutions of marriage and baptism, he appears to have none of
the silent energies of love and understanding that could
give them a sacramental meaning. For marriage—and here,
if anywhere, emerges the main theme of the novel—is the
most conspicuous instance (and the most confounding) of a
form, a symbol, which to experience in its total cultural significance, requires the complete exertion of man. In marriage, Goethe means to say, civilization fulfills itself because
it is there that we are led to recognize and realize the dynamic interplay of reason and submission, of natural instincts and of faith in the presence of the spirit.

It is this profound tension which is in *Elective Affinities*
so superbly represented. We can hardly separate substance
and form, and it is perhaps impossible to say what moves us
more, the spectacle of the ambivalence of existence, of the
double edge of all experience, of the transubstantiation of all
life—or the consummate symbols of Goethe's tragic irony
that makes this novel an unforgettable work of art.

VICTOR LANGE

Princeton, N.J.
July, 1963

PART

1

chapter 1

EDUARD, a wealthy landowner in his early middle years, had been spending the loveliest hour of an April afternoon in his tree nursery, grafting fresh shoots on young stocks just sent him. His task finished, he gathered his tools into their case and was contemplating his work with satisfaction when the gardener approached, pleased by his master's interest and assistance.

"Have you seen my wife, by any chance?" Eduard inquired, just as he was on the point of leaving.

"She is over there on the newly laid out grounds," the gardener replied. "The summer house which she has been building against the rock wall opposite the castle will be finished today. Everything has turned out beautifully and will certainly please Your Grace. The view from there is remarkable: the village is below; a little to the right is the church, whose steeple you can almost look over; and, opposite, the castle and the park."

"Quite so," Eduard said. "Not far from here I could see the men working."

"And, then," the gardener went on, "to the right, the valley opens out, and you look over the meadows with their many trees, far into a serene and bright distance. The path up to

3

the rocks has been very prettily laid out. Her Ladyship is ingenious; it is a pleasure to work for her."

"Please go and ask her to wait for me," said Eduard. "Tell her that I should like to see and enjoy her latest achievement."

The gardener hurried away, and Eduard followed after a little while. He walked down the terraces and, in passing, looked into the greenhouses and at the hotbeds. When he came to the brook, he crossed a foot bridge and arrived at a point where the way branched in two directions. He did not take the path which ran across the churchyard in an almost straight line toward the rock wall, but followed the other, which wound gently upward, leading a little farther to the left through pleasant shrubbery. He sat down for a moment, on a bench where the paths rejoined; and then he started the climb which brought him, by a steep and uneven way, over all sorts of steps and ledges, finally to the summer house.

At the door Charlotte welcomed her husband and led him to a seat where he could take in at a single glance, through door and windows, the different views of the landscape, as though set in frames. He was delighted and expressed his hope that spring would soon bring new life to the surroundings. "I have only one criticism," he added. "The pavilion seems to me rather small."

"Certainly large enough for two," Charlotte answered.

"Yes, and there may be room even for a third person."

"Why not? And for a fourth as well. If we have company, we can always make other arrangements."

"Since we are now here alone and undisturbed, and in a calm and relaxed mood," Eduard began, "I must make a confession concerning something that has been on my mind for some time, something that I should tell you, but for which I haven't yet found an opportunity."

4

"I had the impression that something was troubling you," said Charlotte.

"Then I shall be quite frank in saying," Eduard continued, "that I should probably have kept silent still longer if the mail were not going out tomorrow, so that we must make a decision today."

"What is it?" asked Charlotte, kindly encouraging him.

"It concerns our friend, the Captain," Eduard replied. "You know the unfortunate position in which, like so many others, he has been placed through no fault of his own. How distressing it must be for a man of his education, talents, and abilities to find himself without anything to do. I'll not hold back my personal wish any longer: to have him here with us for a while."

"This needs serious consideration and must be looked at from more than one angle," Charlotte replied.

"I shall tell you my point of view immediately," Eduard answered. "In his last letter he sounded deeply discouraged; not that he is in want—he knows how to live economically, and I have taken care of his necessities—besides, it does not embarrass him to accept money from me. All our lives we have mutually borrowed and lent to such a degree that we cannot any longer figure out the sum of our credit and debit. That he is without any occupation constitutes his real problem. His only pleasure—his passion, really—is to use for the benefit of others, day by day and hour by hour, those manifold abilities in which he has trained himself. To sit idle, or to go on studying in order to acquire still more skill, while he is unable to use what he already possesses to such a high degree—but enough, dearest. It is a humiliating situation for him, and it tortures him the more acutely since he is so much alone."

"I had reason to believe that he received offers from various quarters," Charlotte said. "I myself have written to many influential friends, men and women, to recommend him. And so far as I know, this has not been entirely without effect."

"That is true," Eduard answered. "But even these various opportunities and offers bring him new distress and embarrassment. None of them is at all suitable to the sort of person he is. He has never been asked to play an active part; he is asked to sacrifice himself, his time, his opinions, and his way of life; and that is impossible for him. The more I think about it all, the more I understand his situation and the stronger is my wish to see him here with us."

"It is very noble and lovable of you to feel your friend's predicament so deeply," Charlotte said; "but let me remind you to think also of yourself and of us."

"That I have done," Eduard answered. "For us, his presence certainly promises only pleasure and profit. There is no question of additional expense; this will be even less if he lives with us, especially since his visit will not cause the least inconvenience. He can have his own quarters in the right wing of the castle; everything else will be solved in due time. How much he will gain by this arrangement, and how many agreeable things *we* shall gain from his company—even some profit! For a long time I have wanted the estate and the whole countryside surveyed; he will arrange and supervise this. You have suggested that we take over the farms as soon as the leases of the present tenants have expired. How precarious such an enterprise is! How much preliminary and useful information he will be able to give! I feel very strongly that I should always have had here a man of his kind. Country folk may have practical experience; but what they say is usually vague and not always straightforward. Educated people from the city and the universities may be clear-headed and logical, but they lack the practical approach to the problems. From my friend I can expect both knowledge

6

and experience. I can easily imagine that a hundred other circumstances will develop from this arrangement, and some are in your interest as well; and these will, as I foresee, do immense good. Thank you, first of all, for having listened so patiently. Now have your say, quite frankly and in detail. Tell me everything that is in your mind; I shall not interrupt you."

"Very well then," Charlotte replied. "First let me begin with a general observation. Men always think more of the individual case—of the Immediate; and they are right, because they are called upon to plan and to act. Women, on the other hand, must think more of things in their sequence; and rightly, because their personal destiny—and the destiny of their families—depends on continuity and because it is just this continuity which it is their mission to preserve. Let us therefore briefly glance over our present and our past life; and you will have to admit that the invitation to the Captain does not completely fall in with our original intentions, plans, and arrangements.

"How I enjoy thinking of our earliest relationship! We fell deeply in love with each other when we were young. You were separated from me—because your father, in his insatiable passion for wealth, married you to a rich woman considerably older than yourself. I was separated from you because, being without particular prospects, I was forced to marry a wealthy man whom I respected but did not love. We both regained our freedom—you first, when your wife left you a large fortune; I much later, at the time when you returned from your travels. So we met once more. We could speak of the past without sadness; we enjoyed our memories. We could live undisturbed. You insisted on marriage. I did not immediately consent; although we were about the same age I, the woman, had aged earlier than you, the man. At

7

last, I could not refuse you what you thought your greatest happiness. You wished by my side to find peace from your restless years at court, in the army, and on your travels. You wanted to collect yourself, to enjoy life, but with me alone. I sent my only daughter to a boarding school, where she certainly receives a far more complete education than would be possible here in the country; and I also sent my niece Ottilie to the same school, although she would perhaps have received a better training—under my own supervision—as my companion and a help in our household. All this was done with your consent, for the single purpose that we might live our own lives, one for the other, and enjoy our so long-desired and so late-achieved happiness in peace and quiet. In this way we started our life together in the country. *I* took over the domestic duties; *you* the outside tasks and the general management of the estate. I have arranged my life to comply with all your wishes, to live for you alone. Let us try, at least for a while, to see how long we can be sufficient to each other."

"Since continuity, as you say, is woman's special element, one either should not listen continuously to your words or should admit at once that you are right; and I shall admit that you have been right—until now," Eduard replied. "The plan by which we mapped out our life is a good one; but should we add nothing new to it—should nothing new grow out of it? *My* work in the garden, *yours* in the park—is this for a pair of recluses?"

"You are right, perfectly right!" Charlotte answered. "We should only avoid introducing anything that might interfere with our way of life—any alien factor. Do not forget that our projects, even our diversions, were, in a way, exclusively dependent on our being alone together. You wanted to read to me the daily record of your travels, and doing so, collect and arrange any loose notes; then, with my help, compile

8

from these invaluable but scattered notes and memoranda, a complete Journal which would give pleasure to us and to others. I promised you my help in copying; and we thought it would be so convenient and enjoyable, so delightful and intimate, to travel, in memory, through that world which we had not been allowed to see together. The beginning has already been made. In the evenings, moreover, you have started playing your flute again, while I accompany you at the piano. And there has been no lack of visits to or from our neighbors. I, for one, had promised myself, with all this, the first truly happy summer I had ever imagined."

"Still, I cannot help thinking while I hear you repeat all this so kindly and sensibly," Eduard said, rubbing his forehead, "that, after all, nothing would be changed by the presence of the Captain; on the contrary, everything would be quickened and stimulated. He has accompanied me on some of my wanderings; he, too, has made many notes, and from a different point of view. Only if we put all that together would the work become a perfect whole."

"Well, then, I will confess quite honestly that my feeling is against this plan," Charlotte declared, with a touch of impatience. "My instinct warns me that nothing good will come of it."

"When you speak in this way," Eduard sighed, "you women are indeed invincible. First, you are so sensible that we cannot contradict you; then, you are so charming that we readily surrender; so emotional that we hesitate to hurt you; and so full of forebodings that we are alarmed."

"I am not superstitious," Charlotte replied. "I should not take these dark intimations too seriously if they meant nothing further; but they are usually subconscious recollections of the fortunate or unfortunate consequences which, as we have observed, follow on our own or other people's actions. Nothing is more momentous in any situation than the appearance of a third person. I have known friends—brothers and sisters, lovers, husbands and wives—whose circumstances were completely reversed, whose mutual relationship changed completely through the accidental or intentional intrusion of a new person."

"This may perhaps happen in the case of people who always blindly grope their way through life," Eduard admitted, "but not to those who, once enlightened by experience, possess more self-awareness."

"The conscious mind, dearest, is no adequate weapon; it is even at times a dangerous one for the person who handles it," Charlotte insisted. "From all this, one fact at least becomes clear—that we should on no account act too hastily. Give me a few more days in which to think it over; do not make any decision."

"As the matter now stands, we are bound to act too quickly in any case, even after the lapse of a day or two," Eduard pleaded. "We have exchanged arguments for and against the plan; now it is the conclusion that matters, and it seems to me best to leave the matter to chance."

"I know that, when you are at a loss and must make a decision, you like to resort to a wager or to the dice," Charlotte said, "but in such a serious matter I should consider that a sin!"

"But what am I to write to the Captain?" Eduard exclaimed. "I must sit down and write a letter at once."

"Write him a calm, sensible, and encouraging letter," advised Charlotte.

"That would be as good as none at all," Eduard replied.

"And yet in certain cases it is necessary and kind to write a letter, even if it says nothing, rather than not to write at all," was all Charlotte said.

chapter 2

EDUARD was alone in his room. His sensitive nature had been agreeably excited by Charlotte's summing-up of the different phases of his life and by her evocation of their mutual situation and projects. He had been so happy to be close to her, to be with her, that he now drew up in his mind a warm, understanding, but sensible and noncommittal letter to the Captain. But when, going to his desk, he took up and reread his friend's letter, the sad plight of this talented man again rose vividly before him; the emotions which had distressed him during the last few days rushed on him again, and he felt that it would be impossible for him to leave his friend in such a desperate situation.

Eduard was not used to denying himself anything. The only child of wealthy parents, he had been spoiled from early youth. They had succeeded in persuading him into an unusual but extremely advantageous marriage to a woman much older than himself, who had pampered him in every possible way, trying to repay his kindness to her by extreme generosity. After her early death he became his own master, free to travel anywhere, able to afford any diversion, any change—not caring for extravagant pleasures but for many and varied interests. He was broad-minded, generous, and gallant—courageous when necessary. What in the world could obstruct his desires!

Up to now everything had gone as he wished. Charlotte had become his wife; he had finally won her by his long, obstinate, romantic loyalty; but now he found himself for the first time contradicted, for the first time frustrated at precisely the moment when he wished to have his friend near him in order to make, as it were, the circle of his life complete. He was vexed and impatient; he took up his pen several times only to put it down again, because he could not make up his mind what to write. He did not wish to go against the wishes of his wife, neither could he do what she had advised him to do; in his restless state it would have been impossible for him to write a calm note. It was most natural that he should try to put the whole matter off. In a few words he apologized to his friend for not having written earlier and for not writing today at greater length; and he promised to send him more important and reassuring news soon.

The next day, while they walked to the summer house, Charlotte took the opportunity to return to their earlier conversation, convinced, perhaps, that the safest way to weaken a project is to discuss it repeatedly.

This suited Eduard perfectly. He expressed himself in his usual manner, kindly and pleasant. Although his natural sensitiveness easily flared into anger, although his temperamental desires could become too insistent, and although his stubbornness was at times hard to bear, yet everything he said was always tempered by a perfect consideration for the other person so that it was impossible not to find him charming even if, at the same time, rather difficult.

Accordingly, this morning he began to put Charlotte in a good mood; and later completely disarmed her with all sorts of lover's talk, so that at last she exclaimed, "I know; you

12

want me to grant to the lover what I refused to the husband.

"You can at least be sure, dearest, that your wishes and the warmth with which you express them do not leave me unmoved and do not find me unresponsive," she added. "They force me to make a confession. I, too, have kept something from you all this time. I find myself in a position similar to yours, and I have practiced the same self-control I am now asking of you."

"I am glad to hear this," Eduard answered, "and I see that it is sometimes necessary for a husband and wife to quarrel; they come to know each other better."

"I want to tell you now," Charlotte said, "that I feel about Ottilie just as you feel about the Captain. I hate to see the dear child in a boarding school where she has to face a rather embarrassing situation. My daughter Luciane, born as she is to play a part in society, is being trained in this school for this part. She learns languages, history, and any other subjects, just at a glance, as she plays her piano sonatas and musical variations at sight. With her lively temperament and excellent memory one might almost say that she forgets everything and remembers everything in a flash; she distinguishes herself among all the others by the freedom of her behavior, by her graceful movements when dancing, and by her perfect ease in conversation; and she has established herself as queen of a little circle of girls by her innate domineering nature. The headmistress of the school sees in her a little goddess who can be shaped into something precious under her direction, who is going to be a credit to the school and will gain her reputation and an increase of pupils. While the first pages of the headmistress' letters and monthly reports are always pure hymns to the perfection of such a child—hymns which I am quite capable of translating into my own prose— everything she finally says concerning Ottilie consists of re-

13

current apologies that a young girl, although growing into such great physical beauty, should not show any real development toward either spiritual or manual accomplishments. And the little she says in addition does not puzzle me, because I recognize in this dear child the complete character of her mother, who was my closest friend. She grew up with me, and I am certain that I could educate and train her daughter to become a wonderful human being if I could be her teacher and her guardian.

"But since this does not fall in with our own plan, and because we should never pluck and pull too much at our conditions of life, always introducing something new, I prefer to bear with the situation and even repress an uneasy feeling that my daughter—who knows perfectly well that poor Ottilie is entirely dependent on us—may use her advantage over her with thoughtless arrogance and so to a certain extent blight our kindness.

"But who is so well educated that he does not sometimes show his superiority over others in a cruel way? Who is so superior that he may not suffer at some time or other under such arrogance? Ottilie's character will be strengthened by these trials; but, since I have realized her painful situation more acutely, I have made continued efforts to place her somewhere else. I expect an answer very soon; and then I shall not hesitate. This is *my* care, my dearest. You see that we both have the same kind of worry and the same loyal and feeling hearts. We shall bear our troubles together, for they do not counteract each other."

"Human beings are very strange," Eduard said, smiling. "If we can only dismiss from our thoughts something that troubles us, we believe that it no longer exists. We are capable of making sacrifices in a general way, but we are seldom ready to sacrifice ourselves in particular. My mother was like that: so long as I lived with her, as a boy and a young man, she was not for one moment free of anxiety about me. If I came home later than expected from a ride on horseback, she immediately imagined an accident; if I became soaking wet in a heavy shower, she was sure that I should catch a fever. But when I went abroad, and I was far away from her—then I scarcely seemed to belong to her.

"If we look more deeply into all this," he went on, "it seems evident that we are both acting in a foolish and irresponsible way in leaving two fine human beings—both very close to our hearts—in this predicament and distress, only because we will not take risks. If this is not selfish, what can be called so? I propose that you take Ottilie and let me have the Captain—and let us try it, for Heaven's sake."

"We might take this chance," Charlotte reflected, "if we two alone were to run the risk. But do you think it advisable to bring the Captain and Ottilie together under the same roof—the Captain being a man of about your age, an age— I make this flattering statement to your face—when a man has just become capable of loving as well as of being loved; and a young girl as attractive as Ottilie?"

"I really cannot understand how you come to think so highly of Ottilie," Eduard objected. "I can explain it only by supposing that you have transferred your affection for her mother to her. She *is* pretty, no doubt, and I remember that the Captain called my attention to her when we returned, a year ago, and met you both at your aunt's house. She *is* pretty; her eyes in particular are beautiful; but I do not remember that she made the slightest impression on me."

"That was nice of you," said Charlotte, "for, after all, *I* was there; and, although she is much younger than I, the presence of your old friend had so much attraction for you that you overlooked the promises of a budding beauty. That

15

is the way you are, and it is the reason why it is so pleasant to share your life."

Although Charlotte seemed to speak in all sincerity, she did not betray a little secret—that at the time, when Eduard had just returned from abroad, she had intentionally introduced Ottilie to him in order to make a favorable match for her beloved foster-daughter. She had given up thinking of herself in connection with Eduard. The Captain, too, had been drawn by her into the plot; he was to bring the young girl to Eduard's attention. But Eduard, stubbornly loyal in his heart to his early love, had looked neither to right nor left and had been happy only in the feeling that it was at last possible to secure the highly desired treasure which a former series of events had apparently denied him forever.

Husband and wife were about to descend toward the castle through the newly laid out grounds when a servant hurried to meet them, and, laughing, called from some distance below: "Will Your Grace please come quickly? Herr Mittler has just galloped at full speed into the courtyard. He shouted to us to find you and to ask if he were needed. 'Am I needed?' he called after us. 'Do you hear? Hurry, hurry!' "

"The queer fellow!" Eduard exclaimed. "But does he not come just at the right moment, Charlotte? Quickly!" he ordered the servant. "Tell him that he should stay—that I need him, that we need him badly. Take care of his horse. Show him into the dining hall and give him someting to eat. We shall come at once."

"Let us take the nearest road," Eduard said to his wife, as he chose the path across the churchyard which he usually avoided. Here also he saw, to his great surprise, traces of Charlotte's loving care. With the greatest possible respect for the old memorials, she had had the place leveled and rearranged, creating in this way a pleasant spot where eye and imagination equally could rest with delight. The oldest tombstones had been given a place of honor, ranged along the wall according to their date; either standing, or let into the wall, or otherwise fastened, they surrounded the high foundation of the church like an ornamental frieze. Eduard was strangely moved when he entered by the little gate; he pressed Charlotte's hand, and tears rose to his eyes. But the tears soon disappeared at the sight of their odd guest, who, not being able to sit still in the castle, had mounted his horse and ridden straight through the village and up to the church-yard gate, where he stopped and called out to his friends: "Are you really serious? If you really need me, I shall stay for dinner. But don't keep me too long; I still have a great deal to do today."

"Since you took the trouble to come so far, do ride in, at least," Eduard welcomed him. "We meet here in a solemn place. Look how beautifully Charlotte has softened its sadness."

"I—enter this place? Never!" protested the rider. "Never! Neither on horseback, nor in a carriage, nor on foot. Those who rest in peace are no concern of mine. I must put up with it when I am carried here some day, feet foremost. Well, is it serious?"

"Yes, very serious!" cried Charlotte. "It is the first time in our married life that we have been in trouble and need help."

"It does not look so," he answered, "but I will believe you. If you are deceiving me, I shall not help you another time. Follow me quickly; my horse deserves some rest."

Soon the three were sitting together in the hall; dinner was served, and Mittler told them what he had done that morning and what he still planned to do. This strange man had once been a clergyman and, apart from his untiring activity

17

in his ministry, had distinguished himself by his skill in pacifying and settling quarrels in his own parish as well as in the neighborhood—at first between individuals and then between communities and between landowners. As long as he had been in his ministry, not one married couple had been divorced; and the district courts had never been bothered with quarrels and lawsuits from his part of the country. Early in life he realized the necessity of a thorough acquaintance with the law; and he devoted himself zealously to that science, soon finding himself a match for the shrewdest lawyer. The sphere of his activity widened remarkably, and some people tried to persuade him to move to the city where he could carry on in more influential circles the ministrations he had begun at a lower level. But, having won a large sum in the lottery, he bought with this money a small estate, which he leased and made the center of his activities. He was firmly determined—or rather followed an old habit and his inclination—never to stay in a house where there was no quarrel to settle or no assistance of any sort needed. People who were superstitious about the significance of names insisted that the name *Mittler* ("mediator") had compelled him to choose this strangest of all vocations.

The dessert had been served when the guest seriously pressed his host and hostess not to keep back their news any longer, since he would have to leave immediately after his coffee. Husband and wife than made their confessions in complete detail; but hardly had he heard what it was all about when he jumped angrily from his chair, rushed to the window, and ordered his horse to be saddled.

"Either you don't know me or don't understand me," he exclaimed, "or you merely make fun of me. Is this a question of a quarrel? Does this call for help? Do you think I am in the world to give advice? Of all the stupid occupations ever un-

18

dertaken by man, that is the most stupid. Everyone should listen to his own advice and do what he cannot help doing. If it turns out well, he should be glad of his wisdom and his luck; if badly—I shall be at hand. The person who wants to get rid of an evil always knows what he wants; but one who wants something better than he has is stone-blind. Yes, yes, laugh at me—he plays at blindman's buff; perhaps he'll snatch something—but what? Do as you like; it does not make any difference! Invite your friends or leave them alone; it is all the same! I have seen the most reasonable things go wrong, the most foolish succeed. Do not rack your brains; and should the whole matter turn out badly in one way or another, don't worry either; send for me—I'll help you! Until then, good-bye!"

With these words he jumped on his horse and left, without waiting for his coffee.

"Now you see of how little use a third person really is when two close friends are not completely in agreement," Charlotte said. "You must admit that we now are, if possible, more confused and uncertain than before."

Both would probably have still wavered for some time if an answer from the Captain to Eduard's last letter had not arrived. He had made up his mind to accept one of the positions offered him, although it was by no means worthy of his abilities. He was supposed to share the boredom of some rich people of rank who expected him to keep them amused.

Eduard at once saw the situation as a whole and filled in the picture with unsparing comments. "Could you bear to see our friend in such a sad predicament?" he exclaimed. "You cannot be so cruel, Charlotte!"

"That strange fellow, Mittler, may be right after all," Charlotte admitted. "All such undertakings are gambles. No one can foresee how they will turn out. New combinations can have fortunate or unfortunate results; and we cannot even claim that the outcome is due to our own merit or our own guilt. I do not feel strong enough to oppose you any longer. We will try; but I ask you to promise me one thing: let everything be planned only for a short time. Give me your permission to investigate further with his interest in mind and to use my influence and my connections to find him a position which will really satisfy him or give him at least some satisfaction."

Eduard thanked his wife very warmly and with his usual charm. With a relieved and happy heart he left to send his friend their invitation; and he then asked Charlotte to add a few words in her own handwriting, saying that she approved the plan and joined him in his friendly suggestion. She wrote with an easy flow of the pen, expressing herself affably and politely, but in a sort of haste which was not her habit; and—which was very unlike her—she finally smudged the paper with a blot of ink, to her great annoyance; and the blot only became larger when she tried to dry it up.

Eduard joked about this and added—as there was still space—a second postscript, saying that his friend should take this as proof of their impatience to see him and should match his coming to the haste in which the letter had been written.

The messenger left, and Eduard thought he could not give a more convincing expression of his gratitude than by insisting again and again that Charlotte should immediately send for Ottilie. She asked him to give her some time to decide and that same evening succeeded in stimulating Eduard to playing a duet with her. Charlotte played the piano extremely well. Eduard performed not quite so well on the flute; for, although he practiced diligently from time to time, he was by nature not patient or persevering enough to train such a talent successfully. Therefore he played his part unevenly

—some passages well but perhaps too quickly; in others he had to slow down because he was not familiar enough with the music; and it would have been difficult for any one but Charlotte to go through an entire duet with him. But Charlotte knew how to cope with it; she slowed down, and then allowed him to run away with her, fulfilling in this way the double duty of a good conductor and an intelligent housewife, both of whom always know how to preserve a general moderate measure, even if single passages may not always be in the right tempo.

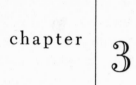

THE Captain arrived. Previously, he had written a letter which had put Charlotte completely at ease. So much frankness about himself, such a clear insight into his own circumstances as well as into the situation of his friends, promised a good and cheerful outcome.

Conversation during the first few hours, as generally happens with friends who have not seen each other for some time, was animated and very nearly exhaustive. Toward evening Charlotte suggested a walk to the new grounds. The Captain was delighted with the entire setting and noticed every beautiful spot which, thanks to the new paths, had come into better view and could now be enjoyed to the full. He had a trained eye but, at the same time, was easily satisfied. Although he could see that all was not perfect, he did not—as is often the case—dampen the good spirits of friends who showed him their property by asking for more than the circumstances allowed; nor did he remind them of anything more perfect he had seen elsewhere.

When they came to the summer house, they found it gaily decorated. Although composed only of artificial flowers and evergreens intermixed with lovely sheaves of wheat and other fruits of field and forest, the whole arrangement showed remarkable taste. "Even though my husband does not wish us to celebrate his birthday or name day, he will not scold me because today I dedicate these few garlands to the celebration of a triple occasion."

"A triple occasion?" Eduard exclaimed.

"Certainly!" Charlotte replied. "Should we not celebrate our friend's arrival; and, then, you both have probably forgotten that today is your name day. Are you not both called 'Otto'?"

The two friends' hands clasped across the small table. "You remind me of our youthful pledge of friendship," Eduard said. "When we were children, we were both called by that name, but later, when we were in school together, the name was the cause of so much confusion that—voluntarily —I yielded my nice laconic name to him."

"Don't boast too much of your generosity," mocked the Captain. "I remember fairly clearly that you liked the name 'Eduard' much better; and indeed it sounds very pleasant, especially when pronounced by pretty lips."

All three were seated around the same little table at which Charlotte had so fervently opposed the invitation to their guest. Eduard, being happy, did not wish to remind his wife of that hour; but he could not refrain from saying: "There is even room here for a fourth person."

At this moment they heard the sound of hunting horns from the castle, affirming and confirming, as it were, the innermost thoughts and wishes of the friends here gathered together. They listened in silence, all three lost in their own thoughts, each moved by his or her own happiness and in perfect harmony with the happiness of the others.

Eduard first broke the silence; he got up and walked out into the open. "Let us take our friend to the top of the hill at once," he said to Charlotte. "He must not think that this narrow valley is our only inheritance and domain; high up there he can have a wider view, and we can breathe more freely."

"This time we have still to climb up the old rather difficult footpath," Charlotte said; "but I hope that my little steps and paths will soon lead us more conveniently to the top."

And so they arrived, over rocks and through bushes and shrubbery at the summit, which was not level but consisted of a succession of grassy ridges. Village and castle, at their back, were no longer visible. Below they saw ponds stretching along the valley, backed by wooded hills; where these ended, steep rocks formed a perpendicular wall behind the last expanse of water, which reflected their magnificent forms on its surface. In a ravine, where a rushing brook poured down into one of the ponds, was a grist-mill; almost hidden among surrounding trees it seemed to offer a pleasant and quiet retreat. In the entire semicircle which they overlooked, a great variety of depths and heights, of thickets and of forests, spread out before them, promising with their early green a future abundant prospect. Here and there single clusters of trees caught their eyes, especially one group of poplars and plane trees directly below them on the edge of the central pond. The trees were all full grown; strong and flourishing, they tapered upward and widely spread their branches.

Eduard asked his friend to take particular notice of them. "I planted those myself when I was a boy. They were saplings that I saved when my father, laying out a new part of the great park, had them removed in the middle of summer. They will, no doubt, show their gratitude again this year by sending out new shoots."

Pleased and in good spirits, the friends returned to the castle. The Captain was assigned comfortable and spacious quarters in the castle's right wing, where he was soon established and where he arranged his books, papers, and instruments in order to continue his usual occupations. But Eduard, during the first days, did not allow him one peaceful moment; he took him, either on horseback or on foot, to see everything about the place; made him acquainted with the surroundings and the estate itself; and told him, on these excursions, his long-cherished plans to improve his knowledge of everything in order to put all to more profitable use.

"The first matter we should attend to is for me to map out the entire terrain with a compass," suggested the Captain. "It is an easy and pleasant task, and, though not entirely exact, it will always be useful and is a good starting point; we can also carry it through without much assistance, and we shall know for certain that it can be finished. If you should ever consider a more precise job of surveying, that can easily be managed later."

The Captain was very skilful at this kind of mapping. He had brought the necessary instruments with him and started at once. He instructed Eduard, as well as some foresters and peasants, to assist him in his work. The weather was favorable. The Captain spent his evenings and early morning hours in making shaded drawings; and in a very short time all was also worked out *au lavis* and in color. Eduard watched while his possessions emerged like new creations upon paper; and it seemed to him as if only now they really belonged to him. Opportunities arose to discuss the environs as a whole and the laying-out of new grounds, which would be much more successful when a map of the entire estate existed than formerly, when they had only experimented with nature in details and according to chance impressions.

"We shall have to explain all this to my wife," Eduard said.

"Don't do it!" warned the Captain, who never liked to impose his own opinions on other people. Experience had taught him that the opinions of human beings are much too varied to be united upon a single point, even by means of the most sensible arguments. "Don't do it! She might easily become uncertain of herself. Like all persons who occupy themselves with that kind of thing as a hobby, she feels that it is more important for her to do something than that something ought to be done. She resembles those who potter about with nature, who have a preference for this spot or that, who do not dare to remove this or that obstacle, who do not have the courage to sacrifice anything, who cannot imagine beforehand what they want to create. They experiment, and this turns out well and that badly; they make changes, changes perhaps where things should have been left as they were, and leave things unchanged which should perhaps have been changed; and in this way everything remains forever a patchwork which is delightful and stimulating but unsatisfactory."

"Now tell me quite frankly—you are not satisfied with her new arrangements?" Eduard asked.

"If the finished effect were equal to the original conception—which is really quite good—I should have nothing to criticize. She has tortured herself with the difficulty of getting through the rocks, and now tortures everyone (if I may say so) whom she takes up to the crest of the hill. For neither side by side, nor in single file, is it possible to walk with any ease. One's step may be interrupted at any moment—and I could make many other objections!"

"But could it have been done in a different way?" Eduard asked.

"Easily," explained the Captain. "She had only to break away one corner of the projecting cliff, which is really quite insignificant, since it consists of small pieces, and she would have gained a graceful sweeping curve for her ascending path and, moreover, plenty of stones which the masons could use to widen the road and to fill the bad spots in it where the path has become narrow and tortuous. But all this is in strict confidence, between friends; any mention of it would confuse and annoy her. What has been done must be left as it is. If you will spend more money and labor, there is still plenty to do from the little summer house up to the crest and beyond; and we can manage this the way we wish."

Even while the two friends were so busy with their present problems, there was opportunity for animated and pleasurable exchange of memories of former times in which Charlotte could share. And they decided to begin the journal of their travels, as soon as the more urgent work was finished, and in this way recall the past.

When Eduard and Charlotte were alone together, they had fewer subjects of conversation than before, especially since the Captain's criticism of the new grounds, which Eduard found to the point, weighed on his mind. He kept silent about it for a long time; but at last, when he saw her toiling up her little steps and paths again from the summer house to the top of the hill, he could no longer refrain and told her, after some evasions, of his new ideas.

Charlotte was completely taken aback. She was intelligent enough to see at once that the friends were right; but her own work, so differently planned, already existed and could not be undone; she had thought it right and liked it; she even liked every one of the details that were criticized. She did not wish to be convinced and defended her little achievements. She blamed the two men for planning everything on too large a scale, for wanting to make an important work out of a playful idea and pleasurable occupation, without considering the expense which a more elaborate plan would inevitably involve. She was upset, hurt, and annoyed. She was unwilling to drop her former plans, although she could not quite deny the advantages of the new ones; but, determined as she was, she stopped the work at once, in order to gain time to think over the whole matter and let it mature in her mind.

Now, while Charlotte was missing her active pastime, the two men were more and more together and looked into everything, especially the nurseries and hothouses. During the intervals of their work they continued their usual country gentlemen's sports—hunting and buying and bartering horses and breaking these into rein and harness; and Charlotte was left more and more to herself. She devoted more of her time to her correspondence and also wrote letters on behalf of the Captain; but she had many lonely hours. She therefore enjoyed the reports she received from the boarding school all the more and read them with great interest.

A long and detailed letter came from the headmistress, who, as usual, after expressing her satisfaction with the progress of Charlotte's daughter, added a short postscript and enclosed a note written by the young man who was her tutor. Both follow:

The Headmistress' Postscript

"In regard to Ottilie, your Ladyship, I can only repeat what I have said in my previous reports. I cannot find fault with her, but I also cannot say that I am happy about her. She is, as she has always been, modest and polite toward others; but I do not quite like her self-effacement and her submissiveness. Your Ladyship the other day sent her a sum of money and material for dresses. She has not touched the money, and the material has not yet been used. Of course, she keeps her things clean and neat and obviously changes her dresses for that reason alone. I also cannot approve of her extreme moderation in eating and drinking. We do not have extravagant meals; but there is nothing I like better than to see the children eat enough good and wholesome food. Everything that is served after careful selection should be eaten, and I never can bring Ottilie to do this. She even manages to find some task to perform, or goes to fetch something that the servants have forgotten or neglected, when she wants to skip some course or the dessert. On the other hand, one must consider that she frequently suffers—as I have only lately been told—from a pain on the left side of her head which is only temporary but probably disturbing and severe. So much for this otherwise dear and lovely child."

Enclosure of the Tutor

"Our excellent headmistress usually passes on to me the letters in which she sends the parents and guardians of her pupils her observations about them. I have always read the letters addressed to Your Ladyship with special attention and pleasure; for, while we congratulate you on having a daughter who combines in herself all those brilliant qualities which will help her to rise in society, I think that you are no less fortunate in possessing in your foster-daughter a child born to be useful and a blessing to others and, without any doubt, destined for happiness, as well. Ottilie is almost our only pupil concerning whom our admirable headmistress and I do not agree. I do not at all blame that untiring lady when she wishes to see the fruits of her efforts appear in a tangible and visible form, but there are some fruits which, although shut into a shell, nevertheless have a sound core, and will sooner or later develop into rich maturity. Your foster-daughter, I am convinced, is such a nature. So long as I have been her teacher, I have seen her ever moving at the same pace, slowly, slowly forward—never back. Just as it

29

is necessary for a small child to start with beginnings, so it is with her. Everything that does not follow from something she has already learned she is unable to grasp. She is incapable, even inaccessible, when confronted with an easily understandable subject—on which, however, she cannot connect with any former experience; but, as soon as one can find the connecting links and explain them to her, nothing is too difficult for her comprehension.

"Because she progresses so slowly, she is far behind her companions, who, with totally different abilities, always hurry on learning everything easily—even unrelated subjects—remember them easily, and can apply them without difficulty. This is not Ottilie's way; she is almost paralyzed when a teacher proceeds too quickly, as happens in a few classes given by excellent but impatient instructors. There have also been complaints about her handwriting and her inability to grasp the rules of grammar. I have looked closely into this. It is true that she writes slowly and tensely, if one may say so; but her letters are neither timid nor badly formed. When I tutored her in French (although that is not my subject), I taught her by going forward step by step; and she easily understood. Of course it is strange, although she knows many things and knows them well, when she is asked questions she does not seem to know anything at all.

"If I may conclude with a general observation, I should like to say that she does not learn like a person who receives an education but like one who herself wishes to educate others; not like a pupil but like a future teacher. Your Ladyship will think it strange that I, a teacher and educator, cannot think of higher praise to give a person than to pronounce her my equal. Your Ladyship's great insight and deeper knowledge of the world and of human nature will read my inadequate but well-meant words with the best understanding. You can be assured that this child, too, is promising. With my best compliments, I ask your Ladyship's permission to write again as soon as I have something important and pleasant to report."

Charlotte was very happy about this note. Its contents closely corresponded to the idea she had herself formed of Ottilie; at the same time, she could not help smiling at the Tutor's warm interest which seemed greater than the perception of good qualities in a pupil usually rouses. In her quiet unprejudiced way of thinking, she looked at this relationship as she had in many similar cases; she appreciated the sympathy felt by this sensible man for Ottilie, having learned from many experiences during her life how precious true affection is in a world where indifference and dislike are so much at home.

chapter 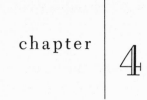 4

THE topographical map of the estate and its environs was finished. In pen-and-ink and colors it showed clearly all the characteristic features on a fairly large scale. Its exactness was well founded on trigonometrical measurements made by the Captain. Hardly anyone but this active man could have gone with so little sleep; his days were always devoted to an immediate purpose, so that every evening showed that something had been accomplished.

"Now let us turn our attention to the rest," he said to his friend; "that is, a descriptive survey of the estate. There must already be enough documents from which evaluation of the leases and other matters will naturally develop. But we should firmly decide on one principle and strictly observe it: to separate business from pleasure. Work requires serious thinking and firmness; life should be lived more flexibly. Work demands a clear sequence; in life one has at times to be inconsequential; this is delightful and even exhilarating. If you are firm in the first, you can be more free in the second; otherwise, if you mix the two, firmness will be swept away and canceled by freedom."

Eduard felt a slight reproach in his friend's remark. Although by nature not without orderly habits, he could never bring himself to arrange his papers in files. His correspond-ence with others and the papers which concerned his per-sonal affairs were not kept separately. In the same way, he was liable to confuse business with mere occupation and con-versation with entertainment. Everything was now easier for him since his friend, acting as a second self, took care of all these matters and brought about a division which the single self often refuses to make.

In the Captain's wing they constructed a depository for their present transactions as well as an archive for past ones. They collected there all the documents, papers, and com-munications received, from different places—from rooms, garrets, and cupboards—where they had formerly been kept; and in no time the chaos was cleared, and the marked files lay in gratifying order in their labeled pigeonholes. The friends found the necessary documents more complete than they had expected. An old clerk was extremely helpful—he did not leave his desk all day, even spending part of the night there—although Eduard had previously found him unsatisfactory.

"He does not seem the same person!" he exclaimed. "He is so active and useful!"

"The reason is that we do not burden him with new work before he has finished the old at his convenience," the Cap-tain explained. "In this way he accomplishes a great deal, as you see; if you disturb him, he can do nothing."

Although they spent their days together in this manner, the two friends never failed to keep Charlotte company in the evenings. If no visitors from the neighboring towns and estates arrived—which was frequently the case—they read and talked, mostly on topics concerned with the improve-ment of conditions, the privileges and the comfort of the middle class.

Charlotte, whose habit was to make use of the present moment, felt that it was to her own personal advantage if her husband was happy and contented. Various domestic arrangements which she had always wished to make but had not known how to start were now realized with the help of the Captain. Her private medicine chest, until now poorly stocked, received new supplies of medicines; and Charlotte herself, aided by popular books on the subject and through discussion, was now in a position to exercise her active and charitable nature more frequently and more efficiently than before. After the three had discussed the usual emergencies, which in spite of their frequent occurrence only too often take us by surprise, they began, first of all, to provide everything which might be required for the resuscitation of a drowned person. This sort of accident happened very frequently in this region, since they lived near so many ponds, lakes, rivers, and mill dams. The Captain took extensive care of this special department, and Eduard let fall the remark that a strange case of this kind had marked a memorable point in the life of his friend. But the Captain said nothing, evidently wishing to avoid sad memories; and Eduard immediately became silent. Charlotte, who had a general knowledge of the incident, passed quickly over the allusion.

"All these precautions are very valuable," the Captain began one evening, "but we lack the most essential factor: a good man who knows their practical use. I can warmly recommend a former army surgeon whom I know well, and whose services are at present available at moderate terms. He is an excellent man in his profession, and he treated me frequently, in the case of a violent internal trouble, more skilfully than a famous physician. Immediate medical care is the thing one misses most in the country."

They wrote to the surgeon at once; and Eduard and Charlotte were glad that a sum of surplus money, set aside for extra expenses, could now be used for essential needs. In this way Charlotte used the Captain's knowledge and his practical judgment for her own purposes; she gradually became completely reconciled to his presence and at ease concerning any possible consequences. She usually prepared certain questions she wished to ask him; and, as she loved life, she wished to eliminate anything harmful or of a fatal nature. The lead glaze of pottery and the verdigris on copper vessels had worried her very often. She asked him to explain all this to her; and they naturally had to go back to elementary physics and chemistry.

Eduard's special liking for reading aloud to others gave an occasional and always welcome motive for this sort of conversation. He had a very musical deep-pitched voice and, in former years, had been famous for his lively and moving recitals of poetry and dramatic prose. At present he was interested in other subjects; and the books from which he now read to them were, for the most part, works on physics, chemistry, or technical problems.

One of his most striking peculiarities—which he very likely shared with many others—was that he could not bear to have anyone look over his shoulder at the book he was reading.

Formerly, when he used to read poems, plays, or stories aloud, this antipathy had been the natural consequence of a desire which is equally strong in the reader, the poet, the actor, and the narrator: to surprise, to pause, and to work up suspense. These intended effects are, of course, thwarted when another person's eyes can run ahead over the page. For this reason Eduard usually chose a seat where no one could sit behind him. In the present case—in their little circle of three—such a precautionary measure was unnecessary; and, as the reading matter offered no cause for emotional excitement or for imaginative surprise, he did not trouble to be particularly careful in his choice of a seat.

One evening, however, when he had seated himself to read, without giving much thought to the place, he suddenly noticed that Charlotte was looking into his book. His old impatience returned, and, speaking in a rather unkind tone, he chided her: "That is one of the annoying habits I wish people would drop once and for all! When I read aloud to you, is it not as though I were speaking directly to you? The written and the printed words take the place of my own thoughts, my own heart. Would I make the effort to talk if a little window had been set into my forehead or breast, so that the person to whom I communicate my thoughts and emotions, one by one, would know all the while, in advance, what I was driving at? If someone glances into the book I am reading, I always feel as if I were being pulled apart."

In a large as well as in a small circle, Charlotte had shown a special talent for quietly passing over any unpleasant, violent, or even any too outspoken remark. She knew how to interrupt a long-winded conversation or, on the other hand, how to stimulate one that threatened to exhaust itself; and now this wonderful gift did not fail her. "I am sure you will forgive me my tactlessness if I confess what occurred to me just now," she said. "I heard you reading about 'relationships' and 'affinities,' and I immediately thought of certain relatives—two cousins who just now are giving me a good deal of trouble. My attention turned again to your reading; I heard that it concerned inanimate matter; and I glanced into your book to pick up the lost thread."

"It is the analogy which misled and confused you," Eduard answered. "The book here deals only with earth and minerals; but man is a true narcissus; he likes to reflect himself

36

everywhere; he spreads himself under the whole world like the foil of a mirror."

"Yes," the Captain added. "He treats everything outside himself in this fashion. His own wisdom and his folly, his will and his whim, he attributes to the animals, the plants, the elements, and the gods."

"Would you explain to me quite briefly—as I do not want to lead you too far away from the present subject—what is meant here by—'affinities'?" Charlotte asked.

"I shall do that with pleasure and as clearly as I can," the Captain, to whom Charlotte had directed her question, answered. "Whatever I have learned and read about these matters dates back about ten years. Whether the scientific world still accepts this theory, or if the theory agrees with modern doctrines, I cannot say."

"It is a pity that nowadays we cannot learn anything to last a lifetime," Eduard exclaimed. "Our forefathers relied on what they were taught in their youth; *we* have to learn something different every five years or so in order not to fall completely behind the times."

"We women are not so particular," said Charlotte. "Quite frankly, I am mainly interested in the exact meaning of the word; nothing makes one more of a laughing stock in society than to use a foreign or a technical term incorrectly. I only wish you would tell me in what sense this term is used in connection with the matters you mentioned. I am quite content to leave its scientific implications to the scholars who will not (by the way) ever agree easily among themselves, as I have had the opportunity to observe."

"How are we to begin, in order to come to the point in the quickest possible way?" Eduard asked the Captain, who, after reflecting for a short time, began:

37

"If I begin farther back, we shall come to the point all the quicker."

"I shall certainly be very attentive," said Charlotte, putting her needlework away.

The Captain then began:

"The first thing we notice in all natural elements is that they have a relation to themselves. It may sound strange for me to state something so obvious; but only if we completely agree about the known, can we proceed together to the unknown."

"I think," interrupted Eduard, "we can make everything clearer for Charlotte and for ourselves if we give a few examples. Just think of water, or of oil, or of mercury—and you will see a unity, a cohesion, of their parts. This unity is never lost except when broken by force or by some other determining factor. If this factor is eliminated, the parts immediately combine again,"

"No doubt that is very true," Charlotte agreed. "Raindrops quickly unite and form a flood. Even as children, we used to play with quicksilver and separate it into small pellets which, to our great surprise, always ran together again."

"Then perhaps I may briefly mention an important point," the Captain added, "namely, that this perfectly clear relation of parts, made possible by the liquid state, always distinguishes itself by a definite globular shape. The falling water drop is round, and you yourself mentioned just now the small mercury pellets; but even a drop of molten lead, if it has time to harden as it falls, lands on the ground in a globular shape."

"Wait a moment and see if I have understood what you are driving at," Charlotte said. "Just as everything relates to itself, so it must have some relation to other things."

"And that relation will be different according to a difference in the elements involved," Eduard eagerly went on. "Some will meet quickly like friends or old acquaintances and combine without any change in either, just as wine mixes with water. But others will remain detached like strangers and refuse to combine in any way—even if they are mechanically mixed with, or rubbed against, each other. Oil and water may be shaken together, but they will immediately separate again."

"From this point it is only a step to imagine that one sees in these simple forms the people one has known," said Charlotte. "I am particularly reminded of the societies in which we have lived. But the strongest resemblance to these soulless elements shows in the groups which confront one another in the world: the trades and professions, the aristocracy and the commoners, soldiers and civilians."

"But just as all these can be unified by common laws and morals, so also in our chemical realm intermediate links exist which join mutually hostile elements," Eduard said.

"In this way we combine oil and water by means of alkaline salt," the Captain interjected.

"Please don't go too fast with your lecture and let me prove that I can keep up with you," Charlotte said. "Have we not by now arrived at the 'affinities'?"

"You are right!" the Captain replied. "In just a moment we shall become acquainted with them in their full force and determination. The tendency of those elements which, when they come into contact, at once take hold of, and act on one another, we call 'affinity.' The alkalis and the acids reveal these affinities in the most striking way—although by nature opposites, perhaps for that very reason they select one another, take hold of and modify each other eagerly; and then together form an entirely new substance. You have only to think of lime, which shows a decided inclination for all sorts of acids—a distinct desire to combine with them. As soon as our chemistry cabinet arrives, we will show you many kinds of interesting experiments which will give you a much better idea of all this than words, names, and technical terms can do."

"I must confess that when I hear you say that these odd things are 'related,' they seem to me not so much blood relations as relations in spirit and soul," Charlotte said. "In just the same way truly deep friendships can develop between people because opposite dispositions are the best basis for a very close union. I shall now wait for the moment when you will show me some of these mysterious effects. I'll not interrupt your reading again," she said, turning to Eduard. "You have taught me so much that now I shall be a more attentive and understanding listener."

"No, my dear," Eduard replied. "You have challenged our instruction, and you will not get off so easily. It is precisely the complicated cases that are most interesting. Only through them can you learn to know the degrees of affinity—the closer and stronger, as well as the more remote and weaker, relationships. Affinities really become interesting only when they bring about separations."

"How terrible!" Charlotte cried. "Is that depressing word, which, unfortunately, we hear so often nowadays, also in nature's textbook?"

"Of course it is," Eduard answered. "The title of honor formerly given to chemists was 'artist in separating.'"

"But that title is probably no longer given, and it is just as well," Charlotte said. "*Uniting* is a greater and more deserving art. An artist in *uniting* would be welcome in any profession, the world over. But, as you both seem to be in a teaching mood, tell me more of your cases."

"We will, then, take up where we left off in our talk," said the Captain. "For instance, what we call limestone is a more or less pure calcareous earth in close combination with a volatile acid known to us in a gaseous form. If we put a piece of this limestone in a weak solution of sulphuric acid, the latter will take possession of the lime and appear with it in the form of gypsum; but the delicate gaseous acid will escape. Here we see a case of separation, and of a new combination, so that we think we are correct in using here the term 'elective affinity,' as it really looks as though one relation had been deliberately chosen in preference to another."

"Excuse me as I excuse the scientist," said Charlotte. "But in this case I should never think of a choice but of a compelling force—and not even that. After all, it may be merely a matter of opportunity. Opportunity makes connections as it makes thieves. As to your chemical substances, the choice seems to be exclusively in the hands of the chemist who brings these elements together. But once united, and they *are* together, God have mercy on them! In the present case I am only sorry for the poor gaseous acid which must again roam about in infinite space."

"The acid has only to combine with water to refresh the healthy and the sick as a mineral spring," the Captain retorted.

"That is easy for the gypsum to say," said Charlotte. "The gypsum is taken care of; it is a *substance;* but that other displaced element may have much trouble until it finds a home again."

"I am very much mistaken if there is not a bit of malice behind your words," said Eduard, smiling. "Out with your mischievous thoughts! Perhaps *I* am (in your eyes) the lime which has been taken into possession by the Captain, who is the sulphuric acid, and am torn away from your amiable company and changed into refractory gypsum."

"If your conscience prompts you to make remarks like that, I have no reason to worry," said Charlotte. "These parables are entertaining, and who does not like to play with analogies? But man is placed many degrees higher than these elements; and if we have here used fine words like 'choice' and 'elective affinity' a little too broadly, we would do well to turn back into our own hearts and, in so doing, think seriously about the value of such terms. Unfortunately, I know enough cases where a close union of two hearts, apparently indissoluble, has been dissolved by the accidental introduction of a third person; and where one or the other of a once happily united couple has been driven out into an uncertain world."

"You see how much more chivalrous the chemists are," said Eduard. "They provide a fourth element, so that no one feels neglected."

"That is true!" added the Captain. "And those cases are indeed the most important and remarkable, wherein this attraction, this affinity, this separating and combining, can be demonstrated, the two pairs, as it were, crossing over; where four elements, until then joined in two's, are brought into contact and give up their former combination to enter a new one. In this dissociating and taking possession, this flight and seeking, we actually imagine we see some higher pre-determination; we believe these elements capable of exercising some sort of willpower and selection, and feel perfectly justified in using the term 'elective affinities'!"

"Why don't you describe such a case!" Charlotte asked.

"Such matters cannot easily be described in words," replied the Captain. "As I said before, as soon as I can demonstrate to you the experiments themselves, everything will become intelligible and simpler for you. As it is I should be forced to put you off with formidable scientific terms which would have no meaning for you. You must see with your own eyes these apparently lifeless but actually very dynamic elements and observe with interest how they attract, seize, destroy, devour, and absorb each other and then emerge out of that violent combination in renewed and unexpected form. Only then will you agree that they might be immortal or even capable of feeling and reasoning, because we feel our own senses to be almost insufficient for observing them properly and our reason too limited to understand their nature."

"I will not deny that the strange scientific terms must seem difficult and even absurd to anyone who has not become familiar with them by direct observation and by general conceptions," Eduard said; "but meanwhile we can easily express in symbols, for this occasion, the relations of the elements we have been discussing here."

"If you will not think me too pedantic, I can very easily sum up the whole matter by using letters," the Captain said. "Imagine an *A* so closely connected with a *B* that the two cannot be separated by any means, not even by force; and imagine a *C* in the same relation to a *D*. Now bring the two pairs into contact. *A* will fling itself on *D*, and *C* on *B*, without our being able to say which left the other first, or which first combined itself with the other."

"Now then!" said Eduard. "Until we have seen all this with our own eyes, we shall take this formula as a useful allegory and draw from it a practical lesson. You, Charlotte, represent the *A*, and I am your *B*; for, to be honest, I completely depend on you and follow you as *B* follows *A*. *C* obviously stands for the Captain, who just at present draws me away from you to some extent. It is only to keep you from escaping into infinite space that we should try to find a *D* for you; and that is, no doubt, your darling Ottilie, whose coming you should really no longer resist."

"Very well!" Charlotte agreed. "Even if, in my opinion,

the example does not quite fit our case, I think it very fortunate that today we all agree for once perfectly and that these natural and elective affinities have encouraged me to tell you, earlier than I had intended, that I made up my mind this afternoon to send for Ottilie, for my faithful housekeeper is about to leave to be married. This decision is in my own interest and for my own sake. Why I decided in Ottilie's interest, you shall read aloud to us. I'll not look into the letter while you are reading. Of course, I already know what it says. Here, read; do read!"

With these words she produced a letter and gave it to Eduard.

chapter | 5

The Headmistress' Letter

"Your Ladyship will excuse me if I am very brief today. I must write reports to all the parents and guardians concerning the results of the public examinations which are just over and which will show what we have accomplished with our pupils during the past year. I may be brief since I can tell you much in a few words. Your daughter has turned out to be in every sense the first in her class. The enclosed certificate and her own letter, with its description of her awards and her delight at her success, will be a great satisfaction and pleasure to you. My own feelings are somewhat sad ones, because I expect that soon there will be no longer any reason for keeping with us a young lady who is so far advanced. I send my compliments to your Ladyship. In my next letter I shall submit my suggestions concerning the best plans for her future. My assistant will write you about Ottilie."

The Tutor's Letter

"Our respected headmistress has left it in my hands to write you concerning Ottilie, partly since she is embarrassed, because of her attitude in these matters, to report

45

what must be reported; partly because she herself feels guilty and prefers that I offer apologies in her name.

"Knowing only too well how inarticulate our dear Ottilie is about herself and the things she really knows, I had been worried about this public examination, for which it is not possible to prepare a student—least of all Ottilie—who could never be prepared for mere show and make-believe, as such preparation is usually made. The result of the examination has only too well justified my uneasiness. She did not receive any award and is, besides, among those who did not receive a certificate. What more can I say? Her handwriting is very good; her letters are better shaped than those of the other pupils, but these others have much more freely flowing pens. They were all quicker with their answers in arithmetic; and no difficult problems—which she can solve better than the rest—came up. In French the others outtalked and outshone her. In history she was not prompt with her names and dates; and in geography she did not show enough knowledge of political division. During the music recital there was neither time nor quiet for her few simple tunes. In drawing she would certainly have received the first prize. Her outlines were clear, the details carefully done and yet full of imagination. Unfortunately, she had set herself too large a task and was not able to complete it.

"After the pupils were dismissed, the examiners went into a conference to which we teachers were also admitted, and where we could say a few words. I soon noticed that Ottilie was either not mentioned at all or mentioned with indifference if not with disapproval. I hoped to improve her chances by frankly describing her personality as a whole, which I could do with great warmth, because I was deeply convinced of what I said and because, when young, I had found myself in a similar predicament. Everyone listened

46

with attention; but, when I had finished my plea, the chairman of the board of examiners said, kindly but laconically, 'Aptitudes are taken for granted; they should become accomplishments. This is the aim of all education; it is the clear and pronounced wish of parents and guardians as well as the unexpressed and perhaps only half-realized wish of the children themselves. It is also the purpose of examinations, where both teachers and pupils alike are tested. From all you have said, there seems to be a possibility of promise in this child; and it is certainly to your credit that you so conscientiously watch the capacities of the pupils. If, during the next year, you can develop her aptitudes into accomplishments, you and this pupil you are so warmly interested in will certainly receive our full approval.'

"I had already resigned myself to the consequences, but I had not anticipated the disturbing scene which occurred soon afterward. Our dear headmistress, who, like a good shepherd, cannot bear to see one of her flock lost or (as was here the case) unadorned, after the departure of the examiners could no longer conceal her disappointment. She said to Ottilie, who was standing quietly near a window, while the other pupils rejoiced in their awards, 'Now for Heaven's sake tell me, how can any intelligent person appear so stupid?'

"Ottilie calmly answered, 'Excuse me, dear Mother. I feel my headache again today, and it is very painful.'

" 'No one could know that,' the headmistress, who is usually so sympathetic, said dryly; and she unkindly turned away.

"Well, it *is* true that no one could realize it, for Ottilie's face does not change; and I have never seen her once move her hand to her temple.

"But this was not all. Your Ladyship's daughter, by nature

47

lively and outgoing, was in high spirits after her triumph, and almost arrogantly so. She danced through the rooms with her prizes and her certificate and waved them in Ottilie's face. 'You have done very badly today,' she cried.

"Ottilie quietly answered, 'This was not the last test.'

" 'But you will always be the last,' the young lady answered and ran off.

"To any other person, Ottilie might have seemed unmoved; but not to me. An inner agitation, against which she fights, always shows in the uneven color of her face: her left cheek flushes for a moment while the right turns pale. I saw this symptom and felt so sorry for her that I talked for a long time with the headmistress alone. We seriously discussed the whole matter, and the kind lady saw that she had made a grave mistake. Without going into details, I shall submit to your Ladyship our final decision and our mutual request that you take Ottilie into your home for a short period. The reasons will gradually become clear to you. If you agree, I shall tell you more about the best way to treat the good child. Your daughter—we expect—will soon leave our school; and then we shall be glad to have Ottilie with us once more.

"One further point which I might forget later. I have never seen Ottilie ask for anything, much less ask for anything urgently. But there are rare occasions when she tries to decline doing something she is asked to do. She does this with a gesture, irresistible to anyone who has caught its meaning. She raises her hands, palms pressed together, and brings them back to her breast, at the same time slightly bending forward and looking into the person's eyes with an expression of such pleading that the asker is glad to give up all he has asked or wished. If you ever see that gesture—

48

which is not likely while she is in your Ladyship's care—remember my words and spare Ottilie."

Eduard finished reading these letters—not without occasional smiles and shaking of the head. They now, naturally, exchanged remarks about the different people involved and the situation as a whole.

"Very well! The long and short of it is that a decision has been made at last; she is coming!" Eduard cried. "You are taken care of, my dear, and now *we* can come out with *our* scheme. It is absolutely necessary that I move into the Captain's wing. The late evening and the early morning are the best time for us to work together. You will then have room enough for yourself and Ottilie in the left wing of the house."

Charlotte did not object to this arrangement; and Eduard thereupon outlined his plans for their future way of living. In the course of so doing, he remarked: "It is really very charming of your niece to suffer from a headache on the left side. I myself feel one sometimes on the right side. If it should happen that we suffer at the same time, and sit opposite each other, I leaning on my right elbow, she on her left, our heads resting on our hands as we look in different directions—what a pretty pair of 'companion pictures' we shall make!"

The Captain thought this highly dangerous; but Eduard cried: "Beware of the *D*, my dear fellow! What would become of *B* if *C* should be captivated by *D!*"

"Well, I should think there would be only one possible solution," replied Charlotte.

"You are right. He would return to his *A*—to his Alpha and Omega," exclaimed Eduard, who jumped up and took Charlotte in his arms.

chapter 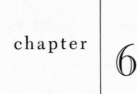 6

THE carriage which brought Ottilie drove up, and Charlotte went out to meet it. The girl hurried to her and knelt before her, clasping Charlotte's knees.

Charlotte was a little embarrassed, and, trying to raise her she asked—"Why so humble?" "This is not meant as a sign of humility," Ottilie answered, and remained on her knees. "I love to think of the time when I did not reach much higher than your knee but I was already certain that you loved me."

She rose to her feet, and Charlotte embraced her with affection. She then introduced her to the two men, and all three immediately began to treat her with particular consideration. Beauty is everywhere a very welcome guest. Ottilie listened to their conversation with great attention but did not join in.

The next morning Eduard remarked to Charlotte, "What a charming and entertaining girl!"

"Entertaining?" Charlotte asked, smiling. "She has not yet once opened her mouth."

"Really?" said Eduard, puzzled. "How strange!"

Charlotte gave the newcomer only a few hints about the management of the household. Ottilie had quickly indeed taken in the whole arrangement with a sort of intuitive grasp. She easily understood what she was to do in general, and what for each person in particular. Everything was done punctually. She knew how to give directions without appearing to give orders. If something had not been done, she did it herself.

As soon as she realized how much leisure she had, she asked Charlotte to allow her to use this spare time for her school work, which she did conscientiously. She worked at her assignments exactly as the tutor had reported to Charlotte. No one interfered, but occasionally Charlotte did resort to indirect suggestions. For instance, she slipped a few worn quill pens among Ottilie's own, to stimulate a bolder sweep to her handwriting; but after a short time these were always resharpened.

The two women had decided to converse in French when they were alone; Charlotte in particular held firmly to the plan, since Ottilie was much more talkative when she spoke this foreign language—which, incidentally, she had promised her teacher to practice regularly. In French she often said more than she apparently intended; Charlotte particularly enjoyed one occasion when Ottilie unexpectedly gave her an accurate and sympathetic description of the school. Charlotte found her an agreeable companion and hoped one day to see her become a trusted friend. She now looked through Ottilie's earlier school reports again, because she wished to refresh her memory about everything the headmistress or the tutor had said about the girl and to compare it with her own observations of Ottilie's personality. It was Charlotte's conviction that we cannot too quickly become acquainted with the disposition of those with whom we have to live, so that we may know what to expect of them, what we can hope to improve in them, and what we have to understand and tolerate, once and for all.

These comparisons did not reveal anything unexpected;

but much that was already known to her now became more significant and obvious. Ottilie's moderate habits of eating and drinking, for instance, really began to worry her.

The most urgent matter which engaged the two women was Ottilie's wardrobe. Charlotte wanted her to dress better and more elegantly. Ottilie, who was never idle, at once began to cut out the materials which had previously been given to her; and, quickly and skilfully, with very little help from others, soon made some dresses that fitted her perfectly. These new and fashionable dresses set off her figure in an admirable way. A woman expresses her natural beauty in her clothes; we imagine we see a new and lovelier person whenever she wears a different dress.

So we can well say that more and more, from the very beginning, Ottilie was, for the two men, a joy to behold. Just as the emerald pleases the eye by its superb color, and may even have some healing power for that precious organ of sight, so human beauty, with a much stronger force, acts on our senses and feelings. He who looks at Beauty is proof against the breath of Evil; he is in harmony with himself and the whole world.

Ottilie's arrival had benefited all of them, in many respects. The two men became punctual, even to the minute, when they were to join the ladies; they were rarely late for dinner, or at teatime, or for their walks together. They did not leave the table so hurriedly, particularly in the evening. None of this escaped Charlotte's notice; and from time to time she watched to see whether one might show more inclination to linger than the other, but she detected none. By and large both men had become more sociable. In their conversation, they seemed to consider what would interest Ottilie, and to adjust their discussions to the scope of her intelligence and knowledge. When they were talking or when reading aloud, they stopped when she left the room and waited for her to return. Their conversation became gentler and less reserved.

In response to all this kindness, Ottilie's wish to be helpful increased day by day. As she became familiar with the arrangements in the household, with its members and with their circumstances, she set to work more eagerly, and even learned quickly to guess the meaning of any expression, movement, half-uttered word, or sound. Her silent attentiveness never changed, nor did her quiet activity. Her every movement, sitting down, getting up, going, coming, fetching, carrying, and sitting down again—all was done without the slightest appearance of restlessness; it was merely a constant change, a perpetual pleasant movement. Indeed, they never heard her walk, so light was her step.

Ottilie's agreeable and obliging behavior was a constant pleasure to Charlotte. There was only one thing of which she did not approve; and one day she spoke to the girl frankly about it. "It is very polite and commendable to stoop down immediately when someone drops something and pick it up. With this gesture, as it were, we show that we feel ourselves obliged to that person; but, in society, we must be careful to whom we show such respect. I do not set up any rules for you about women. You are young. To your superiors and to older persons it is a duty; to those of your own age and class, it is politeness; to those who are younger than you are and to your inferiors, it is an act of kindness and helpfulness; but it is not proper for a young girl to be so eager to do such a service for a man."

"I shall try to rid myself of this bad habit," Ottilie replied, "but you will pardon it when I tell you how I came to adopt it. In our history class I was taught many things that I do not remember as well as I should; I did not realize then how useful they could be later on. Only a few incidents impressed me very much—this one, for example:

"When Charles I of England was facing his so-called 'judges,' the gold top of the stick he carried in his hand fell to the ground. Being used to having everyone do everything for him, he looked about, expecting that this time, too, someone would do him this little service. No one made a move; he himself bent down to pick up the fallen object. I thought this action so pitiful—whether rightly I do not know—that from that moment on I could not see anyone drop anything without bending down to pick it up. Because this is probably not always proper and because," she continued with a smile, "I cannot tell my story on every occasion, I shall be more careful in the future."

Meanwhile, all the useful work which the two men had planned went on without interruption. Every day they found fresh reasons for planning and undertaking something new.

One day while they were walking together through the village, they discussed their dissatisfaction with its backwardness, in so far as order and cleanliness were concerned, in comparison to other villages, where lack of space compelled the inhabitants to pay more attention to such matters.

"Do you remember, on our trip through Switzerland, how we wanted to improve a country estate by laying out a village located as this one is; not in the Swiss style, but with the Swiss order and cleanliness so conducive to a healthier way of living?" the Captain asked.

"It could be done here, for example," Eduard replied. "The hill runs down from the castle in a projecting spur, and the village lies opposite, more or less in a semicircle. All the villagers have tried to protect themselves against the brook which separates the two; some have used stones, some piles and some planks, but none of them has helped his neighbors by these expedients; indeed, they all interfere with each other. And the road is very bad; it runs uphill and down, through water and over the boulders. If all the villagers would cooperate, it should not require a great deal of financial help to build a semicircular dam, and raise the road behind it to the level of the houses. The space this would provide ought to promote cleanliness, and such large-scale planning would make all these petty and inadequate measures unnecessary."

"Let's try it," said the Captain, taking in the entire scene at one glance and quickly appraising its possibilities.

"I don't like to deal with townspeople and peasants unless I can actually give orders," Eduard said.

"You may be right," the Captain agreed. "I have had many annoying experiences on that score myself. How difficult it is for some people to weigh sacrifices against possible gains! How hard it is to desire the ends without despising the means! Many people, as a matter of fact, confuse the means with the end and enjoy the one but lose sight of the other. People set in to remedy evils at the point where they appear; nobody pays any attention to their actual source and origin. This is why it is so difficult to give advice and have it heeded, especially by the general run of men, who are quite reasonable in everyday matters but seldom see beyond tomorrow. And if, in a common arrangement, one person will gain and another lose, you never can persuade anybody to come to terms. Only absolute authority can further the common good."

While they stood and talked, a man approached them, to beg—although he looked more insolent than poor. Eduard, who disliked being interrupted and bothered, shouted at him, after several unsuccessful attempts to get rid of him by using a quieter tone. The fellow slouched away, grumbling and even talking back, claiming the rights of beggars to whom one might refuse alms but whom one should not insult, he being under the protection of God and of the authorities as much as any other man. All this upset Eduard greatly.

The Captain, in trying to calm him, said, "Let us take this incident as an occasion to extend our authority to almsgiving, as well. There is no doubt that we must practice charity; but it is better not to give alms personally, particularly not in our own neighborhood. At home we should be as moderate and sensible in our charity as in everything else. A generous gift attracts beggars instead of speeding them on their way. When we travel, we can allow ourselves the passing luxury of playing Fortuna in person, and throwing a surprisingly large gift to some poor man by the roadside. As a matter of fact, the village and the castle are very favorably located for a planned system of charity; it actually occurred to me some time ago. The inn is situated at one end of the village; at the other is the home of an honest old couple; at both places small sums of money should be deposited. Not the person entering the village but the person leaving it will get something; and as these two houses are also on the road leading up to the castle, everyone who intends to go up there can be directed to one place or the other."

"Come, let's settle that immediately," Eduard said. "The details can be arranged later."

They visited the innkeeper and the old couple, and found them agreeable to this plan.

While they walked back up to the castle, Eduard said, "I am perfectly aware that everything in this world depends upon a brilliant idea and a firm determination. You were a good judge of my wife's projects in the park; you also gave

56

me a hint as to how these might be improved. I must confess that I told her about your advice eventually."

"I suspected that you did," the Captain replied, "and I did not approve of it. You have confused her completely; she has stopped all work up there and on this one point stubbornly refuses to talk to us; she has not invited us up to the summer house again, although she goes there herself sometimes with Ottilie."

"We ought not to let this interfere with our plans," Eduard said. "If I am convinced that a desirable idea can and should be carried out, I cannot rest until it is. Haven't we always been clever enough at turning the conversation as we wished? Tonight, for instance, let us get that book describing English parks, and the engravings that go with it. After we have looked at them for a while, we'll turn to your map of our estate. We'll first discuss it all theoretically as if we were just amusing ourselves; serious consideration of the matter will follow quite naturally."

As agreed, they took out the book and looked at the first drawings together: the basic plan of each English district, its geographical character and its original natural state; followed by the changes which cultivation and landscaping had brought about, to employ and improve inherent advantages. The transition to their own property, to their own region, and to the possible improvements they could make was now very easy. It was convenient to spread out the Captain's map as a basis for their discussion; but it was difficult to abandon altogether the plan by which Charlotte had originally begun the work. They devised, however, an easier ascent to the crest of the hill and also planned to build there a kind of lodge at the top of the slope and in front of a pretty little wood. This structure was to have a special relation to the castle, from the windows of which it would be visible, while the lodge itself would offer sweeping views of the castle and the park. The Captain, having planned and measured every detail with great care, now brought up the problem of the road to the village, the dam at the brook, and the raised road behind it. "Building that convenient path to the hilltop," he said, "will produce exactly the quantity of stone required for the dam. As soon as one project links up with another, both become less expensive and can be carried out more quickly."

"And now to my own part in the project," Charlotte said. "We will have to agree upon a definite sum of money; and, as soon as we know how much we will need, we can divide the sum into regular payments, at least monthly, if not weekly. I have the keys to the cashbox; I shall pay the bills and keep the accounts."

"You evidently do not trust us," Eduard said.

"Not so much in an arbitrary matter," Charlotte replied. "We women know better than you how to keep such things in check."

Everything was settled; the work began at once. The Captain was always about, and Charlotte had daily evidence of the seriousness and firmness of his character. He learned to know her better as well; and it was easy for them to work together and to achieve results.

Work is like dancing: those who keep step become indispensable to each other, and a warm mutual sympathy is bound to result; Charlotte really liked the Captain after she knew him better. Indeed, she calmly allowed him to destroy a particularly lovely spot where a bench stood, which did not fit into his plans; although she herself had selected the site and arranged it with taste, she did not even feel the slightest resentment.

chapter 7

SINCE Charlotte was busily engaged in her work
with the Captain, it was only natural that Eduard looked
more frequently to Ottilie for companionship. He had, in
any case, been attracted to her by a quiet and friendly feeling for some time past. She was helpful and polite to everyone; but his vanity made him believe that she was more attentive to him than to others. There was no question that she
knew by now exactly what food he preferred and how it
should be prepared; how much sugar he liked in his tea;
many other such trifles did not escape her attention. She was
particularly careful to shut out drafts, to which he was
abnormally sensitive and about which he was often at odds
with his wife, who never had enough fresh air. Ottilie also
had a good knowledge of trees and flowers. She tried to accomplish whatever he desired; she tried to prevent anything
that might try his patience. Soon she was as indispensable to
him as a guardian angel; and he became restless when she
was not present. She seemed more talkative and open-
hearted when they were alone together.

Even in maturity, Eduard had about him something of
the child to which Ottilie's youth responded eagerly. They
both liked to talk about the days when they had first seen
each other; these memories went back to the first beginnings

of Eduard's love for Charlotte. Ottilie said that she remembered them as the handsomest couple at court; and, when Eduard expressed a doubt that her memory of her earliest childhood could be so clear, she insisted that she remembered perfectly one particular moment, when he had come into the room and she had hidden her face in Charlotte's lap—not from fear but from childish surprise. She might have added that it was because she had immediately liked him so much.

These conditions had brought to a standstill many things which the two men had been accustomed to do together, and it became again necessary for them to look into matters again, to make some drafts and write letters. To attend to this business, they met at their office, where they found the old clerk in involuntary idleness. They set to work and soon had work for him, without realizing that they now left to him many things which they had once done themselves. The first draft which the Captain attempted was not successful; and it was the same with Eduard's first letter. They fretted for a while over a new idea and a new draft, until Eduard, who was not getting on at all, asked what time it was. The Captain had, evidently for the first time in many years, forgotten to wind his chronometer; and both friends seemed at least to feel, if not to realize, that they had begun to be indifferent to time.

While the two men had more or less relaxed in their work, the women's activity increased considerably. The life of an ordinary family revolving as it does around a given group of people and their pursuits, can generally, like a vessel, hold an unusual attachment or a growing passion; and a considerable period of time may pass before this new ingredient causes a noticeable fermentation and all runs foaming over the rim.

In the case of our friends, the effects of their growing mutual sympathies were most agreeable. Their hearts opened, and a feeling of kindliness sprang up. Each member of the group was happy and did not begrudge happiness to the others.

Such a situation lifts up the soul and expands the heart; and everything one does and undertakes faces toward the Infinite. Consequently, the friends were no longer inclined to stay much at home; and they extended their walks farther and farther. Eduard would hurry ahead with Ottilie, to lead the way and find new paths, while the Captain slowly followed with Charlotte, in serious conversation, frequently enjoying a newly discovered spot or some unexpected vista.

One day their walk led them from the gate at the right wing of the castle down to the village inn, then across the bridge toward the ponds. They walked along their shores as far as they usually followed the water; farther along, it was not possible to walk by the water's edge, because of the thickly wooded hills and, beyond them, impassable rocks. But Eduard, who had often gone hunting in this region, pushed on with Ottilie, along a grass-grown footpath, knowing well that an old water-mill, hidden between the rocks, could not be far distant. The little-used path soon came to an end, and they found themselves lost in the dense thicket, among the moss-grown boulders. But the churning sound of the mill wheel indicated that the place they were seeking was quite close at hand. They stepped out onto a projecting ledge and saw the quaint, old, black wooden building deep down below them, shaded on all sides by steep rocks and tall trees. Impulsively they decided to climb down over the moss and boulders. Eduard led the way, and when he looked back and saw Ottilie above him, stepping lightly—fearless, confident, and perfectly poised as she followed him from rock to rock—he thought he saw a celestial being hovering above him. When, at a difficult place, she grasped his outstretched hand, or even supported herself on his shoulder, he had to admit that she was most exquisitely feminine. He half wished that she might slip or stumble, so that he could catch her in his arms and press her to his heart. But for more than one reason he would not have done this under any circumstance; he would have been afraid to offend or hurt her.

His reason for this will soon be understood. Arriving at the mill, they sat down at a rustic table under the tall trees. They had sent the miller's wife for a glass of milk, and after the miller had welcomed them, they asked him to go and look for Charlotte and the Captain. Then Eduard began to speak, rather hesitantly: "I must ask you something, Ottilie; forgive me even if you should have to refuse my request. You have made it no secret—and why should you?—that you wear a miniature next to your heart. It is a portrait of your father, an excellent man whom you scarcely knew, and who deserves in every sense a place close to your heart, but forgive me if I suggest that the picture is much too large and awkward; the metal frame with its crystal gives me anxious moments whenever I see you lifting a child or carrying something in your arms; when the carriage sways, when we force our way through tangles of underbrush; or when we climb down the rocks, as we did just now. The possibility that some fall, or accident or other, might prove serious terrifies me. For my sake, remove the miniature from your person—not from your affection, not from your room. Treasure it in your heart; give it the place of honor, I beg of you; display it in your room—only do not wear it so close to your breast. Perhaps my anxiety is exaggerated, but I think it dangerous."

Ottilie sat silent and motionless while Eduard was speaking. Then, without haste, but also without hesitation, turning her eyes more toward Heaven than toward Eduard, she unclasped the chain, removed the miniature, pressed it against her forehead, and handed it to her friend with the words, "Do keep it for me until we reach home. I cannot give you a better proof of my gratitude for your kind concern."

Eduard did not dare to raise the picture to his lips; but he took her hand and pressed it to his eyes. They were the two most beautiful hands that had ever joined. He felt a weight lifted from his mind, as if a wall between Ottilie and himself had fallen.

With the miller as their guide, Charlotte and the Captain came down by an easier road. There was a general welcome and exchange of pleasantries; they, too, sat down and took some refreshment. No one wished to return the way they had come; and Eduard proposed to lead them by a path through the rocks, on the other side of the brook, where they could see the ponds again. The walking was not easy at first; they went through woods and thickets, and saw, down in the countryside, a great number of villages, large and small; dairy farms surrounded by green pastures and fertile fields; and, higher up, a farm snugly nestled in the woods. From the height which they had gradually ascended, they had a fine view in all directions of this rich terrain. Here they entered a pretty grove and, on leaving it, found themselves on the rock opposite the castle.

How delighted they were to have arrived there so unexpectedly! They had made a journey round a little world; they now stood on the site planned for the new building and looked once more at the windows of the castle.

They went down to the summer house, and, for the first

time, all four of them sat down together in it. Nothing was more natural than for them all to express the wish that the rather difficult path they had followed today, should be laid out so that they could take a leisurely stroll along it with friends and guests. Each offered suggestions; and they estimated that the road which had taken them several hours to walk, could, if well constructed, bring them in no more than an hour from the castle and back again. But when they began to make plans for a bridge below the mill, where the brook ran into the ponds—a bridge which would shorten the walk and be an added ornament to the landscape—Charlotte gently stopped their inventive imaginings, reminding them of the expense involved in such an undertaking.

"That need not worry us!" Eduard exclaimed. "That pleasant little farm in the woods brings in very little rent; let's sell it and use the money for this project. The interest of well-invested capital will then add to the enjoyment of our delightful walks. As it is now, when we settle our accounts at the end of the year, the pitifully small income from that farm merely annoys us."

Even Charlotte, who was a thrifty housewife, could not say much against this plan. The whole matter of selling the farm had already been discussed. The Captain was for parceling out the land among the peasants of the forest; but Eduard wanted a shorter and simpler transaction. The present tenant, who already had made a first bid for the farm, should have it and pay for it in installments; and gradually, as the money came in, they would carry out the planned construction, step by step.

Such a reasonable and prudent arrangement was approved by all. In their imagination the friends saw the new paths winding along and all the charming retreats and lovely views they were hoping for.

64

In order to bring everything vividly to their minds in complete detail, they spread out the new map again that evening. Now once more they could follow with their eyes the road they had taken; and they wondered whether it could not be improved by relocating it here and there. All previous projects were again discussed and brought into line with their latest schemes. The site of the new building opposite the castle was again approved; and they decided that the circuit of paths leading up to it should end there.

Ottilie had not said one word the whole time, so that Eduard at last moved the map, which had been spread out before Charlotte, over to her, at the same time inviting her to give her opinion. When she still hesitated, he warmly encouraged her to speak out. "Nothing has been settled yet," he said. "We are still just making plans."

"I would build the lodge here," said Ottilie, indicating the highest level of the hill. "It is true that you cannot see the castle from there, since it is hidden by a little grove, but, to make up for that, you will be, as it were, in another and a new world, because the village with all its houses is also hidden. The view of the ponds, the mill, the hills and the mountains, and the country below is extremely beautiful; I noticed it as we came along."

"She is right!" exclaimed Eduard. "How could we have overlooked it! This is what you mean, isn't it, Ottilie?" he said. He took a pencil, and with bold strokes, drew an oblong on the crest of the hill.

It broke the Captain's heart to see his carefully and neatly drawn map defaced in this way; but, after a slight disapproving remark, he controlled himself and took up Ottilie's suggestion. "Ottilie is right," he said. "Don't we enjoy a long carriage ride just to get a cup of coffee or walk a long distance to eat fish which would not have tasted half so well at home? It is a change we seek—and unfamiliar things. Your ancestors exercised good judgment in building the castle on this site; here it is protected against the winds, and everything you need is close at hand. A building designed more for entertainment and recreation than as a residence, however, will be very appropriate on the height and will permit us to spend most agreeable hours there in summertime."

The more they discussed the plan, the better it seemed; and Eduard could not conceal his triumph that it had been Ottilie's idea. He was as proud as though it had been his own.

chapter 8

EARLY the next morning the Captain went up to examine the place they had chosen. He first made a rough sketch and, after all of them had confirmed their decision on the site, he completed a plan, with an estimate of costs and requirements. They began preparations immediately. Negotiations leading to the sale of the farm were taken up again. Both men found renewed energy for their activities.

The Captain reminded Eduard that it would be a courtesy—almost an obligation—to celebrate Charlotte's birthday with the laying of the cornerstone. It was not too difficult to overcome Eduard's former antipathy against such celebrations, for it suddenly occurred to him that then they could celebrate Ottilie's birthday, which came later, as well.

Charlotte took the whole project and everything it involved very seriously indeed, for she thought it important and almost hazardous; she was always busy with estimates, contracts, and payments. The friends saw less of each other during the day, and looked forward with much greater eagerness to their evening meetings.

Meanwhile Ottilie had become almost absolute mistress of the household. With her quiet and reliable ways, how could it have been otherwise! She was, moreover, by nature inclined rather toward the house and domestic affairs than toward social and outdoor life. Eduard soon noticed that she accompanied them on their walks only to be agreeable and that she stayed outdoors longer in the evening only because she thought it the proper thing to do; she sometimes even tried to find an excuse to go inside again because of some household task. He soon succeeded in arranging their excursions together so that they were home before sunset. He also resumed his former habit of reading poems aloud, preferring those which expressed a pure yet passionate love.

In the evening they usually gathered around a small table in their customary places: Charlotte on the sofa, Ottilie opposite her in a chair, the men completing the circle. Ottilie sat at the right of Eduard, who moved the lamp closer to her when he was reading. Then Ottilie would move a little closer to him and look into his book, because she trusted her own eyes more than the lips of another; and Eduard would also move closer, so she could see more easily. He even paused frequently, longer than was necessary, in order not to turn the page before she had finished reading it.

This did not escape Charlotte and the Captain; and they often exchanged a smile over it; but both were really surprised by still another indication which, once, betrayed Ottilie's secret affection.

On one occasion, when boring visitors had spoiled the better part of an evening, Eduard suggested that they not retire quite yet. He felt in the mood to play his flute, which he had long neglected. Charlotte looked for the sonatas they usually played together; when she could not find them, Ottilie, after some hesitation, confessed that she had taken them to her room.

"Then you *can*—you *will*—accompany me at the piano?" cried Eduard, his eyes shining. "I think I can," Ottilie replied. She brought the music and sat down at the piano. Charlotte and the Captain were attentive and were surprised to note how perfectly Ottilie had learned her part but, still more, how well she adapted her accompaniment to Eduard's playing. "Adapt" is not quite the right word in this case. With Charlotte, everything had depended on her skill and her own free will to slow down in one part and accelerate the tempo in another, sometimes hesitating, sometimes racing ahead, to please her husband; but Ottilie, who had heard the couple play the sonata several times, seemed to have studied it entirely from the viewpoint of Eduard's rendition. She had made his shortcomings so much her own that they played in unison; although the tempo was quite wrong, the performance still sounded extremely harmonious and pleasant. The composer himself would have enjoyed hearing his work altered in such a mistaken but sincere way.

Charlotte and the Captain silently observed this strange and unprecedented performance with the emotion we often experience when we watch childish behavior we cannot approve because of its disquieting consequences, but which we cannot condemn, and sometimes even must envy. For between these two, as between Ottilie and Eduard, there was growing a tender affection which was perhaps even more dangerous since they were both more serious, more self-possessed, and more capable of controlling themselves. The Captain had already begun to feel that a strong attachment threatened to draw him irresistibly to Charlotte. He forced himself to avoid her and did not visit the new grounds at the hours she was accustomed to be there. He got up very early, gave his orders, and then retired to work in his wing of the castle. At first Charlotte thought this absence accidental and looked for him in all the places he might possibly be. But later she thought she understood his reasons, and her respect for him increased.

Although the Captain avoided being alone with Charlotte, he was no less eager to push forward the work on the paths, so that all would be ready for the grand celebration of her birthday. When he was constructing the path along the more gentle slope at the bottom, coming up from the rear of the village, he also had a crew of men building the upper part, while he pretended they were merely breaking stones; and he had arranged and timed everything so exactly that the two pathways would be joined on the eve of the birthday. The foundation for the new house on the hill had been started but not completed; and a fine cornerstone had been hewn out, with hollow spaces and a slab to cover them.

These overt activities and many small, covert schemes, as well as more or less repressed emotions, did not make for a very lively conversation when the four were together; so that Eduard, who felt that something was lacking, asked the Captain one evening to bring his violin and play while Charlotte accompanied him at the piano, to which the Captain readily agreed. To the great pleasure of themselves and their listeners, he and Charlotte played a difficult work with feeling, gusto, and ease. They promised to play together more often and to practice.

"They play better than we do, Ottilie!" Eduard said. "We will admire them; but we can have a good time, too!"

chapter 9

THE birthday arrived, and everything was ready. The whole length of the built-up road was now safe from the waters of the brook behind its dam, as was the road past the church, which followed for a time the path Charlotte had laid out, and then, winding through the rocks, ran first below the summer house to the right and later, after curving upward, overlooked it to the left and gradually reached the crest of the hill.

Many guests had arrived for this festive day. Everyone went first to church, where the whole congregation was waiting, dressed in holiday best. After the service, all of them formed a procession, headed by the smaller boys, the young men, and the older men; then came the master and mistress of the castle with their guests and servants, with the little girls, maidens and married women following at the end.

Where the road rounded the curve, the Captain had arranged a seat in the rocks; and he asked Charlotte and her guests to stop here and rest. From this point they could see the whole length of the road, the group of men who walked ahead, and the women who were now passing. The weather was lovely; the entire picture very impressive. Charlotte was surprised and moved; she pressed the Captain's hand affectionately.

They and their guests followed the slowly ascending crowd which was forming a circle around the site of the new building. Eduard, his family and friends, and the most distinguished of the guests were invited to step down into the excavated space where the cornerstone, propped up on one side, lay ready. A mason, in holiday attire, his trowel in one hand, his hammer in the other, made a handsome speech in well-turned verse, which can only be inadequately rendered here in prose.

"Three things are very important in building a house," he began; "first, that it stand in the right place; second, that it be well founded; and, third, that it be well built. The first requirement is really the responsibility of the man who has the house built. Just as in the city the ruler and the community alone can decide where a house shall stand, so it is the privilege of the lord of the manor to say: Here I want my house and nowhere else!"

Eduard and Ottilie did not dare to exchange a glance, although they stood exactly opposite each other.

"The third requirement, the building of the house, is the concern of many crafts and trades; nearly all of them share in the work. But the second requirement, the laying of the foundation, is the mason's affair and, to speak quite frankly, the most important part of the whole undertaking. It is a serious matter, and our invitation to you is solemn, because this festive act takes place in the depths of the earth. Here, in this narrow space we have dug, you do us the honor of appearing as witnesses to an act of mystery. Soon we shall lower this well-hewn stone; and shortly this excavation, now adorned by lovely and distinguished guests, will no longer be accessible; it will be filled in.

"This stone, its corner a symbol of the right angle of the corner of the building, its rectangular shape a symbol of its regularity, and its horizontal and perpendicular position a symbol of the right angles of all the walls and partitions— this cornerstone might now be laid as it is without delay, since its own weight will keep it in place. Nevertheless, we shall use mortar to cement it; just as human beings, drawn to each other by natural inclinations, are better joined when the law binds them, stones, too, even though they are already shaped to fit, are better joined by a binding force. But since it is not becoming to be idle among busy people, you will surely not refuse to assist us here in our work."

With these words he gave his trowel to Charlotte, who threw mortar beneath the stone. Several others were invited to do likewise; and then the stone was put into place. After this Charlotte and the others in turn took the hammer and, with three taps, blessed the union of the stone with the earth.

"The work of the mason," the orator continued, "done openly here, is almost always carried on in obscurity and is destined to remain in obscurity. The carefully constructed foundations will be covered when the ground around them is leveled, and nobody will be reminded of us not even by the testimony of the walls we build above ground. The work of the stone-cutter and the stone-carver is more conspicious; and we masons are even expected to approve that the plasterer completely effaces our handiwork with stucco and paint. Is it not important for the mason, therefore, even more than for other workmen, to turn out work that satisfies himself? Who has more reason to feel his own worth? After the house is built, the floors leveled and tiled, the outer walls adorned with ornaments, he can still discern, beneath all this later work the carefully and accurately joined stones of his masonry, to which the whole building owes its existence and support.

"But just as the man who has done an evil deed must live in fear lest it come to light some day, so the man who has done good in secret may expect to be rewarded openly. And by the same token, we declare this cornerstone to be a memorial stone as well. Here in these pockets of varying sizes hollowed out of the stone, objects will be preserved to bear witness of this act to later generations. These sealed metal cases contain handwritten documents; on these metal plates sundry memorable legends are graven; in these fine bottles we immure the choicest old wine with the date of its vintage; here also are coins of many kinds, minted this year; and all these are contributed by the generous master whose house we build. There is still room left; do some of the guests or spectators care to dedicate something to posterity?"

There was a pause, and the young orator looked around; but, as is so often the case on such occasions, no one was prepared, and everyone was taken by surprise. After a bit a jaunty young officer said, "If I am to contribute anything that is not as yet represented among these memorial objects, it will have to be a button or two from my uniform, and I believe these deserve to be handed down to posterity!" This was no sooner said than done. Soon others began to contribute. The women did not hesitate to drop in sidecombs, scent-bottles and other trinkets and jewelry. Only Ottilie still hesitated; she was preoccupied with watching the others until Eduard roused her. Then she unclasped from her neck the gold chain on which she had carried her father's picture and laid it down gently with the other jewelry; whereupon Eduard hastily ordered the cover to be placed on the cornerstone and sealed.

74

The young mason who had taken an active part in this procedure, resumed the rostrum and continued: "We lay this stone for eternity, as an earnest of a long happy life for the present and future owners of this house.

"But in committing these treasures to the earth so carefully, we emphasize the frailty of human existence! We are thinking that this tightly sealed cover may again be lifted, which could happen only if the whole house, as yet unbuilt, were destroyed.

"But just for that reason—because we are confident that it will be built—let us turn our thoughts from the future back to the present. After this celebration, let us resume our work at once, making ready for the other trades which will build on top of our foundations; so that the house will rise quickly to its completion, and the master of this house, his family and his guests may enjoy the view from windows yet to be provided. And now let us drink to their health and to that of all who are present!" With these words he emptied a fine crystal goblet at one draught and flung it into the air, wishing to express the fullness of his joy by breaking the glass used on this happy occasion. But this time fate would have it otherwise; the glass did not crash to the ground, though it was no miracle that saved it from destruction.

To speed the construction of the building, the opposite corner of the foundation had already been completely excavated; here the walls had been started and scaffolding built.

For today's ceremony boards had been laid across the scaffolding for a number of spectators to stand on; but mainly to accommodate the workmen. The glass flew in that direction and was caught by one of the men, who took this as an especially lucky sign for himself. He kept the glass in his own hands, but he let the bystanders look at it; and all

75

could see the letters *E* and *O* worked into a graceful mono-
gram; it was one of the glasses which had been made for
Eduard as a child.

The workmen had now left the scaffolding, and the more
agile guests climbed up to look about; they expressed themselves enthusiastically about the view. How true it is that
we can discover so many new things from a point of vantage
only a very little higher than the one we have been accustomed to. Deep in the countryside, several new villages
came into view; one could also follow the silvery bends of
the river; someone even insisted that he could see the spires
of the city. On turning round, one saw, behind the wooded
hills, the blue summits of a distant range of mountains rising
into the sky; and the whole country immediately below
could be taken in at a glance. "To make the view perfect,
the three ponds should be made into one lake!" one of the
guests exclaimed.

"That could well be done," the Captain said. "In earlier
times they actually were one lake."

"But I should like to have you spare my grove of plane
and poplar trees, which are so beautiful standing there by
the middle pond," said Eduard. He turned to Ottilie, led her
a few steps forward, and pointed downward. "Look; it was
I who planted those trees."

"And how long ago was that?" asked Ottilie.

"They are just about your age," Eduard replied. "Yes, my
dear child, I planted them when you were still a babe in
arms."

The party returned to the castle. After dinner, they were
invited for a walk through the village, to look at the new
work that had been carried out there. At a suggestion from
the Captain, the villagers had gathered in front of their
houses. They did not stand in a row as if at attention but

rather in natural family groups; some busy with work they usually did in the evening, others resting on the new benches. They had been urged to consider it a pleasant duty to appear at their best on Sundays and holidays, with a special emphasis on order and good behavior.

A congenial atmosphere, such as prevailed among these four friends, is always unpleasantly disturbed by the intrusion of a large number of people. They were much relieved to find themselves alone once more in the big hall. But their regained privacy was soon interrupted when a letter was delivered to Eduard, with the news that yet other guests would arrive on the following day.

"Just as we thought!" Eduard called to Charlotte. "The Count won't stay away; he is coming tomorrow."

"Then the Baroness is not too far away," Charlotte replied.

"You are right!" said Eduard. "She will also arrive tomorrow, from the other direction. Both ask us to put them up for a night, as they will leave together the following day!"

"Then we must begin preparations at once, Ottilie," Charlotte said.

"How do you want me to arrange things?", asked Ottilie. Charlotte gave her some general directions, and Ottilie left the room.

The Captain inquired about the relationship of these two persons whom he knew only casually. Many years ago, these two had fallen madly in love with each other, although both were already married. The wrecking of two marriages had nearly led to a scandal. They resorted to divorce. The Baroness succeeded, but not so the Count. For the sake of appearance, they could not be seen together, but their relationship remained unchanged. Unable to be together in the city during the winter season, they made up for this in

77

the summer, traveling together and visiting the same watering places. They were both a little older than Eduard and Charlotte, with whom they had become close friends at Court years ago. Eduard and Charlotte had remained loyal to the Count and the Baroness, although they did not approve of everything they did. This was the first time that Charlotte had found their visit particularly inconvenient; and if she had examined her reasons closely, she would have discovered that it was on account of Ottilie. She did not want the young girl to be exposed to this sort of informal relationship so early in life.

"They really might have stayed away a few days longer, until we had finished the business about the farm," Eduard said, just as Ottilie returned. "The draft of the deed of sale is ready, and I have one copy of it here; but the second is not yet done, and our old clerk is seriously ill." The Captain offered his assistance, and so did Charlotte, but there were objections to their helping.

"Please, let me do it!" cried Ottilie, eagerly.

"You will not be able to finish it in time," Charlotte said.

"I absolutely must have it early the day after tomorrow; and it is a long document," Eduard added.

"It *will* be ready!" Ottilie exclaimed and took the paper.

The next morning while they watched from an upstairs window for their guests, so that they would be on hand to greet them, Eduard said: "Who is that man on horseback riding so slowly up the road in our direction?" The Captain described him in some detail. "Yes, that is he," Eduard said; "the details which you can see better than I, correspond to what I can make out. It is Mittler! But why is Mittler, of all people, riding slowly, so slowly?" The rider came nearer, and indeed it was Mittler. They welcomed him cordially as he came slowly up the steps to the entrance.

"Why didn't you come yesterday?" Eduard called down to him.

"Noisy parties are not to my liking," Mittler replied. "Instead I have come now to celebrate yesterday's birthday quietly with you."

"Are you sure you can spare the time?" asked Eduard, laughing.

"For my visit you are indebted—if you consider yourselves indebted at all—to a thought that crossed my mind yesterday. I was happily spending several hours in a home where I had restored peace and happiness, when I heard of your birthday celebration. It is downright selfish, I said to myself, for you to insist on enjoying yourself only with people you have persuaded to live in concord. Why don't you go and enjoy yourself, for once, with friends who live peaceably and go on living peaceably? No sooner said than done! I made up my mind, and here I am!"

"Yesterday you would have found a large gathering here; today you will only find a small one," Charlotte said. "We are expecting the Count and the Baroness, who have already given you a great deal of trouble."

At these words the crotchety little man darted out of the circle of his welcoming friends, and looked for his hat and riding crop. "My unlucky star always rises whenever I try to relax and enjoy myself. Why don't I stick to my business? I never should have come here; and I certainly can't stay, for I shall never abide under the same roof with those two! And I warn you all—be careful! They bring nothing but trouble; their nature acts like a ferment that corrupts and contaminates everything it touches."

They tried to calm him, but without success. "He who attacks marriage," he exclaimed, "who undermines by word or by action this foundation of all moral society, is my enemy wherever I find him; and if I cannot defeat him, at least I shall have nothing to do with him. Marriage is the Alpha and Omega of all civilization. It makes the savage gentle; and the gentility of the most civilized finds its highest expression in marriage. It must be indissoluble because it brings with it such an abundance of happiness, that the occasional moments of unhappiness scarcely weigh in the balance. And why all this talk about unhappiness? It is the impatience that grips men from time to time which makes them indulge in a feeling of unhappiness. If you let time cure your impatience you will rejoice at finding this long-standing relationship still intact. There is no plausible reason for divorce. Life is brimming over with pleasure and pain; no married couple can calculate their debt to each other. It is an infinite debt and can only be paid in eternity. Marriage is a burden; I can well believe that, and so it should be. Are we not also married to our consciences; and do we not often wish to rid ourselves of them, because they are even more of a burden, than a husband or a wife could ever be?"

He continued to speak with great vehemence and would not have stopped had not the sound of the postilions' horn announced the arrival of the visitors, who, as if by previous arrangement, drove at the same moment into the castle yard from different directions. When their hosts hurried down to receive them, Mittler slipped away, ordered his horse brought to the inn, and left in a very black mood.

chapter 10

THE guests were welcomed and escorted into the house. They were delighted to be back once more after so long a time in a place where they formerly had spent so many happy days. Eduard and Charlotte, too, were very glad to see them again. The Count as well as the Baroness had that sort of tall and handsome presence which is at its best not so much in youth as in middle life, when, as a compensation for youth's fresh energy, attractiveness is coupled with the ability to inspire confidence. They were very agreeable guests. Their easy way of accepting and shaping the events of their lives, their continued good spirits and evident freedom from any embarrassment, were immediately infectious; and with scrupulous good taste they never overstepped the bounds of decorum while they never seemed to feel the least constraint.

The effect on everyone could be immediately observed. The new arrivals, fresh from the great world, as their dress, their belongings, and everything about them showed, somehow contrasted with their friends' rural life and their hidden emotional state, a contrast which, however, faded in the exchange of old memories and new interests; and they all joined at once in an animated conversation.

But it was not long before they separated. The ladies retired to their own wing, where they found enough to keep them occupied: mutual confidences and the latest styles and patterns in morning robes and hats and such; while the men were busy looking at the new coaches, having the horses trotted out, and beginning at once to bargain and trade.

They did not meet again until dinner. Everyone had dressed, and again the newcomers showed to advantage. Everything they wore was new and rather unusual to their friends, but their way of wearing it made it natural and very becoming.

The conversation was lively and touched on a great variety of topics, for everything and nothing seems interesting in the company of such people. They all spoke French, so they could speak freely in front of the servants; with ease and a touch of malice they discussed great issues and issues not so great. The conversation had dealt with one particular subject for an undesirably long time, when Charlotte inquired about a childhood friend, and heard, with amazement, that she would soon get her divorce.

"It is distressing," Charlotte said, "suddenly to hear of misfortunes which have befallen acquaintances we thought comfortably settled, or that a dear friend we thought provided for is in difficulties and is forced to begin a new life— perhaps an insecure one."

"After all, my dear, it is our own fault if that sort of thing surprises us," the Count replied. "We rather indulge ourselves in imagining that human institutions, and particularly the institution of marriage, are extremely stable. The comedies which we see so often are misleading; they tempt our imagination away from the realities of the world. In a comedy we see marriage as an ultimate goal, reached only after surmounting obstacles which fill several acts; and, at the moment when this goal is achieved, the curtain falls and a momentary satisfaction warms our hearts. But it is quite different in life. The play goes on behind the scenes, and, when the curtain rises again, we would rather not see or hear any more of it."

"It cannot be as bad as that," said Charlotte, smiling. "We often see that people who have made their exit from this stage would very much like to reappear in a new role."

"There is nothing wrong with that," said the Count. "We always like to play a new part, and, knowing the world, we know that the difficulty, in a world which is ever changing, merely arises from the unchanging and unending character of marriage. One of my friends who generally shows his good humor by suggesting new laws, maintained that every marriage should be contracted only for five years. It is, he said, a fine, odd, and sacred number and a period just long enough in which to get to know each other, have a child or two, quarrel, and—the best part!—become reconciled again. He used to exclaim: How happy the first part of that period would be! Two or three years at least would be sheer bliss! After that, one of the partners would probably want to prolong the relationship, and the nearer the end of the five years came, the more amiable he or she would grow. The indifferent or even dissatisfied partner would gradually be reconciled and charmed, and both of them would forget that time was swiftly running out—just as we forget the passage of time in good company—and it would be a pleasant surprise when they realized, only after the term had expired, that they had tacitly extended it."

Charming and amusing as all this sounded—and it had a deeper moral significance which did not escape Charlotte—she was uneasy about the conversation because of Ottilie's presence. She was very well aware that nothing is more dangerous than too candid a discussion of an improper, or at least questionable, situation as though it were not at all unusual, taken for granted, and even praiseworthy; any attack on marriage certainly belonged in that category. In her tactful way she tried to turn the conversation to other subjects; but she was unsuccessful and was sorry now that Ottilie had arranged everything so well that there was no reason for her to leave the table. The quiet and observant girl gave her orders to the butler by a look and a nod; and everything went smoothly and without incident, although there were two new men in servants' livery who were still clumsy at waiting on table.

The Count did not understand Charlotte's covert suggestions and continued to express himself on the same subject. His conversation was not usually tiresome, but the whole matter weighed heavily on his mind; and his difficulties in obtaining a divorce from his wife had made him bitter about everything connected with marriage, even though, after all, he desired just that so passionately for himself and the Baroness.

"The same friend," he went on, "made another legal suggestion. A marriage should be declared indissoluble only if both parties, or at least one of them, had been married twice before, for such persons have conclusively demonstrated that they regard marriage as indispensable. Furthermore, their behavior in their previous marriages would be known, and so would their peculiarities, which actually cause more divorces than do bad dispositions. It is therefore necessary to make mutual investigation and to observe married as well as unmarried people closely, for no one knows how a marriage may turn out."

"That would, of course, make social life more interesting," said Eduard. "As it is now, as soon as we are married, nobody cares any longer about our virtues or our vices."

"Under such an arrangement," the Baroness said with a smile, "Our dear hosts, who already have passed the first two stages successfully, could be making their preparations for a third."

"They have been very lucky," said the Count. "In their case, death was willing to do what the law courts do only reluctantly."

"Let the dead rest!" said Charlotte, rather gravely.

"Why should we," the Count asked, "when we can speak of them with admiration? They were modest enough to be satisfied with a few years, in return for all the good they left behind."

"If only," said the Baroness, suppressing a sigh, "such cases did not require the sacrifice of our best years."

"Quite," the Count agreed. "It would be enough to drive one mad if it were not for the fact that, as a rule, very few things in life turn out as we hoped they might. Children do not fulfil expectations, and young people rarely do—and, if they do fulfil their early promise, the world does not keep its promises to them."

Charlotte, glad that the conversation had at last changed, replied gaily; "Well, after all, we have to get used to enjoying the good things of life as they come."

"Certainly," the Count again agreed. "You two have enjoyed some wonderful years. When I think of the time when you and Eduard were the most handsome couple at Court—nowadays there is nothing to compare with that brilliant time and those distinguished personalities. When you two danced together, all eyes followed you and paid you homage while you only saw each other!"

"So much has changed since then," Charlotte said, "that we can listen to such flattering words in all modesty."

"I admit that I was often privately inclined to blame Eduard for his lack of persistence," the Count continued, "for his unreasonable parents would probably have finally relented; and it is no small matter to regain ten years of one's youth."

"I must defend Eduard," interposed the Baroness. "Charlotte was not completely blameless, nor above occasional coquetry. Although she loved Eduard with all her heart and secretly thought of him as her future husband, I saw how often she worried the life out of him, so that he was easily rushed into an unfortunate decision to travel, to get away from her, to try to forget her."

Eduard nodded to the Baroness and seemed grateful for her defense.

"But I must say something in Charlotte's defense, too," the Baroness went on. "The man who was paying court to her then had long displayed his affection for her and when you knew him well, he was far more lovable than the rest of you want to admit."

"My dear," said the Count with a touch of spirit, "you should also confess that he was not wholly indifferent to you and that Charlotte had more to fear from you than from any other woman. I think it a very charming quality in women that they can be so steadfastly attached to one man and that no sort of separation suspends or banishes such an attachment."

"This charming quality may be even more frequent in men," the Baroness retorted. "In your case, at least, my dear, I have noticed that no one has more influence over you than a woman of whom you once were fond. I have seen you go to more trouble to oblige such a person than you ever would for your present friend."

"I take a reproach like that as a compliment," the Count replied. "And as for Charlotte's first husband—I disliked him simply because he separated two fine persons—a really predestined couple who, once they were married, would have had no reason to be afraid of those five years or to think of a second marriage, much less a third."

"We shall try to make up for what we missed," Charlotte said.

"Then you must stick to it," warned the Count. "Your first marriages were of the kind which is really the most objectionable," he continued, almost passionately. "Unfortunately, most marriages have something awkward about them, if you will forgive my putting it so strongly; they spoil the most delicate relationships, merely because of the gross assurance which at least one of the partners will exhibit. Everything becomes a matter of course; and two people seem to have come together only so that both can then go their own ways."

At this moment Charlotte, who was determined to stop this sort of talk once and for all, managed to change the subject completely. They began a conversation about matters of general interest in which Eduard, Charlotte, and the Captain could join; and even Ottilie was asked for her opinion. They were in an excellent humor when dessert arrived, and the gaiety was greatly stimulated by the table decorations: a profusion of fruit in pretty baskets, and handsome bowls and vases filled with beautifully arranged flowers of all colors.

The changes in the park were also discussed, and, after dinner, they went out to look at them. Ottilie did not come with them; she said she had something to do in the house; but actually she sat down to go on with her copying. The Count fell into conversation with the Captain, and Charlotte later joined them. When they had reached the top of the hill, and the Captain had obligingly hurried back to fetch his map, the Count said to Charlotte, "I like this man very well indeed. He is well informed and has a logical mind. His work, also, seems to be well planned and systematic. Accomplishments of the sort he has achieved here would be very important in a larger field of action." Charlotte listened with secret delight to the Count's praise; she did not betray her feelings but merely agreed calmly and without elaboration. She was, however, completely taken aback when the Count continued: "I have met this man at just the right time. I know of a position which will suit him perfectly and make him happy. At the same time I can do one of my friends, a person of high rank, a great favor."

Charlotte was thunderstruck. The Count did not notice it, for women, used to controlling themselves at all times, maintain an apparent composure even in the most extraordinary circumstances. But she did not hear the Count's next remarks. "When I make up my mind about something, I always act quickly. My letter is already composed in my mind, and I am anxious to write it down. Please order me a mounted courier—I want to send the letter off tonight."

Charlotte's heart was torn by conflicting emotions. She was so overwhelmed by the Count's proposal and by her own reaction to it that she was unable to utter a single word. Fortunately, the Count went on talking about his plans for the Captain; and Charlotte saw their advantages only too clearly. Just then the Captain returned and unrolled his map before the Count. How different were her feelings as she looked at the friend she was soon to lose! She bowed slightly, turned, and hurried back to the summer house. Before she was halfway there a stream of tears gushed from her eyes; she rushed into the little hermitage and, sheltered by its four narrow walls, completely surrendered to a grief, a passion, a despair, which she would not have dreamed possible a few moments before.

Meanwhile Eduard had walked along the shores of the ponds with the Baroness. That astute lady, who evidently liked to know all about everything, soon noticed, when she put out her feelers, that Eduard could not stop singing Ottilie's praises. She drew him out gradually with apparently casual questions, and finally was quite convinced that this was no budding passion, but one already full-blown.

Married women, even though they may not like each other, are always tacit allies, particularly against young girls. Her worldly mind quickly foresaw the consequences of such an attachment as Eduard's. That very morning, in a conversation with Charlotte, she had expressed her disapproval of Ottilie's sojourn in the country, particularly because of the girl's quiet disposition. The Baroness had proposed taking Ottilie with her to the city; she had a friend there who spared no expense in the education of her daughter—an only child—and who was very eager to find a congenial companion for her, who would be treated like one of the family and enjoy the same advantages as her own child. Charlotte had promised to think the matter over.

But now, after this glimpse into Eduard's heart, the Baroness' suggestion changed into a firm resolution; and, as she made up her mind, she appeared to become even more sympathetic to Eduard's desires, for no one had more self-control than the Baroness. Self-control at crucial moments accustoms us to maintain outward composure on all occasions. When we have so much control over ourselves, we are inclined to extend it to others as an external compensation for all our inner privations.

This state of mind is usually connected with a secret enjoyment of the blindness of others who walk unsuspectingly into the trap. We enjoy not only our present success but, at the same time, the other person's future embarrassment. The Baroness, therefore, was malicious enough to invite Eduard to come with Charlotte to her estate at the vintage season; and when he asked whether they might bring Ottilie, she gave an answer which he could take to be affirmative, if he chose.

Eduard immediately began to exclaim about that wonderful region—the great river, the hills, rocks and vineyards, the ancient castles, the boating parties, the merrymaking when the grapes were gathered, the wine-pressing, and so on. In the innocence of his heart he exulted, anticipating the impression these scenes would make on Ottilie's fresh and receptive mind. At this moment they saw her coming toward them; and the Baroness quickly warned Eduard that he must not breathe a word about the plan for this autumn visit, for if we look forward to things with too much eagerness, they usually do not happen at all. Eduard promised, but he made her walk more quickly to meet Ottilie, and, when they were quite close, even hurried on ahead. His whole person expressed a warm happiness. He kissed Ottilie's hand and prssed into it a nosegay of wild flowers he had gathered on his walk. The Baroness felt something like bitterness in her heart as she watched. Although she could not approve of the improper side of this affection, she could not bear to see its sweet and pleasant side wasted on so simple and inexperienced a girl.

When they all sat down for supper, the whole atmosphere had changed. The Count, who had already written his letter and sent it off by messenger, had managed to have the Captain beside him at the table, and talked only with him, drawing him out without appearing impolite or inquisitive. The Baroness, at the Count's right, got little attention from him or from Eduard who, first because he was thirsty and then because he was excited, drank more wine than usual and chatted animatedly with Ottilie, whom he had asked to sit by his side. Charlotte, opposite them and next to the Captain, found it almost impossible to hide her emotion.

The Baroness had sufficient time to make her observations. She noticed that Charlotte was not at ease; and, since she herself was preoccupied with Eduard's relation to Ottilie, she was convinced that Charlotte was likewise worried and hurt by her husband's behavior; and she pondered how she could best gain her ends.

Even after supper the private conversations went on. The Count, who wanted to sound the Captain's mind thoroughly, had to resort to many roundabout methods to get what he wanted to know out of him, for the Captain was quiet, reserved and not at all vain. They walked up and down one side of the salon, while Eduard, animated by wine and hope, chattered gaily with Ottilie near a window. Charlotte and the Baroness walked silently up and down the other side of the room. Their continued silence and aimless standing about eventually affected the others. The ladies retired to their rooms, and the men went to theirs in the other wing of the castle; the day seemed to have come to an end.

chapter 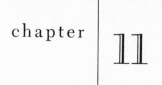 11

EDUARD accompanied the Count to his room and was easily persuaded to stay and talk for a little while. The Count indulged in reminiscences. He had a lively recollection of Charlotte's beauty, and spoke as a connoisseur in describing it. "A pretty foot is a great gift of Nature," he said. "Its graceful charm is imperishable. I watched her as she walked today, and I really felt tempted to kiss her shoe, and to revive a rather barbaric but touching custom of the Slavs, whose highest tribute to a woman they love and admire is to drink to her health from her shoe."

But a pretty foot was not the only object the two old friends praised. From these intimate reflections, they went back to recall old adventures and the difficulties Eduard and Charlotte had met with in those bygone days when they wished to see each other; what efforts they had made, what expedients they had devised to create an opportunity to assure each other of their love.

"Do you remember," said the Count, "how I stood by you as a staunch friend in a certain adventure when Their Highnesses visited their uncle, and we were all together in that big rambling castle? The day had passed with pomp and circumstances and we wanted at least part of the night for a quiet and intimate talk."

"You had made a mental note of the way to the suites of the ladies-in-waiting," said Eduard, "and we arrived safely in my ladylove's room."

"—Who cared more for decorum than for my personal pleasure and had kept a very ugly chaperone with her," sighed the Count, "so that I had a most disagreeable time, while you two enjoyed yourselves, exchanging affectionate looks and words."

"Only yesterday, when we had received word that you were coming, my wife and I reminded each other of that episode and particularly of our retreat," said Eduard. "We took the wrong corridor, and found ourselves in the ante-room where the guards were stationed. Since we knew the way from there, we thought it would be easy to cross the hall and elude the sentinel on duty as well as the other guards. Do you remember our surprise when we opened the door? The whole floor was littered with mattresses on which those giants were stretched out in rows, sleeping. The only man awake was the sentinel on duty; he eyed us with suspicion, but we calmly picked our way among the out-stretched boots—reckless young daredevils that we were—and not one of the snoring Sons of Anak woke up."

"I had a mind to stumble, and sound the alarm," said the Count. "What a strange resurrection we would have wit-nessed!"

At this moment the clock of the castle struck twelve.

"Midnight!" said the Count, smiling. "It is the right hour. Now I must ask a favor of you, my dear fellow. Please guide me, as I once guided you, for I have promised the Baroness to pay her a late visit. During the day we have not had one minute to ourselves. It has been a long time since we have seen each other, and it is only natural that we should long for an hour for privacy. Show me the way; I shall certainly find my way back; in any case, there is no danger of my stumbling over somebody's boots."

"As your host, I'm glad to give you this proof of my friendship," Eduard replied; "but the three ladies are all in the same wing. For all we know, they may be still sitting together, and there is no telling what disturbance we may create."

"Don't worry: the Baroness expects me," the Count said. "At this hour she is most certainly in her room—and alone."

"It is quite easy, anyway," Eduard said, taking up a candle and lighting the Count down a private staircase which led into a long passage, at the end of which he opened a small door. They climbed a winding staircase to a narrow landing, where Eduard gave the candle to the Count and pointed to a concealed door on the right. It opened easily and swallowed up the Count, and Eduard was left in complete darkness.

Another door on the left led into Charlotte's bedroom. He heard voices and listened. Charlotte was talking to her maid: "Has Ottilie gone to bed?"

"No, Madam, she is still downstairs, writing."

"You may light the night lamp and go," said Charlotte. "It is late. I shall put out the candle myself, and I shan't need you any longer."

Eduard was delighted to hear that Ottilie was still at her copying. "She is doing something for me!" he thought proudly. He could almost see her sitting and writing as he stood quite alone here in the enveloping darkness; he imagined himself approaching her, saw her turn her head and look up at him. An irresistible desire to be close to her once more took hold of him. But from where he stood, there was no way down to the floor where she had her room. He was standing directly before his wife's door; a strange confusion of emotions came over him; he tried to turn the knob; he found the door locked and rapped gently. Charlotte did not hear him.

She was nervously walking up and down in the next room, repeating to herself again and again what she had turned over in her mind since she had heard the Count's unexpected suggestion. The figure of the Captain rose up before her. His presence still filled the house; he still enlivened their walks; but soon he would be gone, and nothing left but emptiness. She told herself all the things we can tell ourselves; she even anticipated, as we usually do, the cold comfort that time will heal even such wounds as these. But she dreaded the time needed to heal them, and she dreaded the deadly period when they would be healed.

At last she took refuge in tears, which eased her pain, for she rarely wept. She flung herself on the sofa and completely abandoned herself to her grief. All this time Eduard could not bring himself to move away from the door; he knocked again, and a third time, a little louder, so that Charlotte could hear it quite distinctly in the quiet of the night, and started in alarm. Her first thought was: It could be—it must be—the Captain! Her second: It could not be! She thought it was a delusion; but she had heard it; she hoped she had heard it; and she was afraid she had heard it. She returned to her bedroom and tiptoed to the locked door. She reproached herself for her fears; perhaps the Baroness needed something she told herself, and she called in a composed voice: "Is someone there?"

A hushed voice answered: "It is I."

"Who?" asked Charlotte, not recognizing the voice. For her the Captain was standing on the other side of the door. Now the voice was a little louder: "Eduard." She opened the door, and her husband stood before her. He greeted her with a humorous remark. She managed to answer in the same vein. Then he involved himself in mysterious explanations of his mysterious visit. "Well, let me confess that the real reason for my coming is: I made a vow to kiss your slipper tonight."

"It has been a long time since you thought of doing anything like that," said Charlotte.

"So much the worse," Eduard replied, "and so much the better." She sat down in a deep chair to conceal the lightness of her gown. He knelt down before her, and she could not prevent his kissing her slipper. When the slipper came off in his hand, he clasped her foot, and pressed it lovingly to his heart.

Charlotte was one of those temperate women, who even after marriage continue to behave in the modest manner of loving girls. She never sought to charm her husband; she scarcely encouraged desire; yet without coldness or austerity, she was always rather like an affectionate bride who feels a certain shyness even toward that which is sanctioned. Tonight Eduard found her doubly shy. She fervently wished that her husband would leave, for she kept envisioning the reproachful image of her friend. But her mood rather than repelling Eduard, attracted him all the more strongly. Her expression betrayed her emotions. She had been crying, and tears so unbecoming to weak persons, make those who are normally strong and composed so much the more attractive. Eduard was gentle, affectionate, insisting—he implored her to allow him to stay—he did not demand but, half-serious and half-laughing, tried to persuade her. At last, he simply blew out the candle.

And immediately, in the dim light of the night lamp, their passions and their imaginations asserted their rights over reality. It was Ottilie who was closed in Eduard's embrace;

while the Captain's image—now clearly, now vaguely—hovered before Charlotte. The absent and the present, strangely interwoven, blended in their blissful ecstacy.

But the present will assert itself. They spent part of the night in playful small talk which was quite unrestrained as their hearts had no part in it. But when Eduard woke the next morning, at his wife's side, the day before him seemed ominous; and the sun seemed to illumine a crime. He stole away; and Charlotte found herself alone when she woke.

chapter | 12

WHEN they all met again at breakfast, an acute observer would have been able to discern the innermost thoughts and emotions of each one of them from his or her behavior. The Count and the Baroness conducted themselves like a pair of happy lovers who, after a forced separation, have reassured each other of their mutual affection. Charlotte and Eduard, on the other hand, were almost embarrassed and conscience-stricken as they faced the Captain and Ottilie, for it is the nature of love to recognize no rights but its own; and all other rights vanish before it. Ottilie was as happy as a child; she was almost talkative. The Captain was in a serious mood. Things that had lain undisturbed, even dormant, in him for some time had been stirred up by his conversation with the count, and he had come to realize only too clearly that he was actually neglecting his vocation, wasting his time in idleness disguised as petty activity.

Almost immediately after the Count and the Baroness had left, other visitors arrived. They were quite welcome to Charlotte, who wished to escape from herself and to be diverted, but unwelcome to Eduard, who felt a redoubled desire to devote himself to Ottilie; unwelcome also to Ottilie, who had not yet finished her copy of the document which had to be ready early the next day. She therefore hurried to her room as soon as the last of the visitors had made a late departure.

It was now evening. Eduard, Charlotte, and the Captain walked part of the way with their visitors and saw them into their carriage. They then decided to walk on to the ponds. A boat, which Eduard had ordered at considerable expense from a distant place, had arrived; and they wanted to see if it handled easily.

The boat had been tied up by the shore of the middle pond, not far from a clump of old oak trees which figured in the landscaping plans for this spot. They intended to build a dock here and an elaborate stone seat which could serve as a landmark for people crossing the water.

"And where shall we build the landing on the other side?" Eduard asked. "Near my plane trees, I should think."

"They are a little too far to the right," the Captain replied. "If we can land further down, we shall be nearer the castle. But we must think it over."

The Captain was already standing in the stern of the boat and had taken one oar. Charlotte got in, and Eduard followed, taking the second oar; but as he was just about to shove off, he suddenly thought of Ottilie and realized that this boating trip would delay him and that there was no telling when he would get home! He made a quick decision, jumped back to the shore, passed the oar over to the Captain, and with a casual excuse hurried toward the castle.

When he arrived there, he was told that Ottilie had locked her door and was writing. Although it was agreeable to know that she was working in his behalf, he was most disappointed not to see her. His impatience increased from moment to moment. He paced up and down the big hall; he picked up this and that; but nothing held his interest for

99

long. He wanted to see her, to see her alone, before Charlotte and the Captain returned. Night had fallen, and the candles were lighted. At last Ottilie came in, radiant with loveliness. The feeling that she had done something for her friend had given her a certain pride in herself. She laid the document and her copy on the table before Eduard. "Shall we check this together?" she asked, smiling. Eduard was at a loss for an answer. He looked at her; he looked at the copy. The first pages were meticulously written in a delicate feminine hand; but then her writing seemed to have changed, to have become less cramped and more flowing; and how surprised he was when he ran his eye over the last pages.

"For heaven's sake!" he exclaimed. "What's this? It's my own handwriting!" He looked at Ottilie and again at the written pages; the end, particularly, looked as though he had written it himself. Ottilie did not utter a word, but in her eyes was an expression of deep happiness. Eduard stretched out his arms. "You love me!" he cried out. "Ottilie, you love me!" And they were in each other's arms. It was impossible to tell who had embraced the other first.

From this moment the world was changed for Eduard. He was not the same, and life was not the same. They stood face to face; he held her hands. They lost themselves in each other's eyes and were on the point of embracing again when Charlotte entered with the Captain; both of them were apologizing for having been delayed so long. Eduard smiled to himself. "Oh, how much too early you did come!" he thought.

They sat down to supper and talked about the day's visitors. Eduard, elated by love and happiness, had a good word to say for everyone—always kind and often favorable. Charlotte, who did not entirely agree with him, noticed his generous mood and chaffed him that he who usually made such biting comments after visitors had left was so mild and tolerant today.

Eduard exclaimed, with passionate sincerity, "If only you love one person with all your heart, everybody seems lovable."

Ottilie did not look up, and Charlotted looked straight ahead. Then the Captain took up the subject: "I think the same thing is true of our feelings of respect and admiration. Only after we have had a chance to experience such feelings in respect to one particular object do we learn to recognize what is really valuable in the world."

Charlotte retired to her room as early as she could, for she wished to abandon herself to the memory of everything that had happened tonight to her and the Captain.

When Eduard had jumped from the boat and shoved it off, leaving his wife and his friend to the mercies of the unstable element, Charlotte found herself face to face in the twilight with the man for whom she had secretly suffered so much, and who was now rowing the boat about easily with both oars. A deep sadness, such as she had seldom felt, overcame her. The boat's circling movement, the splash of the oars, the faint breeze rippling the mirror of the water, the rustle of the reeds, the last hovering flight of birds, the flickering of the stars and their reflections in the water—all this seemed unreal in the surrounding stillness. It seemed as though her friend were rowing her far away and would set her on shore somewhere and leave her there alone. Strange feelings stirred in her, but she could not weep.

Meanwhile the Captain was explaining to her his ideas for further improvements to the estate. He praised the boat, which handled easily with one person at the oars. He suggested that if she learned to row, she might find it very pleasant, at times, to float on the water alone—her own boatman and pilot.

When he said this, she was struck again by the threat of imminent separation from him. "Is he saying all this on purpose?" she wondered. "Does he know already, or did he just happen to say that, without realizing that his words seal my fate?" A deep melancholy descended on her, mixed with impatience. She asked him to pull to shore as soon as possible and return to the castle with her. It was the first time the Captain had been out on this pond, and, although he had taken some soundings of its depth, he was not familiar with all of its parts. Darkness fell quickly, and he set his course toward the spot near the footpath to the castle where he thought it would be easy to land. But he changed his mind when Charlotte repeatedly implored him, almost in a panic, to get her to the shore quickly. He approached it with vigorous strokes but unfortunately ran aground some distance out in the water. His efforts to pull the boat free were unsuccessful. What could he do? He had no choice but to step out into the water, which fortunately was shallow, and to carry Charlotte to dry land. He carried his precious burden easily, being strong and steady on his feet, so that she had no reason to be afraid; but she put her arms around his neck and clung to him anxiously. He held her firmly and pressed her close to him. He released her only after they had arrived at the grassy bank; he was moved and confused. She still clung to him; and he folded her in his arms again and kissed her. The next moment he was at her feet, pressing his lips to her hand and crying, "Charlotte, will you forgive me?"

The kiss, which came so unexpectedly from her friend and which she had almost returned, brought Charlotte to herself. She pressed his hand but did not help him to rise.

Leaning forward, she laid her hand on his shoulder and said, "We cannot keep this moment from being a memorable one; but whether we shall be equal to it depends on us. You must leave, dear friend, and you shall leave. The Count has made plans for a better future for you. This makes me happy and sad. I didn't want to say anything until it was all decided; but this moment forces me to tell you my secret. I can forgive you—and forgive myself—only if we have the courage to change the situation, for it is not in our power to change our feelings." She drew him up and supported herself on his arm. They returned to the castle in silence.

Now Charlotte was standing in her bedroom, where she could not help feeling and remembering that she was Eduard's wife. In this inner conflict her character, strengthened by the many experiences of her life, came to her aid. She was accustomed to recognizing and controlling her feelings, and so she very nearly regained her usual composure without difficulty; indeed, she smiled when she thought of the previous night's surprising visit. But suddenly she was filled with a strange presentiment, a happy though tremulous agitation which was slowly transformed into quiet hope. Deeply moved, she fell on her knees and repeated the pledge she had given to Eduard before the altar. Consoling thoughts of friendship, affection, and resignation passed through her mind. She felt her old self once more. Overcome by a sweet drowsiness, she fell peacefully asleep.

chapter | 13

EDUARD, on the other hand, was in a quite different mood. He felt so little like sleeping that he did not even think of undressing. Again and again he kissed the copy of the document—at least the first pages, which were written in Ottilie's childish and timid hand. He hardly dared press his lips to the last pages, which he thought so strangely resembled his own hand. "If it were only a different document!" he thought to himself, but it was, all the same, a delightful assurance that his most fervent wish had been fulfilled. He would keep it and always carry it next to his heart, even though it would be sullied by the signature of a third person. The waning moon rose behind the wood. The warm night tempted Eduard to go out of doors. He strolled about, the most restless and happy of men. He walked through the gardens, and found them too confining; he ran across the fields, and found them too open. He was drawn back to the castle and stood under Ottilie's windows; he sat down on the steps of the terrace below. "Walls and locks divide us, but our hearts are not divided," he said to himself. "If she were standing here now, she would fall into my arms, and I into hers; and is not this certainty enough for us?" Around him all was quiet—not a breeze stirred. It was so still that in the ground beneath him he could hear the burrowing of busy animals, to whom night and day are alike. He was wrapped in happy dreams; at last he fell asleep and did not waken until the sun came up in all its splendor and scattered the early mists.

He was the first person awake on the whole estate. It seemed to him that the workmen should be already there. They finally arrived. He thought there should be more of them; the work planned for the day was too trifling for his eager desires. He insisted that more workmen be hired; it was promised and they arrived later in the day. But even this extra help was insufficient to carry out his projects quickly enough. He had lost interest in the work itself; what he wanted was to see it finished; and for whom? The paths should be smoothed, so that Ottilie could walk on them in comfort; and benches should be placed everywhere, so that Ottilie could rest. He also speeded up the work on the new building; the carpentry work was to be completed on Ottilie's birthday. There was no moderation in anything Eduard thought or did. The certainty of loving and of being loved in return banished all restraint. How changed everything seemed to him: all the rooms, all his surroundings. He no longer felt at home in his own house. He was completely absorbed in her—he had no other thought; his conscience was dumb. Everything that had been subdued in him burst forth, and his whole being rushed toward Ottilie.

The Captain watched this frantic activity and wished to avert unfortunate consequences. The exaggerated haste with which part of the new work was being done had upset the plans of the Captain, who had expected their gradual completion to occupy months of their quiet and friendly life together. He had concluded the sale of the farm; the first instalment had been paid and entrusted to Charlotte, as agreed. But even during the first week she had to be consistently firm, patient and orderly, for the sum set aside for the work would not last long at the present rate.

A great deal had been started, and still more had to be done. How could the Captain leave Charlotte in such a situation? They discussed the matter and came to the conclusion that it would be wisest to speed up work on the whole project, and, for that purpose, to borrow money which would be repaid by the instalment payments from the sale of the farm. This could be done with almost no loss by a transfer of the title deed. They would then have a freer hand and could get more done, since everything was now well under way; they had as many workmen as they needed; they could soon complete the entire project. Eduard gladly assented, since the plan coincided with his own wishes.

Meanwhile, deep in her heart Charlotte clung to her resolution, and her friend was staunch in his support of this spirit, but this only increased their intimacy. They talked frankly about Eduard's passion and discussed what they should do. Charlotte spent more time with Ottilie and observed her closely; but, the more she understood her own heart, the more deeply she understood Ottilie's heart. She saw no other way out; she must send her away.

It was fortunate that her daughter Luciane had excelled at school, because her great-aunt, on hearing this, decided to take her into her household permanently and bring her out into society. Ottilie could now go back to school; the Captain would leave for a better post; and everything would once more be as it had been a few months before, perhaps even better. Charlotte hoped soon to mend her relationship with Eduard, and she explained everything to herself so reasonably that she kept strengthening her delusion that a disturbed situation can be restored to its earlier tranquillity—that what has been violently released can be suppressed again.

Eduard was acutely aware of the obstacles which were put in his way. He soon noticed the arrangements which kept Ottilie and him apart, so that it became difficult for him to speak to her alone, or even to approach her, except in the presence of others. He resented this and many other things as well. When he succeeded in exchanging a few words with Ottilie, he not only reassured her of his love but also complained to her about his wife and the Captain. He did not realize that his own unreasonable actions were about to exhaust their funds. He blamed Charlotte as well as the Captain for not keeping to their first agreement; but he forgot that he had consented to the second agreement and had, in fact, been the cause of it himself.

Hate is partial but love is even more so. Ottilie's attitude toward Charlotte and the Captain also changed. One day when Eduard complained about the Captain to Ottilie, saying that under the circumstances he did not act quite honestly, as a friend should, Ottilie thoughtlessly replied, "I have been displeased before when he was not quite honest with you. I once overheard him say to Charlotte, 'If only Eduard would spare us his wretched tootling; he'll never be a good flutist, and it is painful to listen to him.' You can imagine how this hurt me, for you know how I love to accompany you."

As soon as she had said this, some instinct told her that she should have held her tongue; but it was too late. Eduard's expression changed. Nothing had ever hurt him more; his weakest point had been attacked; he knew that he had cherished a childish kind of ambition, without wishing to make the slightest pretension. He expected his friends to be tolerant of the things which amused and pleased him.

He forgot how unbearable it is for a listener to have his ear irritated by an amateurish performer. He was offended—furious—unforgiving. He felt himself absolved from any obligations of friendship.

His overmastering need to be with Ottilie, to see her, to whisper to her confidentially, became more urgent every day. He decided to write her, asking her to correspond with him in secret. The slip of paper on which he had written his brief request was lying on his desk, and the draft blew it off when his valet entered the room to dress his hair. The valet was in the habit of picking up any scrap of paper lying on the floor to test the heat of his curling iron. This time he got hold of Eduard's note, which he pinched quickly with the iron, singeing it. Eduard, seeing his error, snatched the note from him. He sat down a few minutes later to rewrite the message, but it did not sound as well the second time. He felt a little uneasy, even doubtful; but he overcame this feeling. He pressed the slip of paper into Ottilie's hand the first moment he could approach her.

Ottilie wasted no time in replying. He put her note in his waistcoat without reading it. The pocket of his short waistcoat, cut fashionably, was too shallow to hold it. It slipped out and fell to the floor without his noticing it. Charlotte saw it, picked it up, and after a quick glance gave it to him. "Here is something you have written down," she said; "you probably would not like to lose it."

He was puzzled. "Is she pretending?" he thought. "Did she read what was written on it, or did the similarity of the handwriting deceive her?" He hoped and believed that the latter was the case. It was a warning to him in a double sense; but he did not heed these accidental hints which some higher Being seems to give us. On the contrary, the further his passion drove him, the more intolerable did he find the restraint which he felt was forced upon him. He avoided the company of his friends. He hardened his heart, and, if it was necessary for him to be together with his wife and his friend, he could not recapture the pleasure he had once found in their company. He could not help feeling guilty about it, which, in turn annoyed him and he resorted to a kind of humor which, lacking affection, also lacked its usual charm.

In all these trials, Charlotte was sustained by her own integrity. She did not relax her determination to renounce her affection for the Captain, however pure and noble she knew it to be.

And she was also sincerely anxious to help the others. She knew only too well that separation alone is not enough to heal such wounds. She made up her mind to speak frankly with the girl about the whole matter; but she could not bring herself to do it; the memory of her own conflict stood in her way. She tried to refer to the matter in general remarks; but again, these fitted her own situation—a situation she hesitated to discuss. Any hint she wished to give Ottilie touched her own heart. She wanted to warn her and felt that perhaps she herself was in need of some warning.

She merely tried to keep the two lovers apart as before, without saying anything; but she gained nothing by this. Gentle hints, which sometimes slipped out, had no effect on Ottilie, who had been assured by Eduard that Charlotte loved the Captain and that Charlotte herself wanted a divorce which he would try to arrange in the fairest possible manner.

Ottilie, confident in the feeling of her own innocence and seeing herself on the road to supreme happiness, lived for Eduard alone. Strengthened in goodness by her love for him, still happier in her work, more communicative with others than formerly, she felt herself in a heaven on earth.

And so all four continued their normal daily life, each in his own way, with or without reflection. Everything seemed to go on as usual, just as, in troublous times, when all hangs in the balance, everyone goes on living as though nothing at all could happen.

chapter | 14

MEANWHILE, a letter arrived from the Count, addressed to the Captain—two letters, actually: one with splendid promises for the future, which he could show his friends; the other with the definite offer of an immediate important position at Court, including the rank of Major, a good salary, and other advantages; but the Count requested him to keep this to himself for a while, as there happened to be reasons for secrecy. The Captain, therefore, told his friends only about the remote expectations and kept the imminent decision to himself.

He continued his present occupations with great zeal and quietly made the necessary preparations so that, even in his absence, all would go on without interruption. Now he, too, was eager to set a final date for the end of the work and wished that as much as possible should be ready for Ottilie's birthday; as a result the two friends really enjoyed working in agreement, although the agreement was tacit. Eduard was very pleased that more funds were available, because they had raised the money in advance, and that all the projects moved ahead rapidly.

The Captain would have liked to put an end to the plan of combining the three ponds into one large lake. The lower

dam would have to be reinforced, and the middle ones de-
molished; and all this was, from more than one point of
view, a large and precarious task. Both projects, however,
interrelated as they were, had already been started. A young
architect had arrived—a former pupil of the Captain—who
was a very desirable addition, for he pushed the work
ahead, partly by employing skilled laborers, partly by letting contracts, when possible. All this promised security and
stability for the project. It also gave the Captain a feeling of
quiet satisfaction to know that his own absence would not
be so keenly felt. It had always been his principle not to
abandon any work he had started before it was finished unless his position was satisfactorily filled by someone else.
Indeed, he despised those who, in order to make their departure felt, leave everything in chaos, wishing, like uncivil-
ized egotists, to wreck anything they are no longer allowed
to work at.

And so everyone exerted himself to prepare for a splendid
celebration of Ottilie's birthday, although no one ever mentioned it or even admitted it to himself. Charlotte, while
not at all jealous, did not approve of a conspicuous celebration. Ottilie's youth, her circumstances of life, her relation
to the family, did not qualify her to appear as the queen of
such a day; nor did Eduard wish the date to be mentioned,
since he wanted everything to happen spontaneously, to be
a surprise and, of course, a delightful one.

For all these reasons, they tacitly agreed on the pretext
of having the carpenters' festival at the new house on that
day, without any mention of the birthday, which would en-
able them to invite their friends and the villagers for the
occasion.

But Eduard's passion knew no bounds. His longing to call
Ottilie his own was as immoderate as were his gifts and

promises to her. Charlotte's suggestions about birthday presents for Ottilie seemed to him much too modest. He talked with his valet, who, taking care of Eduard's wardrobe, had connections with tradespeople and dealers in luxuries. This man knew what gifts would please and how they ought to be given, and immediately ordered a handsome, even elegant, red morocco traveling case, studded with brass nails, and filled it with gifts worthy of the case itself. The valet made another suggestion; there were some fireworks which had never been set off. It would be easy enough to add to them. Eduard took up this idea with great enthusiasm; and the valet promised to attend to everything and keep everything a secret.

As the day grew near, the Captain made arrangements with the constabulary for guards, a precaution he thought necessary whenever a crowd was attracted or called together. He had also taken precautions against the beggars and rowdies who are likely to be a nuisance at a festival.

Eduard and his confidant, on the other hand, busied themselves mostly with their fireworks. They planned to set them off near the middle pond under the tall oaks. The guests would stand on the opposite shore, under the plane trees, where, safely and conveniently, they would have a good view of the display, the reflections in the water, and the pieces set afloat on the water.

On another pretext, Eduard gave orders to have the ground under the plane trees cleared of underbrush, grass, and moss. Only then did the beauty of the trees, magnificent in height and spread, come into full view on the cleared ground. Eduard was delighted. "It must have been just about this time of year when I planted them. I wonder how long ago it was?" he pondered. As soon as he returned home, he got out the old diaries his father had kept so methodically, especially when he was at this country seat. Eduard's planting of the trees was probably not recorded, but he was sure to find another important family event, which he still remembered clearly as having happened on the same day. He skimmed through several volumes. Sure enough, the event *was* mentioned! But how amazed and happy Eduard was when he discovered a strange coincidence. The day and the year when he had planted the trees was the day and year of Ottilie's birth.

chapter 15

AT last the radiant morning of the day Eduard had so eagerly awaited had come. Gradually the guests arrived. Invitations had been sent to the whole neighborhood, and many who had not been present at the laying of the cornerstone, but had heard how memorable that occasion had been, did not want to miss this second celebration.

Before they sat down to dinner, the carpenters marched into the courtyard to the music of a band. They carried a huge floral piece made of several wreaths of foliage and flowers, swinging loosely one above the other. The carpenters greeted the company and asked the ladies, in the traditional way, for silk handkerchiefs and ribbons to decorate their garland. While the guests had dinner in the castle, the procession went on its way with sounds of rejoicing; it lingered for a time in the village, where the women and girls also had to sacrifice many ribbons. It eventually arrived on the hill, accompanied by a large crowd which joined the one already waiting beside the half-finished lodge.

After dinner Charlotte detained her guests in the castle for a little while. She wanted to avoid a solemn and formal procession; therefore, they all arrived on the hill in separate groups walking slowly and without regard to distinctions of precedence. Charlotte lagged behind with Ottilie, but her stratagem did not improve matters, for Ottilie turned out to be the last person to arrive on the scene, and it seemed as though the trumpets and drums had only been waiting for her and the festivities seemed to start immediately upon her arrival.

To cover its bare appearance the house had according to the Captain's directions been decorated with green branches and flowers; but, without the Captain's knowledge, Eduard had directed the architect to outline the date in flowers on the cornice. There was nothing really objectionable about that; but the Captain arrived just in time to prevent Ottilie's name from being displayed in bright colors on the gable as well. He cleverly managed to prevent this and have the flowery letters which had already been prepared put aside.

The wreath was raised and was visible far and wide. The gay scarves and ribbons fluttered merrily in the breeze, which also blew away the greater part of a speech. When the ceremony was over, the dancing began on a level space in front of the building enclosed by arbors made of branches.

A spruce young apprentice introduced a lively village girl to Eduard and asked Ottilie, who was standing next to Eduard, for a dance. The two couples were immediately followed by others, and soon Eduard changed partners, caught Ottilie, and danced the round with her. The younger guests mixed gaily with the villagers and workmen, while the older ones looked on.

Then, before everyone began to stroll about, it was agreed that all the guests should meet again at sunset under the plane trees. Eduard arrived there first and made all necessary arrangements with his valet, who, together with the man who had made the fireworks, was to attend to the aerial magic on the opposite shore.

These arrangements did not altogether please the Captain. He tried to have a word with Eduard concerning the expected crush of spectators; but his friend asked rather nervously that this part of the festivities be left to him.

A great crowd had already gathered on the dams, where the ground was uneven and unsafe, because the sod had been removed. The sun went down, and it grew darker. As they waited for complete darkness, the guests were served refreshments under the trees. Everybody thought it an incomparable spot, and anticipated with delight the view they would eventually have from here over a wide lake with a variety of scenery along its shores.

A perfectly calm evening with not the slightest breeze stirring promised success for the spectacle. But all at once loud and terrified cries were heard. Large sections of earth had broken off the dam, and several people had been plunged into the water. The ground had given way under the trampling and pushing of the rapidly increasing crowd. Everyone had tried to get the best point of vantage, and now no one could move forward or back.

All crowded forward, more to see what had happened than to help, as it was impossible to reach the unfortunate victims. With the assistance of a few resolute men, the Captain ran to the scene of the disaster and cleared the crowd off the dam onto the shore to make more room for those who were trying to help the people in the water. These were soon on dry land again, partly through assistance, partly through their own efforts, except for one boy whose violent struggles carried him far out into the water instead of back to the dam. His strength was visibly failing; and only now and then did a hand or a foot appear above the surface. The boat, unfortunately, was on the opposite shore, filled with fireworks; the unloading of these went slowly and help was delayed. The

Captain came to a quick decision; everyone watched him throw off his outer clothing, and was inspired with confidence in his physical strength, but a cry went up from the crowd when they saw him jump into the water. All eyes followed the skilful swimmer who, in a short time, reached the boy and brought him, seemingly dead, to shore.

Meanwhile the boat had arrived, and the Captain stepped into it and asked those about him if everyone had been saved. The physician arrived and took care of the still unconscious boy. Charlotte had come over, and implored the Captain to think of himself—to go back to the castle and change his clothes. He hesitated, until he was assured that everyone had been saved. The people who told him that were sensible and reliable, and had helped him in the rescue.

When Charlotte saw the Captain going back to the castle, it suddenly occurred to her that such necessaries as wine and tea had been locked up, and that people are likely to get hold of the wrong thing on such occasions, in any case. She hurried past the rest of the guests, who were still standing under the plane trees in scattered groups, and found Eduard busy urging everyone to stay for a little while: he was about to give the signal for the beginning of the fireworks. Charlotte went up to him and begged him not to go on with an entertainment which would be out of place this moment and which no one would enjoy. She reminded him of their duty toward the boy and the one who had rescued him. "The doctor will manage all right," Eduard replied. "He has everything he needs, and we would only be in the way." Charlotte insisted and made a sign to Ottilie, who started to follow at once. But Eduard took her hand and protested: "This day shall not end in a hospital! I'll not have Ottilie playing the sister of mercy. The half-dead will be wakened without our help, and the living will rub themselves dry."

Charlotte did not answer and left. Some of the guests followed her; others stayed; finally, as no one wished to be the last, they all left. Eduard and Ottilie were now alone under the plane trees. He insisted on staying, although Ottilie was uneasy and implored him to return with her to the castle. "No, Ottilie," he cried, "extraordinary things do not happen in an ordinary way. This startling incident tonight unites us all the more quickly. You are mine—I have said that to you so often and sworn it. Let's stop talking and promising; let it now be a fact!"

The boat crossed over from the other shore. The valet was in it, and asked with some embarrassment what should be done with the fireworks. "Set them off," Eduard called to him. "They were meant for you, Ottilie, and you alone shall see them. Let me sit beside you and share your pleasure!" He sat down by her side, without touching her.

Rockets rose roaring into the sky; cannonades thundered; star shells climbed high; firecrackers flashed like hissing serpents and exploded; pin wheels whirled—first separately, then in pairs, then in masses—blazing brighter and brighter, one after the other, and then merging. Eduard, his heart on fire as well, watched the fiery phantoms with eager and happy eyes. Ottilie, with her sensitive emotional disposition, was more frightened than delighted by this deafening and flashing rise and fall. Timidly she leaned against Eduard, who felt her nearness and confidence to be a pledge that she belonged to him completely. Hardly had the night closed around them once more, when the moon rose, lighting their way back to the castle. A man, his hat in his hand, stepped into their path and begged alms, claiming that he had been forgotten on this festive day. The moon shone full

119

on his face, and Eduard recognized the insolent beggar he had met before. But in his present state of happiness, he could not possibly be angry with anyone. He had also completely forgotten that on this particular day begging had been forbidden. It did not take him long to search in his pocket and find a gold coin. He wanted to see everyone happy, for his own happiness seemed to be boundless.

In the castle, all had turned out well. With the help of the doctor's skill, the provision of everything he needed, and Charlotte's assistance, the boy had been restored to life. The guests had scattered, some to catch a glimpse of the fireworks from a distance, and some to return to their quiet homes after all the excitement.

After quickly changing his clothes, the Captain had also helped where he was needed. All was quiet again, and he was alone with Charlotte. With his characteristic kindness he now told her that he would be leaving very soon. She had gone through so much tonight that this disclosure made almost no impression on her. She had seen her friend risk his life and save the life of another without suffering any harm himself. She saw in these miraculous happenings a propitious omen for his future and felt that fate would be kind to him.

When Eduard returned with Ottilie, he was also told of the Captain's imminent departure. He suspected that Charlotte had known all about this for some time; but he was too preoccupied with himself and his own plans to resent it.

On the contrary, he listened with attention and pleasure to the description of the fine and honorable post which had been offered the Captain. His own secret desires raced ahead of all these changes. He already saw his friend married to

Charlotte, and himself married to Ottilie. He could think of no finer gift he might have received on this festive day.

And how surprised Ottilie was when she entered her room and found on her table the handsome traveling case. She opened it at once. Everything in it was so beautifully packed and arranged that she did not dare to remove or even to touch anything. Muslin, batiste, silk, scarves, and lace vied with each other in their beauty, elegance, and costliness. Nor had jewelry been forgotten. Although she understood perfectly that it was intended to provide her with a more varied wardrobe, everything seemed to her so lavish and strange that she did not dare, even in her thoughts, to claim these things as her own.

chapter | 16

On the following morning the Captain had disappeared, leaving behind a note for his friends filled with expressions of his gratitude. The night before, he and Charlotte had said a vague and almost wordless goodbye. She felt that it was a final separation and had resigned herself to it, for in the Count's second letter, which the Captain had at last given her to read, the prospect of a favorable marriage had also been touched upon; and, although the Captain had not stressed this point, Charlotte accepted the arrangement as settled and gave him up for good with a pure heart.

But she also felt that now she had a right to demand of others the same self-control which she had practiced herself; it had not been impossible for her, and it should not be impossible for them. In this mood she began to talk to her husband, and she was able to do this openly and confidently, because she was determined that the matter should be settled once and for all.

"Our friend has left us, and we are once again in our old situation," she said. "It is now entirely up to us whether or not we wish to return to the old state of things."

Eduard, who heard only what flattered his passion, thought that Charlotte's remark referred to the earlier period when she had been a widow and that in a veiled way she wished to give him some small hope for a separation. He therefore answered, with a smile, "Why not? The only important thing would be to come to an understanding."

But from Charlotte's answer he saw that he was mistaken. She said, "Now we have only to choose between two possibilities, both very desirable, to change Ottilie's situation as well. Either she can go back to school, since my daughter has left there and is staying with her great-aunt; or she can be received into a very good family where she will enjoy all the advantages of an education suitable to her station, together with an only daughter."

"But living with us so long in a congenial atmosphere has spoiled Ottilie, and leaving us will not be pleasant for her," Eduard replied, trying to hide his feelings.

"All of us have been spoiled; certainly you have," Charlotte replied. "We are now at a turning point, where we should stop and look back and think what would be best for all the members of our little circle; and we should be willing to make some sacrifices."

"But I do not think it is fair to sacrifice Ottilie," Eduard argued, "and that is just what we would be doing if we banish her to live among strangers. The Captain was called away by his good fortune; we could see him leave with no qualms and even with pleasure. But who knows what Ottilie will have to face? And why such haste?"

"What you and I are going to face is quite clear," Charlotte replied with some emotion. Determined to speak her mind once and for all, she went on: "You love Ottilie, and every day you become more attached to her. Her affections, too, are centering more and more on you. Why not speak frankly of something which is clear and obvious at every moment? Should we not have enough foresight to ask ourselves how it will all end?"

"A precise answer to that question, of course, is impossible, but if we cannot be sure how things will turn out, the best decision is always to wait and see what the future will bring," Eduard said, trying to control himself.

"It takes no great wisdom to see the future clearly in our case," said Charlotte. "At least we know this much: both of us are too old to walk blindly into something we should not and must not do. There is no one to take care of us; we have to be our own friends and our own advisers. People expect us not to go to extremes; we can't afford to expose ourselves to criticism or ridicule."

"Can you blame me for having Ottilie's happiness at heart? Can't you understand that?" said Eduard, embarrassed for an answer to his wife's straightforward words. "And I do not mean her future happiness, which is quite beyond our calculation, but her present situation. Imagine for a moment, honestly and without deceiving yourself, Ottilie torn away from us and at the mercy of strangers; for my part I am not cruel enough to let her suffer such a change."

Charlotte clearly recognized the firm determination behind her husband's dissembling. For the first time she realized how far apart they had grown. Almost trembling, she cried, "Can Ottilie be happy if she comes between us, if she takes my husband from me, if she takes their father from his children?"

"I should think that our children are well taken care of," Eduard said, with a killing smile; but he added in a kindlier tone, "Why go to such extremes?"

"Extremes border on passion," Charlotte said. "While there is still time, do not reject my advice, but help me to help both of us. In uncertain situations, the person who sees most clearly ought to act and help. This time it is I! My dear, dearest Eduard, let me prevail! Can you expect me simply to give up my well-deserved happiness, my most precious rights—can you ask me to abandon *you*?"

"Who has asked you to?" Eduard answered, rather embarrassed.

"You have," Charlotte replied. "Is not your wish to keep Ottilie near you an acknowledgement of everything which must come of it? I do not wish to press the matter, but, if you cannot master yourself, you will at least not be able to deceive yourself much longer."

Eduard knew how right she was. It is a shock to hear in plain words what our heart has cherished secretly for a long time. Simply to change the subject for the moment Eduard said, "I do not even know what your plans exactly are."

"I intended to talk over the two possibilities with you. Each has its good points. In Ottilie's present stage of development, the school would be better for her. But when I think of her future, I see that the other situation promises more opportunities and a wider scope." Charlotte went on to tell her husband all the details of the two proposals, and then she summed up: "My own feeling is, that, for several reasons, the lady's household is preferable to the school, particularly because I should not like to encourage the affection, if not passion, which the young Tutor feels for Ottilie."

Eduard seemed to agree, but he did this only to gain time. When Charlotte, who wanted to come to a final decision, met with no pronounced opposition, she seized the opportunity to fix the date of Ottilie's departure; she had already made quiet preparations for Ottilie to leave a few days later.

Eduard was horrified. He believed himself betrayed and suspected behind his wife's affectionate words subtle plans to separate him forever from his happiness. On the surface he seemed to leave the whole matter to her; but in his heart his decision was already made. Only to get a breathing spell, and to prevent the threatening and unimaginable disaster of Ottilie's being sent away, he decided to leave home. He told Charlotte that he was going, but he was able to deceive her by explaining that he did not wish to be present when Ottilie left; that he did not even want to see her again. Charlotte, believing that she had won, encouraged him warmly. He ordered his horses, gave his valet the necessary instructions about packing and following him, and then, at the last moment, he sat down and wrote:

Eduard to Charlotte

"The misfortune which has befallen us, my dear, may be curable or it may not—I am sure of only one thing—if I am not to be driven to despair—I must gain some time for myself, and for all of us. Since I am making a sacrifice, I am entitled to require something in return. I am leaving my home, and I shall return only when there are prospects happier and more peaceful. Meanwhile, you are to remain in possession, but together with Ottilie. I want to be sure that she lives with you and not with strangers. Take care of her; treat her as you always have and even more affectionately, more gently. I promise you that I shall not try to get in touch with her without your knowledge. At least for a short time, please do not let me know how you are getting on; I shall assume the best; do the same about me. One promise only I implore you most fervently, most urgently to give me—not to make any attempt to send Ottilie away, into new surroundings. Once she is out of your castle, your park, and entrusted to strangers, she belongs to me, and I shall take her. But if you have any regard for my affection, my wishes, and my suffering, if you leave me to my illusions and hopes, I shall not resist a cure if it should offer itself. . . ."

The last phrase came from his pen, not from his heart.

Indeed, when he saw it on paper, he began to weep bitterly. That he should ever renounce in the slightest, the happiness, or even the misery of loving Ottilie! For the first time he realized fully what he was doing: he was going away without knowing what his action might lead to. At least he would not see her again *now;* would he ever see her again? What assurance did he have of that? But the letter was written; the horses were ready at the door; and he was afraid that at any moment he might see her somewhere and be shaken in his resolution. He pulled himself together and reflected that it would, after all, be possible for him to return at any time and that his very absence might bring him closer to his heart's desire. On the other hand, he pictured Ottilie's being forced to leave if he were to stay. He sealed the letter, ran down the stairs, and mounted his horse.

As he rode past the village inn, he saw the beggar to whom he had been so generous the night before. The man was sitting outside under the trees, comfortably eating his dinner, but he rose and bowed to Eduard respectfully and almost reverentially. It was the figure that had stepped out in their path last night, as Eduard had walked arm in arm with Ottilie. He now reminded Eduard painfully of the happiest hour of his life. His agony increased, the consciousness of what he was leaving behind became unbearable; he turned to look at the beggar and cried, "You lucky fellow! You can still live on yesterday's alms, but I cannot live any longer on yesterday's happiness."

chapter 17

OTTILIE went to the window when she heard someone riding off and was just in time to see Eduard's back. She thought it odd that he was leaving the house without having seen her or without having wished her "Good morning." She was uneasy and became more and more perturbed when Charlotte invited her for a long walk and talked about many things without ever mentioning her husband—apparently on purpose. When they returned to the castle it was a still greater shock to Ottilie to find the table only set for two.

We do not even like to lose apparently unimportant things to which we are accustomed; but the loss of something vitally important is actually painful. Eduard and the Captain were not with them. Charlotte, for the first time in months, had ordered the meal herself, and Ottilie almost felt herself supplanted. The two women sat opposite each other. Charlotte talked quite freely about the Captain's post and how unlikely they were to see him again soon. At the moment, Ottilie was able to comfort herself only with the belief that Eduard had ridden after his friend in order to keep him company part of the way.

But, when they left the table, they saw Eduard's traveling coach standing under the window; and when Charlotte, rather annoyed, asked who had given orders to bring it there, she was told that it had been the valet, who wished to load some things into it. It took all Ottilie's self-control to hide her astonishment and anguish.

The valet came in and asked for some small objects: his master's cup, a few silver spoons, and some other things, which Ottilie took to mean that a long journey and a prolonged absence had been planned. Charlotte simply dismissed the valet's request, saying that she did not understand what he was talking about, since he himself had everything which belonged to his master under lock and key. The shrewd fellow only wished to speak to Ottilie and was seeking a pretext to get her out of the room, so he made an excuse and persisted in his request, which Ottilie was quite willing to grant; but, since Charlotte refused, the valet was forced to leave, and the coach drove off.

It was a terrible moment for Ottilie. She understood nothing; she grasped nothing; she realized only that Eduard was parted from her for a long time. Charlotte knew how she felt and left her alone. It is impossible to describe Ottilie's agony or her tears; she suffered beyond measure. She prayed God to help her live through this one day; she lived through the day and the night, and, when she was able to think clearly once more, she felt she was a changed person.

She had not entirely recovered from the shock, nor was she resigned; but, having survived such a great loss, she still had something to fear. Her immediate anxiety, after she had collected herself, was: would she, too, be sent away, now that the men were gone? She did not know about Eduard's threats, which had insured her continuing to stay with Charlotte, but Charlotte's own behavior helped to calm her. Charlotte tried to keep the young girl occupied, and only rarely and reluctantly let her out of her sight. Although she knew how little words can accomplish in the face of a powerful passion, she also knew the power of reflection and reason; and therefore she talked with Ottilie about many subjects.

It was a great comfort to the girl, when Charlotte on one occasion casually but intentionally made the wise observation: "How grateful people are, when our calmness helps them through an emotional crisis," she said. "Let us cheerfully devote our energies to the projects the men have left unfinished. We can make the prospect of their return all the more pleasant, since our moderation will have preserved and improved the work that their violent and impatient natures might well have ruined."

"When you speak of moderation, dear aunt, I cannot help thinking of the lack of it in men, particularly in regard to wine," Ottilie replied. "I have often been distressed and upset to see them, for hours on end, lose their clarity of judgment, their consideration for others, their charm and their good manners, when confusion and disaster threaten to spoil all the pleasure to be found in the company of cultivated men. It must have been the cause of many a rash decision!"

Charlotte agreed, but she did not continue the conversation, for she felt sure that Ottilie was simply thinking of Eduard again. Although he was not a habitual drinker, he took wine more often than was desirable when he was working or engaged in animated conversation, or in low spirits.

If Charlotte's remarks had reminded Ottilie of the two friends and of Eduard in particular, she was all the more surprised when Charlotte spoke of the Captain's impending marriage as something settled and generally known, which put an entirely different complexion on everything Eduard's earlier assurances had led her to imagine. All this made

Ottilie keenly watchful of every remark, every allusion, every step and action of Charlotte's. Ottilie, without being aware of it, had grown wise, alert, and suspicious.

All this time Charlotte conscientiously looked after every detail in her domestic domain and went about her work with her usual efficiency, constantly urging Ottilie to participate in her activities. She resolutely economized in her household. On deeper reflection, as a matter of fact, she considered the emotional incident as almost providential. At the rate they had been spending money, they might easily have lost all sense of proportion; if they had not stopped and considered before it was too late, their ample fortune would have been depleted, if not dispersed by their extravagant life and diverse projects.

She did not interrupt the work in the park, and, indeed, went on with everything that might serve as a basis for future development, but that was all. She wanted some pleasurable occupation to be available for her husband on his return.

In all this work and planning she could not sufficiently praise the methods of the young Architect. In a short time the lake lay stretched before her eyes, and the new shores were turfed and planted in excellent taste. All the rough work on the new houses was soon finished, and everything necessary had been done to protect it against wind and weather. She stopped the work at a point where it would be a pleasure to take it up again in the future. She was always calm and in good spirits; Ottilie was calm, too, but only on the surface. She watched everything only in search of indications of Eduard's return. She had no interest in anything but that.

For this reason she welcomed a plan to recruit a group of peasant boys and train them to keep the enlarged park always neat. This had earlier been Eduard's idea. A kind of bright uniform was made for the children, which they had to put on in the evening after having washed and cleaned themselves thoroughly. The uniforms were kept at the castle in the care of the most responsible and reliable of the boys. The Architect supervised the group; and in a very short time they all did their work quite efficiently. They were easy to train, and they performed their chores almost like a military exercise. When they marched along with their scrapers, garden shears, rakes, their small spades and hoes and brooms, while others marched behind with baskets for stones and weeds, and still others pulled along the heavy iron roller, it was a cheerful and pretty procession indeed, and the architect sketched a series of attractive poses and actions for the frieze of a garden pavilion. But to Ottilie it was only a kind of parade that would welcome the returning master of the castle.

This encouraged her to arrange something else of the same kind to receive him. For some time the girls of the village had been taught to sew, knit, spin, and engage in other forms of feminine industry. The gradual improvement in the cleanliness and beauty of the village had stimulated these domestic virtues. Ottilie had occasionally lent a helping hand whenever she had time or felt so inclined. Now she began to work more consistently and systematically. But it is more difficult to form girls into corps than boys. She used her common sense, and, almost unconsciously, merely tried to inspire each girl with a feeling of devotion for her home, her parents, and her brothers and sisters. In a good many instances she was successful. She heard only complaints about one lively little girl, who, people said, was utterly useless and refused to do anything around the house. Ottilie did not have the heart to be angry with this child, who was always friendly and especially attached to her, walking with her and running after her, if permitted. In Ottilie's company the child was helpful, gay, and never tired. The devotion to a lovely mistress seemed to be all she needed. At first Ottilie tolerated her companionship; later she became attached to her, at last they became inseparable; and Nanni accompanied her mistress wherever she went.

Ottilie frequently visited the garden and was pleased to see how everything thrived and grew. The season of berries and cherries was almost over; but Nanni in particular feasted on the last late fruit. All the other trees promised a rich crop in autumn; and the gardener constantly talked about his master and wished to see him at home again. Ottilie loved to listen to the good old man. He was an expert in his profession and could not stop talking to her of Eduard.

When Ottilie showed her delight that the shoots which had been grafted in the spring had developed so well, the gardener said doubtfully: "I only hope that my good master will be pleased with the results. If he were here this autumn, he could see what wonderful fruit we are going to get from the trees in the old park which our late master, his father, planted. The present nurserymen are not as reliable as the Carthusian monks used to be. In the catalogues we find, of course, only the most respectable firms. We buy from them their shoots, graft them, but in the end, when the trees bear fruit, we find our orchards full of trees which were not worth all that trouble."

Whenever this faithful servant met Ottilie, he asked her if his master were coming back and when. And if Ottilie could not give him any information, the old man let her feel by his behavior, and by his barely concealed sadness, that he thought she did not trust him. The feeling of being in the dark herself, which such occasions emphasized, was unbearably painful. And yet she could never stay away from these

133

borders and flowerbeds. What she and Eduard had sown and planted together was now in full bloom. The flowers hardly needed any special care, but Nanni was always willing to water them. With what emotions did Ottilie look at the late flowers that were just beginning to bud. Their brilliant abundance was intended to decorate the celebration of Eduard's next birthday, to express her own love and gratitude. Sometimes she tried to imagine this birthday as a gala day; but her hope often faded. Doubt and anxiety always haunted the poor girl.

A genuine and candid understanding between Charlotte and herself could, perhaps, never be completely restored. The situations of the two women were, of course, very different. If it had been possible to return to the old state of things, and restore their life to normal, Charlotte would have been happy for the present and hopeful for the future, but for Ottilie all would have been lost. We may say *all*, because with Eduard she had found real life and happiness for the first time, and in her present condition she felt an emptiness so complete that she could never have conceived of it. A heart which longs for love may feel that it lacks something; but a heart that has lost love is desolate. Thus longing changes into disappointment and impatience, and a woman's heart, used to waiting and hoping, seeks a new sphere, wishing to do something, to attempt something for its own happiness.

Ottilie had not given Eduard up. How could she, even though Charlotte, against her inner convictions, was wise enough to take it silently for granted that a friendly and calm relationship would be possible between her husband and Ottilie? How often at night, behind her locked door, did the girl kneel before the open traveling case, absorbed in contemplation of the birthday presents she had never touched! She had never used this cloth, never cut it or sewn a stitch! How often did the young girl hurry out of the house at sunrise—she who formerly found all her happiness indoors. She now felt a desire to be out in the open, in the countryside, which never had had any attraction for her. She did not even like to stay long on dry land but would jump into the boat and row out to the middle of the lake. There she would take out a book of travel and let herself be rocked by the rippling waves, reading and dreaming that she was in a far country where she always found her friend —forever close to his heart, as he was to hers.

chapter

I⊤ can be imagined that Mittler, about whose odd and busy career we already know, was very eager to show his friendship and exercise his skill in this particular case. He had been informed of the crisis in the life of his friends, although neither of them had as yet asked for his help. He thought it advisable, however, to wait for an opportunity, as he well knew that it is more difficult to help educated people in their moral entanglements than the uneducated. He therefore decided to leave them alone for a while; but presently he could not bear to wait any longer, and hurried to see Eduard after he had tracked him down.

His route took him to a pleasant valley with a bottom of green, richly-wooded meadow, through which a purling brook twisted and sped. Fertile fields and rich orchards covered the whole extent of the gently sloping hills. The villages were not too close to one another, and the whole landscape had a peaceful character. Although it would not have attracted a painter, every part of it seemed to offer pleasant living.

At last Miller came upon a well-kept farm with a neat and unpretentious farmhouse, surrounded by gardens. He suspected that this was Eduard's refuge, and he was right.

Eduard in his seclusion had completely abandoned himself to his passion, while turning over in his mind innumerable schemes and cherishing all sorts of hopes. He could not deny that he longed to see Ottilie here, that he would like to bring her to this place or to tempt her to come; he also permitted himself other seemly or unseemly thoughts. He lost himself in all sorts of speculations. If he could not make her his own, if she could not be legally his, he would present her with this farm. Here she could live quietly and independently; here she would be happy, and—to such extremes did his self-torturing imagination sometimes carry him—she might even be happy with another man.

So the days passed for him, in an eternal conflict between hope and suffering, tears and happiness; among plans, preparations, and despair. He was not surprised to see Mittler. He had expected him all along and was almost glad when he arrived. If Charlotte had sent him, Eduard was prepared for excuses and postponements as well as more definite proposals; but, if Mittler was bringing him news from Ottilie at last, he would welcome him as a messenger from Heaven.

Eduard was, therefore, rather upset and annoyed when Mittler told him that he did not come from the castle, but on his own impulse. Eduard promptly lost interest, and at first the conversation lagged. But Mittler knew only too well that a person in love wants nothing more than to pour his feelings into the ear of a friend. After a little casual conversation, therefore, he allowed himself for once to drop his usual role and to play the confidant instead of the mediator.

Later, when he gently reproached Eduard for having buried himself in this solitude, his friend replied, "Oh, I do not know how I could spend my time more agreeably! I am always thinking of her; I am always close to her. I have the invaluable advantage of being able to picture in my mind where Ottilie is at any given moment; where she is going, where she is standing, where she is resting. I see her before me, moving and working as usual, doing and planning this or that; always something, of course, principally to make *me* happy. But that is not all: how could I be happy far from her! So then I begin to imagine what Ottilie could do to get in touch with me; I write loving and confiding letters from her to me; I answer them and keep both letters together. I have promised not to take any steps to communicate with her, and I shall keep my promise. But what has *she* promised that keeps her from turning to me? Was Charlotte cruel enough to demand a sworn promise from her that she would not write or send me one word about herself? It would be only natural, and it is very likely what happened; but still I think it outrageous; it is unbearable. If Ottilie loves me, as I believe she does, as I know she does, why doesn't she make up her mind, why doesn't she have the courage to run away and throw herself into my arms? She ought to do it; I some-times think she might do it. If I hear the slightest noise in the hall, I look toward the door. I think—I hope—she must be coming. Alas, just as the possible is impossible, I imagine that the impossible could become possible. When I wake up at night and see the flickering lamp fill the room with shadows, I expect her image, her spirit, a breath of her presence, to float past me, approach me, and touch me for one brief moment—to give me some kind of assurance that she thinks of me, that she is mine. There is only one thing left to make me happy. When I saw her constantly, I never dreamed of her; but now that I am far away from her, we are together in my dreams. Strangely enough, only since I have met other attractive people in this neighborhood, she seems to want to say to me in all my dreams, 'Look about you! You will not find anyone more beautiful or more lovely than me.' And so her image slips into all my dreams. Every-thing that happened to us runs together. Sometimes we sign a contract together: there is her handwriting and mine, her signature and mine; each blots out the other; both inter-twine. These delightful ephemeral fantasies are not without pain. Sometimes she does something inconsistent with the pure conception I have of her; only then do I feel how much I love her, for I suffer indescribable agonies. Sometimes she teases and torments me, which is quite unlike her; but then the image changes; her lovely, round, angelic face becomes drawn; it is a different person. But I still feel tortured, un-satisfied, and exhausted.

"Do not smile, my dear Mittler; or do smile if you like. I am not ashamed of my attachment, my foolish and mad passion, if you choose to call it that. Indeed, I have never loved before; only now do I feel what it means. Up to now, everything in my life has been only a prelude, an anticipa-tion—a pastime—time wasted—until now that I have met her and loved her; loved her alone with all my heart and soul. Some people have accused me, not exactly to my face but certainly behind my back, of being a dilettante in most things. This may be true, but before this I had not found anything in which I could prove myself a master. I should like to meet the man who excels me in the art of loving. True, it is a miserable, sorrowful, and tearful gift, but for me it is so natural, so instinctive, that I do not think I can ever part with it."

This impassioned and frank unburdening of his heart relieved Eduard greatly; but he had also suddenly compre-hended his strange condition fully; so that, overwhelmed by a terrible inner conflict, he burst into tears, which flowed all the more freely because his heart was softened by his confession to his friend.

Eduard's violent and passionate outburst diverted Mittler

from his purpose in coming, and made it even harder for him to suppress his own quick temperament and stubborn common sense; and he expressed his disapproval frankly and without mincing words. He advised Eduard to pull himself together and to realize what he owed to himself as a man; he should not forget that it does a man the greatest credit when he can control his feelings in misfortune, when he can suffer pain with equanimity and dignity; he will be respected, admired, and held up as an example.

To Eduard in his agitation, racked by the most distressing emotions, words like these could only sound hollow and meaningless. "For the man who is happy and untroubled, it is easy to talk in this way," he snapped back, "but he would be ashamed if he knew how unbearable he sounds to the person who is suffering. The stubborn optimist who demands infinite patience refuses to acknowledge the existence of infinite agony. There are cases—yes, there are—when consolation is an offense, and despair a duty! Even a noble Greek who well knew how to portray heroic characters did not disdain to let his heroes weep when they suffered such agony. He said: Noble are the men who can weep. Leave me alone—you who have a dry heart and dry eyes! I curse the happy for whom the unhappy is only a spectacle. They wish him to act nobly even in the cruelest situation, when he is in physical and spiritual distress, if he is to win their applause; and if they are to applaud him at his exit, he should die before their eyes with the proud dignity of a gladiator. My dear Mittler, I thank you for your visit, but you would do me a great favor if you would take a walk around the garden and look at the countryside. We'll meet later again. I shall try to quiet down and become more like you."

Mittler preferred to change his tactics rather than to break off a conversation it would be difficult to take up again.

Eduard also was quite ready to go on talking, for their conversation was tending toward the point he wanted to discuss.

"There is no question that brooding and arguing over a problem leads nowhere," Eduard said; "but, while we were talking, I understood myself for the first time and realized clearly what decision I should reach and have reached. I see my present and my future life before me; the only alternatives are misery or happiness. Dearest friend, try to bring about a separation which is necessary, which already exists; persuade Charlotte to consent. I shall not tell you now the reason why I believe she will. Go to her, my dear man, and bring us all peace and make us happy."

Mittler was taken aback. Eduard continued, "My fate and Ottilie's are inseparable, and we shall not be destroyed. Do you see this glass? Our initials are engraved on it. At a merry celebration some gay fellow flung it into the air so that no one would drink out of it again. It was expected to shatter on the rocky ground, but someone caught it. I paid a high price for it and use it daily, to convince myself every day that all human relations predestined by Fate, are indestructible."

Mittler wailed, "The patience I must have with my friends! Now you bring in superstition—of all things—the most hateful and harmful of all human stupidities. We play with prophecies, premonitions, and dreams in order to give everyday life some significance. But as soon as life itself becomes significant, when everything about us begins to heave and roar, then the gathering storm becomes all the more terrifying because of these ghosts."

"In the uncertainties of my life, suspended between hope and fear, leave my poor heart at least a guiding star to which I can turn, even if I cannot steer by it," Eduard exclaimed.

"There is nothing wrong with that," Mittler replied. "If only I could see some logic in all this—but I have always found that nobody pays attention to warning symptoms. People only heed only flattering and promising signs and portents and believe firmly in them."

Mittler had allowed this conversation to tempt him off into dark regions where he felt more and more uncomfortable the longer he remained in them, so that he was now more than willing to comply with Eduard's urgent wish that he should go to see Charlotte. What else could he say to Eduard now? The best he could do at the moment was to gain time and ascertain how the two women felt about the situation, which accorded with his own inclinations.

He hastened to Charlotte, whom he found calm and cheerful, as usual. She was quite ready to tell him about everything that had happened; Eduard's conversation had not really told him anything except the effect of events on Eduard. Mittler approached the matter most cautiously and could not bring himself to mention the word "divorce" even in passing. He was, therefore, surprised, amazed, and, for his part, delighted when at last Charlotte said to him, after a series of depressing disclosures: "I hope and firmly believe that all this will pass and that Eduard will come back to me. How could it be otherwise, since you find me expecting?"

"Do I understand you correctly?" Mittler interjected.

"Perfectly," Charlotte answered.

"A thousand blessings on this news!" he cried, striking his palm with his fist. "I know the force of this argument on a man's heart. How many marriages have I seen hastened, strengthened, or restored by it! Such a happy expectation has greater force than a thousand words; it is indeed the best expectation we can have. But as for me," he continued, "I should have every reason in the world to be annoyed, for I see that this case will not flatter my vanity. My service in your case will not be appreciated. I feel like a physician—a friend of mine—who was always successful when he treated the poor out of Christian charity but was seldom able to cure a rich patient ready to pay a large fee. Fortunately, here, things will take care of themselves, whereas my efforts—my attempts to persuade—would have been unsuccessful."

Charlotte then asked him to give Eduard the news, to take a letter from her to him, and to see what could be done. But he refused. "Everything has been done already," he exclaimed. "Write your letter; any messenger will do! I must go where I am needed more. I shall come back only to wish you happiness; I shall return for the christening."

Charlotte was again disappointed in Mittler, as she had often been before. His impetuous nature accomplished much good; but his rashness led to many failures. No one was more prone to act on impulse.

Charlotte's messenger found Eduard, who received him almost with trepidation. The letter might well contain a "No" instead of a "Yes." For a long time he hesitated to open it; and he was speechless after he had read the note—almost stunned by the passage with which it ended:

"Do you remember those hours of the night when you visited your wife like a lover in quest of adventure, when you drew her irresistibly to your heart, and closed her in your arms like a beloved, like a bride? Let us revere this strange accident as an act of Providence, which provided a new bond for our relationship at a moment when the happiness of our lives was threatening to dissolve and vanish."

It would be difficult to describe the tumult of emotions which filled Eduard's soul. In such a crisis old habits and old inclinations are again revived to kill time and fill the emptiness of life. Hunting and wars are always convenient escapes for a nobleman. Eduard longed for some external danger to counteract the inner one. He longed for death, for his life threatened to become unbearable; it even comforted him to think that he would not be long in this world and that by his very departure from it he could make his loved ones and his friends happy. No one dissuaded him, since he kept his plans a secret from everyone. When he had observed all the necessary formalities for making his last will and testament, he was very happy that he could transfer the ownership of his farm to Ottilie. He made provision for Charlotte, for the unborn child, for the Captain, and for all his servants. The resumption of hostilities forwarded his plan. In his youth military incompetence had greatly annoyed him, and he had left the service for that reason. Now he was delighted at the prospect of serving under a commander with whom he knew that death would be likely and victory certain.

When Ottilie was told of Charlotte's secret, she was just as stunned as Eduard had been, and even more so. She withdrew into herself completely. There was nothing for her to say. She could not hope and must not wish. Her diary alone will allow us a glimpse into her heart; and we intend to quote some passages from it later.

PART

2

In ordinary life we are often confronted with something which, in an epic poem, we are accustomed to admire as a poetic device, namely, that after the principal characters have left the scene or have withdrawn into inactivity, a second and even a third person, until then hardly noticed, comes forward at once to fill their places. These persons, as they display their whole activity, then seem to us also worthy of our attention, our sympathy and even of our praise and admiration.

So it was with the young Architect, who, after the Captain's and Eduard's departure, became from day to day a more important figure. The direction of a number of plans and their execution now depended entirely on him; and he proved himself exact, reasonable and energetic in everything, as well as useful to the ladies on many occasions. He was also inventive in entertaining them during their leisure hours, when time hung heavy on their hands. His whole appearance was of a kind that gives confidence and arouses sympathy. He was a young man in the true sense of the word —handsomely built, slim, perhaps a little too tall; modest without being timid, and natural without being forward. He took upon himself any work or duty; and since he was very good at accounts, the household soon held no secrets for him, and his good influence was felt everywhere. He usually received strangers who came to the castle, and was clever at either refusing an unexpected visitor, or at least warning the two women in time, so that the visit caused them no inconvenience.

One day a young lawyer gave them some trouble. He had been sent by a neighboring nobleman, to confer about a matter which, though of no particular importance, yet touched a special chord in Charlotte's heart. We must mention this incident because it set in motion several other matters which otherwise might not have come up for some time.

This incident concerned the change Charlotte had made in the churchyard. All the gravestones had been removed from their places and ranged along the walls and around the foundation of the church. The remaining space had been levelled; and with the exception of a broad path that led up to the church and beyond it to a little gate, all the rest had been sown with different kinds of clover, which was now a lovely green and in flower. New graves were planned to start in a certain order from the farther end; but these plots were to be kept level and also sown with clover. No one could deny that this arrangement offered a pleasant and dignified sight to churchgoers on Sundays and holidays. Even the aged clergyman, although attached to old customs and at first not too pleased with the new grouping, now enjoyed it all and took his rest, like Philemon with his Baucis, under the old linden trees at his back door, seeing before him, not irregular mounds and hillocks, but a lovely colorful carpet, which would, moreover, be a profit to his household; for Charlotte had secured the produce of this place for the benefit of the parsonage.

But in spite of all this, several members of the congregation had for some time disapproved of the fact that the markings of the plots where their forefathers rested had been removed, and that their memory had, as it were, been obliterated by this action. For although the well-preserved gravestones indicated *who* had been buried, they did not say *where;* and this *where* was, as many maintained, really the thing that mattered.

This opinion was shared by a family in the neighborhood who, several years before, had reserved for themselves by contract a plot in this general place of rest, and in exchange had made a small endowment to the church. Now they had sent the young lawyer to announce that they cancelled this endowment, and would stop further payments, because the stipulation under which things had been done until now, had been eliminated by one party, in spite of all warnings and objections. Charlotte, who was the originator of these changes, wished to speak personally to the young lawyer who now presented, fervently but not too impolitely, his own and his client's reasons, thereby giving his audience food for some serious thoughts.

After a few introductory words, in which he gave a sound justification for his intrusion, the lawyer said: "You see what great importance the lowest and the highest attach to the marking of a spot that has received members of their families. The poorest farmer who buries his child feels a kind of comfort when he places a flimsy wooden cross on its grave, and hangs a wreath over it, in order to keep memory alive as long as his grief is alive; even if such a memorial is finally effaced by Time along with the mourner's grief. Well-to-do people change these crosses of wood to iron, and they fasten and protect them in many ways that may promise durability for at least some years. But because these crosses, too, will in the end collapse and lose their lustre, the wealthy are eager to set up a memorial of stone which promises to last for generations to come and can be renovated and restored by their descendents. It is not the stone which attracts us but that what lies beneath and has been received by the earth. It is not only a question of the monument, but also of the person; not only of a memory of the past but also of the present. The beloved departed is much closer to us when we see the mound before us—the mound rather than the monument, which is in itself of small significance. But around a grave as around a memorial husband or wife, relatives and friends are meant to gather after the dead have passed away; and the living should also have the right to keep off and turn away any strangers or ill-disposed people from the side of the beloved person who sleeps there. For all these reasons, therefore, I think my client is perfectly right in withdrawing the endowment; and it is a fair enough act, because the members of his family have been so offended that they can never be compensated. They are deprived of the bittersweet feeling that it is possible for them to bring their tributes to their dead; and they are also deprived of the fond hope of resting at some later day by their sides."

"The whole matter is not important enough to provoke a law-suit," Charlotte replied. "I regret so little what I have done, that I am willing to indemnify the church for its loss. But I must tell you quite frankly that your arguments have not convinced me. The pure feeling of a final, universal equality, at least after death, seems to me a greater comfort than this obstinate, rigid persistence upon our personalities, our attachments and the circumstances of our life. And what is your opinion?" she asked, turning to the Architect.

"In such an issue, I should prefer not to argue nor to have

my own notions influence the decision. Allow me modestly to mention something which pertains to my own art and therefore to my own point of view. We are no longer fortunate enough to be able to press to our hearts an urn with the ashes of our beloved, nor are we nowadays either rich or naïve enough to expect that we can preserve beloved remains from decay in large, elaborately ornamented sarcophagi. We are also no longer allowed to appropriate a place in a church for ourselves and our families but are banished into the open. For all these reasons we may, I think, approve of the ways and means Your Ladyship has introduced here. When the members of a congregation lie buried in one cemetery, they rest together as families, and if it is our destiny to be received one day by the earth, I do not think anything could be more natural than to level the mounds. They were, in any case, raised for a short while and will gradually disappear again; so that the covering now borne by all will be lighter for each."

"Do you mean to say that everything should pass away without a sign to evoke a memory?" Ottilie asked, in wonder.

"By no means!" the Architect continued. "We should not give up the memorial itself, only its position. The architect and the sculptor are extremely anxious for men to demand enduring evidence of their lives from them, from their art, from their handicraft. That is why I should like to see well-designed and well-executed monuments, not standing by themselves or scattered here and there at random, but set up together in a place which promises permanence for them. Since even the good and the great have renounced the privilege of being laid to rest in churches, we should at least set up monuments and hang up tablets with inscriptions in the churches or in beautiful arcades surrounding the cemeteries. Thousands of forms exist, which might be taken as patterns for these, and there are thousands of ornaments with which they might be adorned."

"If the artists are really so rich in models, please tell me why we never see anything but a mediocre obelisk, a broken column and an urn," Charlotte challenged him, "Instead of the thousands of forms which you boast of, I have never seen anything but a thousand repetitions of the same thing."

"That is perhaps the case in our country but not everywhere," the architect replied, "and a difficult problem probably always exists between intention and proper application. Especially in a case like this, the great difficulty lies in trying to enliven a melancholy subject and not to render unpleasant an unpleasant one. Regarding the designs for monuments of all sorts, I have collected many of these and will show them to you on occasion. But I believe that the best memorial for a man is his portrait. More than anything else it gives an idea of what he was; it is the best text to all that can be said about him in a few or many words; but it should be done only in his best years, and this is usually neglected. While people are still alive, no one thinks of preserving their human forms, and if it *is* done, it is mostly done inefficiently. Sometimes a cast is taken in a hurry after a person's death; and such a death mask is set up on a pedestal and called a portrait bust. How rarely has an artist the skill to make it completely lifelike!"

"Perhaps without intention and purpose you have turned the scales of this discussion entirely in my favor," Charlotte remarked. "The portrait of a person is, without any doubt, quite independent; in whatever place it stands, it stands by itself and need not necessarily mark the burial place proper. But I have to confess to a strange sort of emotional aversion to portrait busts. They always seem to me like a silent reproach; they point toward something far away and passed away, and remind me how difficult it is really to be just to the present. If we recall how many people we have seen and known, and confess to ourselves how little we have meant to them, how little they have meant to us—what must then be our feelings! We meet a man of genius without talking with him, a scholar without trying to learn from him, a widely-traveled person without broadening our knowledge, a person full of love without showing him any kindness.

"Unfortunately, this does not happen with casual encounters only. Societies and families behave in the same way toward their dearest members, cities toward their most deserving citizens, peoples toward their best sovereigns, nations toward their most distinguished men.

"I once heard someone ask: Why has everyone good words only for the dead, while there is always some caution in the case of the living? The answer was: because we have nothing to fear from the former, whereas it is still possible that we may meet the latter. Our concern for the memory of the others is often insincere and for the greater part only a selfish game; but we should be absolutely serious in keeping our relations with those who are still living always cordial and active."

chapter 20

STIMULATED by this incident and by the discussion arising from it, they went the following day to the churchyard, where the Architect made several happy suggestions. But the church itself was also to be entrusted to his care—a building which had aroused his interest from the moment of his arrival.

This church, built in the early German style, had been standing here for many centuries; its proportions were good, and its ornaments remarkable. One could clearly see that the master-builder of a monastery in the neighborhood had left, on this smaller building, authentic traces of his judgment and taste. It still made a solemn and peaceful impression on the observer, although the new arrangements for a Protestant service had deprived the interior of some of its calm and grandeur.

It was not difficult for the Architect to ask for, and to receive, from Charlotte, a small sum of money which he intended to use for the restoration in the old tradition, of the exterior as well as of the interior of the church and bring it into harmony with the "resurrection field" in front of it. He possessed considerable manual skill; and some men who were still busy at the new lodge could be kept on until this pious task was also finished.

They could now begin to make a thorough examination of the whole building with all its grounds and annexes; and in the course of this the Architect discovered, to his great surprise and delight, an almost forgotten little side-chapel of still more ingenious and balanced proportions, with still more beautiful and carefully worked out ornaments. This chapel also contained many carved and painted remnants of that earlier service which had marked the different church festivals with various vessels and vestments, and had celebrated each in its traditional way.

It seemed impossible to the Architect not to include the chapel in his project; and he decided to restore this narrow space with particular care, as a monument of earlier times and of their taste. He already imagined how he would like to see the empty wall spaces decorated, and looked eagerly forward to practicing there his talent for painting. But for the time being he kept this a secret from the others.

Before he began his restoration, he showed the two women, as he had promised, different reproductions and designs of ancient monuments for the dead, of urns and other objects to the same purpose. When the conversation turned upon the primitive *tumuli* of the Northern peoples, he also showed them his collection of various weapons and tools found in these places. He kept everything very neatly, and easily to be carried, in drawers and compartments, on partitioned and cloth-covered trays, so that, by the way he treated them, these grim old things appeared almost like precious trinkets. It was a pleasure to look at them, as though one were looking into the boxes of a dealer in jewels.

Since he had begun this display of his treasures, which formed an entertainment for the two lonely women, he got into the habit of producing every evening another part of his collection: objects mostly of German origin. Among these were thin mediaeval plates of silver, large silver coins, seals, and other things of this nature. All these objects directed the imagination toward ancient times; and as he finally illustrated his talks with the first examples of the art of printing, with wood-cuts and the earliest copper-plate prints; and as the church, developed from day to day, in decoration and color, in the spirit of the same age,—the question quite naturally arose: Were they actually living in modern times? Was it not a dream that they were surrounded by quite different habits, customs, modes of life and ideas?

After such preparation, a large portfolio which he finally produced made the strongest impression on them. It contained for the most part mere outlines of figures, but these had been traced from the original pictures, and therefore had completely preserved their ancient character—and how charming this character was, in the eyes of the spectators! All the figures breathed a perfect purity of heart; all were, if not noble, certainly full of goodness. Serene composure, willing recognition of a Divine Being above us, silent devotion full of love and hope, were expressed on their faces and in their gestures. The bald-headed ancient, the boy with his profusion of curls, the buoyant youth, and the serious man; the Saint transfigured, the angel hovering in the air,—all seemed to be in a state of heavenly bliss, happy in an innocent, contented, pious expectation. The most ordinary scenes had a touch of heavenly beauty; and every being seemed to be worthy of a part in the divine service. Most people, very likely, look with yearning toward such a realm, in the way we look back toward a vanished Golden Age, a paradise lost. Ottilie was perhaps the only one who felt at home in that world.

After all this, who could have rejected the Architect's offer to paint the wall spaces between the pointed arches of the chapel in the manner of the original pictures—murals he wished to leave as his own memorial in a place where he had spent such happy days. He said this with a touch of sadness, for he knew that, as matters stood, his stay in this delightful company could not last forever: it might very soon come to an end.

Although not very much happened during these days, there was always occasion for serious conversations. We take this opportunity to set down some of the comments, written by Ottilie in her diary; and we cannot find a more suitable transition than a comparison which struck us as we were looking through her moving pages.

There is a curious custom in the British Navy: all the cordage of the Royal Fleet, whether heavy or light, is twisted so that a red thread runs through whole ropes, by which even the smallest piece can be recognized as Crown property.

In the same way a thread of love and deep attachment seems to run through Ottilie's diary, connecting everything she writes, and giving it a distinctive character. Because of this thread, the young girl's comments, observations and quotations bear a special mark, and convey a particular meaning. Each passage we have selected and recorded is definite proof of this.

From Ottilie's Diary

That we shall some day rest by the side of those we love, is the most comforting thought we can have, when we think about the Hereafter. "To be gathered to our fathers"—are extremely heart-warming words.

So many different kinds of monuments and memorials exist, which bring those who have died, and friends who have left us, closer to our hearts. But nothing is as significant as a portrait. To talk to the picture of a person dear to

157

us, though it may not be a good likeness, is as delightful as an occasional quarrel with a friend. We have the pleasant impression of being two who still cannot be separated.

Sometimes we speak to a person who is in our presence, as though we would speak to a picture. It is not necessary that he should speak to us or look at us or pay us any attention: it is *we* who look at him and deeply feel our relation with him, which may become even closer, without any action on his part, without his even being aware of it, since for us he is nothing but a picture.

We are never satisfied with the portraits of people we know. I have therefore always felt sorry for portrait-painters. Though we rarely expect from anyone the impossible, we expect it from them. They are supposed to include in their portraits everyone's relation to the original, whether it be sympathy or antipathy, and to paint him not only as *they* see him but as everyone else does. I am not surprised that such artists become, little by little, stubborn, indifferent and intractable. This would not matter so much, if it did not frequently deprive us of the portraits of many persons, dear to us.

It is certainly true, and borne out by the Architect's collection of weapons and tools, once buried with the dead under high mounds of earth or stones, that man's careful provisions for the preservation of his personality after death, are entirely useless. And how inconsistent we are! The Architect admits having himself opened such burial mounds of forebears, yet he keeps on occupying himself with monuments for their descendents.

But why should we be so critical? Is perhaps all we do done for eternity? Do we not put on our clothes in the morning, only to take them off in the evening? Do we not travel in order to come back again? And why should we not wish to rest by the side of our families and friends, though it may be only for a century?

When we see the many sunken tombstones, worn by the footsteps of churchgoers, and the churches, collapsed over their own memorial—tablets for the dead—life after death seems to us, indeed, a second life which man enters in the form of the portrait and the inscription, in which he exists longer than in his actual life-span. But this memorial, this second existence, will also be effaced—sooner or later. Time does not relinquish its rights, either over human beings or over monuments.

chapter 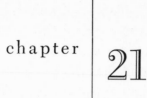 21

BECAUSE it affords us so much pleasure to occupy ourselves even with something we can do only imper-
fectly, we should not perhaps blame the dilettante for dabbling in an art he will never master; not should we blame
the artist who feels inclined to trespass, beyond the bound-
ary of his own field, on a neighboring one.

With these tolerant feelings we shall watch the Architect's
preparations in the chapel: he mixed the colors, took the
measurements and designed the preliminary cartoons. He
made no claim to originality, but kept strictly to his sketches.
His only concern was the skilfull composition of the seated
or floating figures and their decorative effect within the giv-
en space. Scaffolding was set up, and the work moved forward. As soon as something definite could be seen, he no
longer objected when Charlotte and Ottilie came over to
look at his work. The lifelike faces of the angels, their robes
billowing against a background of celestial blue, delighted
them, and the serene composure of their devotion touched
their hearts and filled their minds with peace.

They joined the artist on the scaffolding; and as soon as
Ottilie saw how easily and with how little effort the work
proceeded in just the manner it had been planned—every-

thing she had learned in school came back to her, and she understood its meaning. She took up a brush and some paint, and, after a few directions, touched in a richly folded drapery with accuracy and taste. Charlotte, who was always happy when she saw Ottilie busy or in some other way diverted, left the pair to their painting and went home alone, to follow the train of her thoughts and to work out on her own all the deliberations and worries which she could not confide to any other person.

When ordinary people are moved to strong emotions of passion and anxiety by common daily predicaments, we may smile indulgently, but we look with awed admiration on a mind which carries the seed of a great destiny, are forced to wait for the development of this seed, and must not and cannot hasten the good or the evil, the happiness or the misery, which is destined to come from it.

Eduard had sent an answer to Charlotte by the same messenger she had dispatched to him in his seclusion. His words had been kind and sympathetic, but at the same time more calm and grave than intimate and affectionate. Shortly afterward, Eduard disappeared, and Charlotte had not been able to obtain any news from him until, quite by accident, she saw his name in the newspaper, where he was mentioned with honor among those who had distinguished themselves in an important military engagement. She now knew where he had gone and that he had escaped great danger. But she was also convinced that he would expose himself to still greater danger, and she understood only too well that it would be impossible to restrain him from extreme action. She carried this constant anxiety in her thoughts, and no matter how she might look at it, she could find no comfort.

Ottilie had not the slightest suspicion of all this—she had become very much interested in her work in the chapel and

had easily obtained Charlotte's permission to continue painting there regularly. The work was progressing rapidly, and
soon the azure sky was filled with suitable figures. Through
continued practice Ottilie and the Architect worked with
more independence on the later pictures, which were distinctly better than the first. The faces, which had been left
to the Architect, increasingly revealed a very peculiar quality: they all began to resemble Ottilie. To be so close to her
had obviously made so strong an impression on the young
man, who had not yet formed a preference for any one
natural or artistic facial type, that on the way from his eye
to his hand, nothing was lost—eventually, both worked together in perfect accord. One of the last little countenances
he painted was a perfect likeness—it seemed that Ottilie herself looked down from the heavenly spaces.

The vaulting was finished; the walls were to be left un-
decorated and only painted a lighter umber tint; the slender
pillars and the ingeniously carved ornaments were to be contrasted in a darker shade. But since, in such cases, one thing
leads to another, they decided at the last moment to add
festoons of flowers and fruit, to unite, as it were, heaven and
earth. Here Ottilie was in her element. The gardens supplied
them with the loveliest motifs; and although the wreaths
turned out to be very luxuriant, all was completed much
earlier than it had been planned.

But everything else still looked very untidy and unfinished. The scaffolding had been piled up helter-skelter,
planks thrown one on top of the other; the uneven floor
looked worse than ever because of the paint they had
dropped on it. The Architect now asked the two ladies for a
week's time and for their promise not to enter the chapel
until then. One fine evening he finally invited them both to

go and see for themselves: he himself did not wish to accompany them and left immediately.

"Whatever surprise he may have in store for us, I am not, at the moment, in a mood to go see it," Charlotte said, after the young man's departure. "You won't mind going alone and telling me all about it later? I am sure he has created something beautiful. I shall enjoy it first in your description and then, with much greater pleasure, in reality."

Ottilie, who was well aware that Charlotte was now in many respects very careful—she avoided anything that might upset her and in particular disliked being surprised—started out at once. She looked, instinctively, for the Architect but could not see him anywhere—he was possibly hiding. The church was finished, cleaned and consecrated earlier. It was open and she entered. She stepped to the chapel door; its heavy bronze weight opened easily, and she was surprised by the unexpected sight of the familiar place.

A solemn many-colored light fell through the symmetrical panes of the one high stained-glass window. The whole space had taken on an unfamiliar quality and induced a peculiar mood. The beauty of the vaulting and the walls was heightened by the decorative design of the floor, paved with specially shaped bricks which were joined by mortar to form a beautiful pattern. These bricks as well as the stained-glass panes had been secretly assembled by the Architect and then been put together in a very short time. He had also looked about for seats. Among the ecclesiastical antiques, mentioned before, he had found some exquisitely carved chancel stalls and had arranged them along the walls.

Ottilie was delighted to see these familiar pieces now forming an unfamiliar whole. She stopped here and there and walked up and down, examining and re-examining

163

everything; at last she sat down in one of the seats: looking above and around her, it almost seemed to her that she existed and yet did not exist; that she felt and did not feel— as if all this might vanish before her eyes and she might vanish too. Only when the sun left the window through which it had shone so brightly, did Ottilie waken from her dream and hurry back to the castle.

The fact did not escape her that this surprise had occurred at a strange moment. It was the eve of Eduard's birthday. How differently had she hoped to celebrate it—how she had wished to decorate everything for this occasion! But now the wealth of autumn flowers stood ungathered. The sunflowers still turned their disks to the sky; the asters looked about them with their quiet modesty, and the only flowers which had been made into wreaths had served as models for the decoration of a place, which, if it were not to remain merely an artist's whim but was to be used for any true purpose, seemed appropriate only for a family tomb.

She could not help remembering the noisy festivities with which Eduard had celebrated her own birthday; and she recalled the events at the newly finished house, under whose roof they had hoped to spend many hours. The fireworks flashed and sputtered again before her eyes—the lonelier she was, the more vividly she saw everything in her imagination, but she also felt a deeper loneliness. She no longer leaned on his arm; and she had lost all hope ever to be thus supported again.

From Ottilie's Diary

I must make a note of a remark made by the young artist: we observe quite distinctly in the case of the craftsman as well as of the creative artist, that man is least able to appropriate to himself what is truly his own. His works utterly desert him, as birds desert the nest in which they have been hatched.

In this connection, the architect's fate is the strangest of all fates. How often does he give his intelligence and his entire devotion to the creation of buildings from which he is excluded! The halls of royal palaces owe their magnificence to him, but he does not enjoy them in their full splendor. In places of worship he draws a line between himself and the Holy of Holies: he is no longer allowed to ascend the steps which he has built for the heart-stirring celebration—like the goldsmith who only from a distance worships the monstrance whose enamel and precious stones he has set together. It is to the rich man that the masterbuilder gives, together with the key of the palace, all the luxury and opulence he will never enjoy. Is it not obvious that in this way his art will gradually withdraw from the artist, when his work, like a child who is well provided for, need no longer fall back on its father? And how much had art to do for its own advancement in the days when it was destined to work almost entirely in the public interest, with matters which belonged to all and consequently to the artist as well!

One conception of the ancients is solemn and almost frightening. They imagined their ancestors sitting in huge caves in a circle on thrones, in silent communion. When a newcomer entered, they rose and bowed their heads to welcome him, if he deserved it. Yesterday, when I was sitting in the chapel in my carved seat and saw opposite me other seats arranged in a circle, I remembered this, and it was a comforting and happy thought. Why can you not remain here? I said to myself,—remain here, quiet and lost in your thoughts for a long, long time, until your friends arrive at last and you will rise, and with a friendly gesture direct them to their places. The stained-glass panes transform the day into somber twilight; someone should donate an everburning lamp, so that here even the night would not be complete darkness.

We may imagine ourselves in any situation we like, but we always think of ourselves as *seeing*. I believe that the reason man dreams is because he should not stop seeing. Some day perhaps the inner light will shine forth from us, and then we shall need no other light.

The year moves toward its end like a sound toward silence. The wind sweeps over the stubble, and there is nothing for it to stir. Only the red berries of those slender trees seem to wish to remind us of gaiety; just as the rhythmic beat of the thresher's flail reminds us how much nourishment and life lie concealed in the sickled ear.

chapter 22

THESE incidents had filled Ottilie with a sense of instability and impermanence, and it was therefore a strange and unexpected shock to hear the news, which could no longer be kept a secret from her, that Eduard had exposed himself to the chances of war. Unfortunately, none of the possibilities involved escaped her; but, fortunately, we can absorb disastrous news only up to a certain point—anything beyond that destroys us or leaves us indifferent. There are situations in which hope and fear become one, cancel each other out, and are lost in dull apathy. How could we, otherwise, bear knowing that our distant loved ones are in continual danger, and yet go on as usual with our everyday life? It was therefore as though a benevolent spirit was caring for Ottilie by introducing into this quiet atmosphere, in which she seemed alone and inactive, a sudden flood of visitors; these gave her enough work to do, and at the same time drew her out of her seclusion and restored to her an awareness of her own strength.

Hardly had Luciane, Charlotte's daughter, left school to come out in society, to find herself surrounded by friends and admirers in her great-aunt's house, when her pleasing disposition found favor in the eyes of a very rich young man, who fell violently in love with her and wished to marry her. His large fortune gave him a right to own the best of everything, and he seemed to have everything except a perfect wife whom the whole world would envy him.

This domestic event had already kept Charlotte busy for some time; she devoted to it all her attention and all her correspondence, with the exception of the letters written to obtain more detailed information concerning Eduard. This was also the reason why Ottilie had been lately left to herself more than usual. Although the young girl knew about Luciane's expected arrival and had made the most necessary preparations, no one expected the visit so soon. Charlotte was about to write another letter to settle some details and to suggest a definite date, when the storm suddenly broke over the castle and over Ottilie's head.

The ladies' maids, the valets, and the *brancards* with trunks and boxes were the first to arrive, and even then it seemed as though two or three families were already in the house; but only now did the guests themselves arrive: Luciane with her great-aunt, some friends, and her fiancé, who had brought along a group of his own friends. The hall was littered with bags, portmanteaus, and all sorts of leather cases. It took some time to sort out all the smaller boxes. More luggage was brought in and moved about. In addition, it began to rain, causing much inconvenience. Ottilie met all this tumult and confusion with complete calm, and her cheerful efficiency was shown to advantage. In the shortest possible time she had arranged, and disposed of, everything. Everyone had been shown to a room, and felt well taken care of.

The moment came when everybody wished to rest after the tiring journey. Luciane's fiancé wanted to talk with his future mother-in-law, to assure her of his affection and good will; but Luciane herself would not rest. For the first time she had experienced the joy of riding horseback, and her fiancé had excellent horses which she wished to try without delay. Wind and weather, rain or storm, did not matter; the one thing in life that did seem to matter was first to get soaking wet and then dry again. When she felt in a mood for walking, she did not care how she was dressed or what shoes she wore; she had to inspect the new grounds of which she had heard so much. What she could not do on horseback, she did on foot—but always running. In a very short time she had seen everything and—criticized everything. She had such a quick temper that it was not easy to contradict her. The other guests had a great deal to bear, most of all her maids, who were continually washing, pressing, ripping things up, and sewing them together again.

As soon as she had finished exploring the castle and its immediate surroundings, she felt it her duty to make calls on all the neighbors. Since she and her friends rode and drove very fast, the area of neighborhood was extended on all sides. The castle was soon swamped with people returning the visits; and, in order that hosts and guests should not miss one another, special days were agreed upon when the hosts would stay at home.

While Charlotte tried to settle the financial arrangements with her aunt and the fiancé's agent, and Ottilie was busy with the servants, taking care that nothing was lacking for so many, and setting hunters and gardeners, fishermen and shopkeepers in motion, Luciane was behaving like the blazing heart of a comet which drags a long tail in its wake. The ordinary entertainment offered to visitors soon became boring to her taste. Even the oldest persons, peacefully sitting at their card-tables, were not safe from her restlessness. Anyone who could still move a limb—and who could resist moving when coaxed by her charming insistence?—had to join her, if not to dance, then to play at forfeits and puzzles. But although all these games, particularly the redeeming of forfeits, were calculated for her own personal interest, no one, on the other hand (particularly no man, of any sort) ever went entirely unrewarded; and she was even successful in winning over to her some elderly distinguished persons, when she discovered the dates of their birthdays or name days and then celebrated these with special courtesy. On every such occasion, her personal skill in showing kindness to all was very useful, since she gave every single person to believe that he was the most favored: a weakness of which even the oldest man among the guests conspicuously proved himself guilty.

If it seemed to be her firm determination to conquer every man of importance,—or rank, character, fame or of whatever repute; to defeat wisdom and moderation and even to cause the sedate to forgive her wild, strange ways—the younger people were by no means losers in all this; each one received his share, his day and his hour, when she would deliberately set out to delight and captivate him. It could be expected that she would soon single out the Architect,—who, however, looking innocently from under his long dark hair, stood quite unmoved, at a quiet distance, and answered all her questions briefly and sensibly, without seeming to show the least inclination to go any farther; so that one day she decided,—half in anger and half in cunning—to make him that day's hero, and to win him over to her court of admirers by a trick.

Not unintentionally had she brought so much luggage with her, and had even sent for more. She had provided an endless array of dresses for herself since she liked to change three or four times a day from an ordinary gown to something more elegant—and this went on from morning to night.

170

But in between she now and then appeared in actual fancy-dress—as a peasant-woman or a fisherman's wife; as a good fairy or a flower-girl. She was not even afraid of disguising herself as an old woman, if only to show her young, fresh face framed in a cowl; and she mixed so much of the actual with the fantastic that one might have thought one's self to be related directly, or by marriage to a nymph of the river Saale.

But her principal purpose for all these costumes was their use in pantomimes and dances, in which she was very good at expressing different characters. One of her admirers had arranged with her to accompany her performance with incidental music on the piano. They needed only to exchange a few words of explanation to understand each other at once.

One day, during an intermission of a gay ball, Luciane was asked for such a performance. The question seemed to come on the spur of the moment; but she herself earlier had secretly dropped a hint. Now she pretended to be embarrassed and taken by surprise; and she was also for a time reluctant, which was quite unlike her. She seemed undecided, wished the others to choose her rôle, and asked for a theme, as an improviser does, until at last her accompanist, with whom she had very likely arranged everything beforehand, sat down at the piano and, beginning to play a funeral march, asked her to do the *Artemisia*, which she had studied so admirably. She let herself be persuaded, and, after a short absence, again appeared as the royal widow carrying an urn in her arms and walking with measured steps to the tender and mournful sound of the funeral march. Behind her, a large blackboard was carried in, together with a well-sharpened stick of chalk fastened in a golden drawing-pen holder.

One of her admirers and aides, into whose ear she whispered, approached the Architect and asked—or rather, forced—him, while pushing him toward her, to draw, as a masterbuilder would, the tomb of Mausolus; adding that he should not consider himself by any means a supernumerary, but one of the actual performers. The Architect who, in his black tight-fitting modern civilian dress formed an odd contrast to all Luciane's gauze, crêpe, fringes, jet, tassels and crowns, looked very embarrassed at first, but soon regained his composure; still, it was a strange sight! With the greatest seriousness, he took his stand in front of the blackboard, which was supported by two pages, and slowly and carefully executed a drawing of a tomb which, although more appropriate for a king of the Langobards than for one of Caria, had such beautiful proportions, was so serious in all its details and so ingenious in its ornaments, that everyone present watched the drawing grow with delight; and all were full of admiration when it was finished.

All this time the Architect had almost never looked in the direction of the Queen, but had given his whole attention to his task. When he finally bowed to her, to indicate that he believed he had carried out her orders, she offered him the urn, suggesting her wish to see it portrayed on the top of the tomb. He did this, although unwillingly, since it did not fit into the character of the rest. Luciane was now at last satisfied; it had certainly not been her intention to have him do a meticulous drawing. If he had done a hasty sketch in a few strokes, something approximately resembling a monument, and had occupied himself with her for the remainder of the time, it would have been much more to her liking. His behavior had made matters very difficult for her; she tried to vary somehow the expression of her grief, her commands and suggestions as well as her approval of the growing design, and even—in order to focus his attention on her—almost pushed him about. He, in turn, behaved so stiffly that she had to shift the urn much too frequently, pressing it to her heart and gazing up to heaven. Since a performance of this sort is bound to demand ever increasing intensity, she soon resembled a widow of Ephesus rather than a queen of Caria. For all these reasons the entertainment lasted much too long; the pianist, who had been very patient, was at a loss into what key he should modulate. He thanked God when he saw the urn standing on top of the pyramid, and involuntarily, just when the queen was on the point of expressing her gratitude, struck up a merry tune. This changed the whole character of the performance but cheered up the party, which at once divided into two groups—one expressing their delight and admiration to the lady for her excellent acting, the other showing the Architect their appreciation of his fine and artistic delineation.

The fiancé was particularly enthusiastic. "I am sorry that your drawing is so impermanent," he said. "Won't you at least allow me to have it brought to my room, so I can discuss it with you later?"

"If you are interested, I can show you elaborate drawings of monuments and buildings of that kind compared to which this is only a casual and imperfect sketch," the Architect replied.

Ottilie was standing not far away and now came nearer. "Don't forget to show your collection to the Baron," she said. "He is a friend of art and antiquity, and I wish you two would become better acquainted with one another."

Luciane swept up and asked: "What are you talking about?"

"Of a collection of works of art which this gentleman possesses and will show us some time," the Baron answered.

"Go and get it immediately," Luciane exclaimed. "You *will* bring it at once, won't you?" she added, touching him kindly with both hands.

"I do not think that this is the right moment," he replied.

"What! You refuse to obey the orders of your queen?" Luciane cried in a commanding tone. Then she began to coax him like a child.

"Don't be stubborn!" Ottilie said in a low voice.

The Architect left them with a slight inclination of his head, neither "yes" nor "no."

He had hardly gone when Luciane began to chase through the room with her greyhound. "Alas! How unhappy I am," she exclaimed, brushing against her mother by accident. "I did not bring my monkey with me; everyone advised against it; it is only the laziness of my servants that deprives me of my fun. But I am going to have it brought here—I shall send someone to fetch it. It would even cheer me up to see his picture. I must have his portrait done, and I'll never again let it leave my side."

"I can perhaps cheer you by sending to our library for a whole volume filled with the most extraordinary pictures of monkeys," Charlotte said. Luciane shrieked with joy, and the large folio was brought. The sight of these hideous creatures, resembling men and, as drawn by the artist, exaggeratedly so, gave Luciane the greatest pleasure. But she was particularly happy in discovering in every single animal a resemblance to a person known to her. "Does he not look like my uncle?" she cried, mercilessly "and this one like M . . . our dealer in trinkets, and that one so like Parson S . . .; but this one is really the very image of Mr. So-and-So. After all, monkeys are the true "Dandies," and it is difficult to understand why they are excluded from good society."

All this was said in the presence of the best society; but no one resented it. Everyone was so used to allow her charm all possible liberty that they finally permitted her naughtiness, too.

Meanwhile Ottilie talked with Luciane's fiancé. She hoped that the Architect would return and, with his more serious and tasteful collection, rescue the company from this disgraceful fuss about monkeys. With this expectation in mind she talked to the Baron and told him more about the collection. But the Architect did not at once return; and when he at last appeared, he lost himself among the guests. He had not brought anything with him, and behaved as though no one had ever asked him for anything. Ottilie was for a few moments—how shall we describe it?—annoyed, angry, hurt; she had spoken kindly to him and she had also wished to give the Baron a pleasant hour, since she felt that, in spite of his deep love for Luciane, he quite evidently suffered because of her extravagant behavior.

The monkeys had to make way for supper. Social games, even more dancing, and finally a bored sitting about, and several attempts to stimulate an almost exhausted desire for pleasure, dragged out this time, as usual, until long past midnight. For it had already become a habit with Luciane never to get out of bed in the morning and never to get into it at night.

During these weeks Ottilie rarely recorded actual events in her diary; but she wrote down, more frequently, maxims and aphorisms which either referred to life or were taken from it. Since the greater part of these are probably not her own thoughts, it is likely that someone had given her a book, from which she copied those which corresponded to her feelings. But many of her own thoughts, related to the deep experiences of her heart, will easily be recognized by the red thread.

From Ottilie's Diary

We love to look into the future, because we should dearly like, by our silent wishing, to guide in our own favor the Undetermined that wavers there.

In a large gathering of people the thought seldom leaves us, that Chance, which brings so many together, may also lead our friends here.

However secluded we may live, sooner or later, and before we realize it, we become either debtors or creditors.

Whenever we meet a person who owes us a debt of gratitude, we instantly remember it. But how often do we meet someone, to whom *we* are indebted, without remembering it.

To communicate our thoughts to others is nature; to assimilate what is communicated to us, with understanding, is culture.

No one would talk much in society, if he knew how often he misunderstands others.

When we repeat what we have heard others say, we change a good deal; no doubt only because we did not really understand everything, to begin with.

He who talks alone and at length before others without flattering his audience, arouses antipathy.

Every word that is spoken provokes its contrary.

Both contradiction and flattery make poor conversation.

The most agreeable societies are those, governed by an easy mutual regard of their members.

Nothing reveals people's character more than their reaction to what they consider laughable.

The ridiculous arises from a moral contrast, by which, in a harmless way, two matters become connected in our mind.

The natural man often laughs, when there is no reason for it. Whatever stimulates him, it is his inner well-being that comes to the surface.

The reasoning man considers almost anything ridiculous; the reasonable man almost nothing.

An elderly man was sharply criticized for continuing to pay court to young women. "It is the only way to keep young," he replied, "and that is certainly everybody's desire."

We can bear being criticized for our faults, and even bear to be punished and to suffer on their account; but we become impatient, when we are expected to give them up.

Some faults are necessary to the life of the individual. We would be sorry if old friends gave up certain peculiarities.

People say "He will die soon," when someone acts in a way that is not characteristic of him.

What kind of faults are we permitted to keep, even to indulge in? Those which flatter rather than hurt others.

Passions are weaknesses or virtues, but intensified.

Our passions are true phoenixes. As soon as the old bird consumes itself, a new one rises at once from the ashes.

Great passions are incurable diseases. What might cure them, makes them all the more dangerous.

Passion becomes ennobled and calmed by confession. Nowhere is a middle course more desirable than in the choice of what we confide to, or conceal from, those we love.

chapter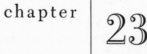

AND so the intoxication of living kept driving Luciane ever deeper into the vortex of social amusements. Her court of admirers daily increased, partly because her drive animated and attracted many; partly because she knew how to attach others to herself by her acts of kindness and her generosity. She was indeed generous to a high degree; and since her great-aunt's affection and her fiancé's love had flooded her so suddenly with so much that was beautiful and precious, it seemed as if nothing she possessed really belonged to her, and as if she did not know the value of the objects which accumulated around her. Therefore she never for a moment hesitated to take from her shoulders an expensive shawl and wrap it around a young woman who, in her opinion, was poorly dressed compared to others; and she did this, moreover, in such a droll and clever way that no one could refuse a gift, because of the way it was given. One of her followers always carried with him a sum of money, and had been instructed to inquire, in whatever place they stopped, after the most sick and the oldest persons, and to relieve their situation at least temporarily. In this way she made herself a great reputation in this part of the country; but this practice was also sometices a great nuisance, since far too many needy persons were attracted to her.

Nothing increased her popularity more than her extraordinary and unwavering kindness to an unhappy young man who had given up all social life because he, otherwise handsome and well built, had lost his right hand, although with honor, in action. This disability had made him so melancholy, and the fact that each new acquaintance had to be told the story of his accident was so annoying, that he preferred to hide himself, devoting all his time to reading and studying, and not wanting to have anything to do with society.

Luciane had, of course heard of this young man. She did not rest, until he came first to small parties, then to larger ones, and finally to the largest. She paid more attention to him than to anyone else; and because of her eagerness to help him and her determination to compensate him for his loss, she even succeeded in making it valuable to him. At dinner she made him sit next to her and cut up his food for him, so that he needed only to use his fork. If he had to give up his place to older people or persons of higher rank, she extended her attention across the entire table, and the servants had to run and render him the services of which his distance from her deprived him. Finally she encouraged him to learn to write with his left hand; he had to address all his attempts to her, so that she was, far or near, constantly in touch with him. The young man did not know what had happened to him, and from this time on really started a new life.

One would have imagined that Luciane's fiancé might not have been pleased with such behavior, but just the opposite was true. He thought it much to her credit that she took all this trouble; he was not worried, since he knew her almost exaggerated fear of being entangled in anything in the least risky. She wanted to handle everyone according to her mood; at one time or another everyone was in danger of being pushed or pulled about, or otherwise teased by her; but no one was allowed to do the same with her—no one dared to touch her if she was unwilling; no one could take the slightest liberties with her in return for those she herself had taken. In this way she kept the others within the strictest bounds of proper behavior, whereas she herself seemed to trespass continually upon this propriety.

One might really have believed that it was a matter of principle with her to expose herself equally to praise and to blame, to affection and to dislike. For, although she tried in all sorts of ways to win people, she offended them at the same time by her sharp tongue which spared no one. After her visits to near-by castles and country houses, where the kindest hospitality had been shown to her and her guests, she would make the most reckless comments, which indicated that she saw all human relationships and conditions from a ridiculous angle only. There were, for example, the three brothers, who from sheer politeness as to who should marry first, had been overtaken by old age; there was the little young wife with the big old husband; and there was the jolly little man and the clumsy giantess. In one of the houses they had at every step stumbled over a child; another never seemed to be crowded—even with a host of guests—because there were no children at all. Old husbands should hurry to get themselves quickly buried, to give people an opportunity to laugh, since there were no legitimate heirs. Young couples should travel, because keeping house did not become them. She even treated objects in the same way as persons—house, furniture, the various articles of a dinner service. The wall decoration of a room provoked her in particular to merry remarks. From the oldest tapestry to the latest wallpaper, from the most venerable family portrait to the most frivolous new copper-plate engraving—they all had to suffer, pulled to pieces, as it were, by her sarcastic remarks; and it was almost a miracle, that for five miles around, anything continued to exist at all.

Her tendency always to be negative was not really malicious; usually she was prompted by an egotistic love of mischief; but true bitterness had developed in her relationship with Ottilie. She looked down with contempt on the younger girl's quiet, consistent activity, which was noticed and admired by all; and when Ottilie's great interest in the gardens and her good care of them and of the hothouses was mentioned one day, Luciane ridiculed it, pretending to be surprised—although it was now the depth of winter—that she could see neither flowers nor fruit. She also ordered from this time on so much green stuff, so many branches, even those in bud, for the daily decoration of the rooms and of the dinner table that Ottilie and the gardener were extremely distressed to see their hopes for the coming year, and perhaps longer, destroyed.

Luciane also begrudged Ottilie the quiet round of her domestic life in which she moved with so much ease. She forced her to join excursions and sleigh rides and to attend the balls which were arranged in the neighborhood; she was not supposed to mind the snow or the cold or the heavy night storms because, after all, other people did not die of such things. The delicate girl suffered under the strain, and Luciane gained nothing from all this; for although Ottilie was always very simply dressed, she was always—or so at least the men seemed to think—the most beautiful. Her gentle charm gathered all the men around her, whether she was in the foreground or in the background. Even Luciane's

181

fiancé often talked with her, especially because he wanted her advice and assistance in a matter which occupied his mind.

He had come to know the Architect better, and, looking at his collection, had talked to him about its history. On other occasions, particularly when he saw the chapel, he had learned to appreciate the young man's talent. The Baron was young and wealthy; he was himself a collector and he wished to build; but, although his love for the arts was strong, his technical knowledge was limited. He now thought he had found in the Architect the man who could help him attain more than one purpose at the same time. He had told Luciane of his intention, and she had applauded it, delighted with the proposal, more, perhaps, because she hoped she could take the young man away from Ottilie—for she believed she had detected in him signs of a fondness for her—than because she wished to use his talents properly. Although he had proved very useful at her improvised entertainments and had made many intelligent suggestions, she always believed that she herself could do things better; and as her own inventions were for the most part very primitive, the skill of a clever valet would have served her as well as that of a superior artist. Her imagination was not capable of much more than an altar on which something could be sacrificed, or a wreath to crown some head (whether living or of plaster) on the occasions of a birthday or other day of honor.

Ottilie was best able to give the Baron the desired information, when he asked her about the position of the Architect at the castle. She knew that Charlotte had already taken steps to find him a new position. If the visitors had not arrived, the young man would have left immediately after finishing his work in the chapel, for during the winter all construction work would necessarily come to a standstill.

It was therefore very desirable for him to find employment with a new patron.

Ottilie's personal relationship to the Architect was entirely innocent and natural. She had always keenly enjoyed his pleasant and active presence like that of an older brother. Her feeling for him remained on the quiet dispassionate level of a family relationship, for there was room in her heart for Eduard alone: it was filled to the brim with her love for him, and only the Deity that pervades all things could share her heart with him.

As winter advanced, the weather became inclement, and the roads more impassable; and the charm of spending the shortened days in congenial company increased. After brief periods of quiet, a tide of visitors would, now and then, flood the house again. Officers from distance garrisons were drawn to the castle; the educated among them were a welcome addition, while the ruder ones were frequently a nuisance. There was also no lack of civilians, and—quite unexpectedly—the Count and the Baroness arrived together one day.

Their visit created for the first time a real Court atmosphere. The men of rank and distinction formed a circle around the Count, and the ladies paid due homage to the Baroness. No one was surprised to see the couple together in such high spirits, for they now learned that the Count's wife had died and that the new marriage would take place as soon as propriety permitted. Ottilie thought of their first visit and remembered every word that had then been said about marriage and divorce, about uniting and separating—about hope, expectation, renunciation and resignation. Both these persons, at that time facing a hopeless future, were now standing before her, close to their hoped-for happiness; and an involuntary sigh escaped her.

No sooner had Luciane heard that the Count was fond of

music than she made arrangements for a concert, at which she planned to sing and to accompany herself on the guitar. This soon took place. She did not play the instrument badly and she had a pleasing voice; but it was impossible to understand the words, as is so often the case when a German beauty sings to the accompaniment of a guitar. However, everyone assured her that she had sung most expressively, and she could be satisfied with the loud applause. But now a strange mishap occurred. Among the listeners was a poet on whom Luciane wished to make a special impression, because she wanted him to dedicate some of his poems to her. With this in mind, she had sung many songs to which he had written words. He was polite to her as everyone else was; but she had hoped for more. She threw out a few hints but received no response. Impatiently, she sent at last one of her admirers to ask him if he had not been delighted to hear his wonderful poems sung so wonderfully. "My poems?" the poet asked in amazement, and added, "I am sorry, sir, but I heard nothing but vowels, and even those not always. But, of course, I feel bound to express my gratitude for such kind intention!" Luciane's messenger said nothing, and kept his secret. The poet tried to extricate himself from this embarrassing situation by means of a few well-turned compliments. Luciane now openly showed her desire to have something written especially for her. If it would not have been too malicious, the poet might really have presented her with the alphabet, so that she could have made for herself any eulogy she liked, to any existing tune. But this incident was not to be without humiliation for her. A short time afterward she heard that that same evening the poet had written a very lovely poem to one of Ottilie's favorite tunes—a poem that was more than a complimentary gift.

Like all people of her kind, who can never discriminate between something that becomes them and something that does not, Luciane now decided to try her luck at recitation. She had a good memory, but her declamation was not very intelligent, being vehement without passion. She recited ballads, stories and the usual pieces in a performer's repertory. But she had fallen into the unfortunate habit of accompanying her recitations with gestures, thereby confusing more than blending in an unpleasant way the purely epic or lyric style with the dramatic.

The Count, who was an intelligent man, very soon saw through the whole company—their dispositions, passions, and their amusements; and, fortunately or unfortunately, suggested to Luciane a new kind of performance, extremely suitable to her personality. "I see here so many handsome people who are certainly capable of imitating picturesque poses and movements," he said. "Have you really never tried to represent well-known paintings? Such imitation, although it requires much careful preparation, produces, on the other hand, an unbelievably charming effect."

Luciane quickly saw that this would be completely in her own field. Her beautiful stature, her full figure, her regular yet expressive features, her light-brown braided hair, her slender neck—all these were really made for a painting. And had she only known that she was more beautiful when she stood still than when she moved (since in this latter case something ungraceful inadvertently spoiled the effect) she would have devoted herself with still more eagerness to this kind of natural plastic art.

They now searched for prints of famous paintings, and selected for the first *tableau vivant* the *Belisarius* of Van Dyck. A tall, well-built man in his middle years was picked to represent the seated blind general; the Architect would be the sympathetic soldier, standing sadly before him—a figure he in fact somewhat resembled. Luciane, almost modestly, had chosen the part of the young woman in the background, who counts generous alms from a purse into the palm of her hand, while an old woman seems to try to prevent her, and to point out that she is giving too much. Another woman, who actually hands Belisarius alms, had not been forgotten.

With this picture and others as well, they occupied themselves very seriously. The Count made a few suggestions to the Architect about the style of the settings, and the latter at once set up a kind of stage and made all the necessary arrangements for the lighting. They were already deeply involved in these preparations before they became aware that such an undertaking requires considerable expenditure; and that here in the country, in the middle of winter, it would be very difficult to procure many things that they needed. Therefore, to prevent any delay, Luciane had almost all her dresses cut to pieces to supply material for the different costumes which the painters had rather arbitrarily designed.

The evening came, and the performance took place in the presence of a large audience and met with general applause. Music of a characteristic kind raised the highest expectations. The curtain rose on *Belisarius*. The figures were so perfect, the colors so successfully distributed, the lighting so ingenious, that all seemed transported into another world, except that realism instead of illusion produced a kind of uneasiness.

The curtain fell, and was raised more than once by general request. A musical interlude kept the company diverted, since it had been planned to surprise them with a picture of an even higher order. This was the well-known painting by Poussin: *Ahasuerus and Esther*. This time Luciane had chosen a better part for herself. As the queen, who has fallen into a swoon, she displayed all her charms; and she had cleverly selected, as the maids who surrounded and supported her, only pretty and well-shaped figures. But among them not one was the slightest match to hers. From this picture as from the others, Ottilie remained excluded. They had selected, to sit on the golden throne as the Zeus-like king, the most vigorous and handsome man of the party, so that this tableau was really perfect and beyond comparison.

For the third picture they had chosen the so-called *Paternal Warning*, by Ter Borch; and who does not know Wille's magnificent copper engraving of this painting? A noble knight sits, with crossed feet, evidently severely lecturing his daughter, who faces him. A superb figure in a white satin dress with rich folds, she can only be seen from the back; but her whole posture seems to indicate that she is controlling herself. The expression and gesture of her father tells us, however, that his reproof is not too violent or humiliating; and the mother seems to hide a slight embarrassment while she gazes into the glass of wine she is about to sip.

This was an opportunity for Luciane to appear in her highest brilliance. Her braided hair, the shape of her head and of her neck and shoulders were perfectly beautiful— and the waist, which in women's modern dresses modelled on classical patterns, is hardly visible, in her case was very shapely, slim and graceful, and showed much to advantage in the medieval costume. The Architect had taken special care to dispose the rich folds of the white satin in the most artistic naturalness, so that this living reproduction without any question exceeded the original by far, and excited general delight. There was no end of requests for a repetition of the performance; and the entirely natural wish to see the face of the beautiful girl, after having seen her back for so long, became so urgent that general applause broke out when a witty fellow impatiently shouted the words which we sometimes write at the end of a page: *"Tournez, s'il vous plaît!"* But the performers knew their advantage too well, and had grasped so perfectly the idea of these artistic illusions that they did not yield to the general challenge. The evidently embarrassed daughter did not make a move, and did not allow the audience to see the expression of her face; the father remained seated and kept to his admonishing gesture; and the mother removed neither her nose nor her eyes from the transparent glass in which the wine never diminished although she seemed to drink. It is not necessary to describe the other pictures: small night-pieces, chosen from Dutch tavern-, fair-, and market-scenes.

The Count and the Baroness again left, promising to return in the first happy weeks of their approaching marriage; and now Charlotte hoped to get rid of the rest of the party, too, after the strain of the last two months. She was certain of her daughter's future happiness, as soon as the first emotional excitement of her engaged state had subsided; for Luciane's fiancé considered himself the happiest man in the world. Although his fortune was large and his character sensible, he seemed to feel strangely flattered to become the privileged husband of a woman whom the whole world must find lovely. In a peculiar way he related everything to her; and only through her related things to himself. Therefore he had always a bad moment when any newcomer did not instantly give her his whole attention and (as often happened in the case of older people), because of his fine qualities—turned to give some attention to him—without taking special notice of her.

The business with the Architect was soon settled. He was supposed to follow the Baron on New Year's Day, and spend the carnival season with him in the city, where Luciane promised herself the most heavenly time because of a repetition of the beautifully studied *tableaux vivants*, as well as of a hundred other matters; and all the more since her great-aunt and her fiancé seemed to think little of any necessary expense incurred to keep her amused.

The hour of departure drew near; but this could not possibly happen in any ordinary way. Someone remarked rather audibly and in fun, that the guests would soon have eaten up Charlotte's provisions for the winter. The nobleman who had taken the part of *Belisarius*, a rich man, completely swept away by Luciane's charm, which he had long been admiring, thoughtlessly exclaimed: "Why not then act in the Polish fashion? *You* come now to *my* house and eat me out of house and home; and then we shall go on and make the rounds of the countryside." No sooner said than done. Luciane enthusiastically agreed. The next day they all packed their things, and the swarm invaded another estate. Here there was also ample room, but less comfort and accommodations. All this created many unsuitable situations, which only contributed to Luciane's happiness. Life became every day more disorderly and wilder. Hunting parties with beaters through the deepest snow, and whatever other inconvient sport could be invented, were arranged. Neither men nor women were allowed to excuse themselves on any account; and in this manner they roamed about, hunting and riding in sleighs with great clamor, from one estate to another, until they finally arrived at the capital, where news and gossip about amusements at Court and in the city gave their imaginations another direction, and Luciane with all her following (her great-aunt having gone home some time before) was irresistibly drawn into a new sphere of life.

From Ottilie's Diary

In society we accept everyone as he appears to be, but he must appear to be something. We tolerate difficult people more easily than insignificant ones.

Anything can be imposed upon society except those matters which have consequences.

We never learn to know people by letting them come to us; we must go to them in order to find out how matters stand.

It seems to me a rather natural trait to find fault with guests and to criticize them after they have left, though not always charitably; for we have, so to speak, a right to measure them by our own standards. On such occasions even sensible and impartial persons are likely to be extremely censorious.

But when we have stayed in the homes of others and have seen our hosts in their own surroundings, have watched their habits and the way they adapt or do not adapt themselves to the necessary and inevitable circumstances of their lives —we would show a want of understanding, or even malice, if we found ridiculous that which is worthy of our respect in more than one sense.

We should gain, by what we call good behavior and polite manners, something which is otherwise gained only by force, and perhaps not even by force.

To move in the society of women creates good manners.

How can the character, the particular personality of a man survive the conventions of well-bred behavior? Good manners should enhance personality. We desire the unusual, but it should not be embarrassing.

The educated soldier possesses the greatest advantages in life in general and in society in particular.

Crude soldiers do not, at least, behave out of character; and since good nature is usually concealed behind their strength, it is possible to get along with them, if necessary.

There is no greater nuisance than an ill-mannered civilian. We have a right to expect a certain refinement from a person who is not engaged in rough action.

When we are living with people who have a fine sense of propriety, we are alarmed if something improper occurs in their presence. I always suffer with and for Charlotte when someone rocks back and forth in his chair, a habit which she loathes.

No man would ever dare to enter a drawing-room with glasses perched on his nose, if he realized that women instantly lose any desire both to look at and to talk to him.

Familiarity is always ridiculous when it should be deference. No man would put down his hat immediately, after having paid his respects, if he knew how ridiculous it looks.

Any outward sign of politeness is founded on a deeper moral reason. True education should give us the outward sign and its underlying reason, at the same time.

Behavior is a mirror which reflects the image of everyone.

There is a politeness of heart which is akin to love. The most natural politeness which we outwardly show, springs from this inner source.

Voluntary dependence is the most beautiful condition of life, and how could it possibly exist without love?

We are never so far from our wishes as when we imagine that we possess what we wished.

No one is a greater slave than he who imagines himself free when he is not free.

We have only to declare ourselves free, instantly to feel bound. If we have the courage to declare ourselves bound, we feel that we are free.

Against the superiority of another person there is no other remedy but love.

It is shocking to see a superior man surrounded by fools who plume themselves on his friendship.

It is said that "no man is a hero to his valet," the meaning being that a hero can only be recognized by another hero. The valet, however, is, no doubt, capable of recognizing his own equal.

There is no greater consolation for mediocrity than the knowledge that a genius is not immortal.

The greatest human beings are always connected to their own century by some weakness.

We usually consider people more dangerous than they are.

The fools and the wise are equally harmless. It is the half-fools and the half-wise who are very dangerous.

Art is at once the surest escape from the world and the surest link with the world.

Even in moments of extreme happiness or of extreme misery we need the artist.

The concern of art is the Difficult and the Good.

To see the Difficult treated, as it were, without effort, gives us an idea of what is impossible.

Difficulties increase, the nearer we come to the goal.

To sow is not as difficult as to reap.

chapter 24

CHARLOTTE was in some way compensated for the turmoil this visit had created, by having obtained a deeper insight into her daughter's nature—in this her knowledge of the world gave her much help. It was not the first time she had come face to face with such a peculiar character, although she had never come across one quite so fully developed. Yet her own experience had taught her that people like her daughter, once they have been educated by life, by various experiences and by their environment, can mature and become perfectly agreeable and charming human beings; they become less self-centered, and their haphazard activities find a definite direction. Charlotte, being her mother, could be more lenient toward Luciane's eccentricities which were perhaps unpleasant to others; for parents are justified in being hopeful, where strangers only expect gratification or, at least no annoyance.

But after her daughter's departure, she suffered a strange and unexpected shock: people spoke indignantly of Luciane, not so much because of her faults, but because of certain traits in her behavior which might have been thought praiseworthy. She had apparently made it a rule not only to be merry with the merry but also to be sad with the sad; and giving full sway to a spirit of contradiction, to put sometimes the merry into a bad humor and make the sad cheerful. In every family she inquired at once about the sick or the infirm who could not appear in society. She visited them in their rooms, played the doctor and urged on each of them drastic medications which she always carried in her own traveling medicine chest. Such treatments, naturally, either succeeded or failed, as good or bad luck would have it. She was almost cruel in the exercise of her charity and never listened to advice, being utterly convinced that what she did was right. But in one attempt in the moral field she failed completely, and it was this case which gave Charlotte grave concern, because it had serious consequences, and everybody talked about it. She heard of it only after Luciane had left; and Ottilie, who had been at the party in question, had to tell her the story in all its details.

One of the daughters of a respected family had been so unfortunate as to have caused the death of one of her younger sisters, and she had never been able to recover from the shock. Ever since the day of the tragedy, she had kept to her room. She could bear to see members of her family only if they visited her one at a time, because, if several of them came together, she immediately suspected them of discussing her and her condition. To each of them singly she would speak reasonably enough and would converse with that person for hours.

Luciane had heard about all this and at once made up her mind that she would visit the house, work, as it were, a miracle and lead the girl back into the world. She behaved on this occasion with more caution than usual and succeeded in getting to see the depressed girl alone, whose confidence she apparently gained by playing the guitar for her. Only in the last stage of her plan did she make a fatal mistake; because she longed to create a sensation and thought her patient prepared, one evening she suddenly led the lovely pale child into a gay and brilliant group of visitors. Even this might have perhaps been successful, had not the guests themselves, out of curiosity and apprehension, behaved very unwisely. They crowded around the invalid and then drew back again and confused and agitated her by putting their heads together and whispering. To the girl's sensitive nerves this was unbearable. She screamed and ran away, as though something horrible pursued her. Frightened, the guests also fled in all directions, and Ottilie carried, with the help of others, the poor creature, who had fainted, back to her room.

Luciane had meanwhile severely lectured the group—as she was likely to do—without being in the least aware that she alone was to blame. She never learned from this or her many other mistakes to refrain from this kind of experiment.

The condition of the sick girl had become worse since that evening, and her mental disturbance had increased so seriously that her parents could no longer keep the poor child at home but had to commit her to an institution. Charlotte could only try, by being particularly tactful toward the family, to soothe, to a certain degree, the grief her own daughter had caused them. The whole incident had made a deep impression on Ottilie, who felt sorry for the unfortunate girl, especially since she was convinced—as she said frankly to Charlotte—that with careful treatment she might have been cured.

Since we usually talk more of unpleasant events in the past than of past pleasures, Ottilie and the Architect finally came to discuss a slight misunderstanding between them. It concerned the evening when Ottilie had been puzzled by the Architect's refusal to show his collection, although she had begged him to. His bland refusal had left a slight sting in her heart ever since: why, she did not herself know. Her feeling was perhaps justified: whatever a young woman like Ottilie requests, a young man like the Architect should not refuse. But now, when she, somewhat reprovingly, brought up the subject, his excuses were quite plausible.

"If you knew how rudely even educated people handle the most valuable works of art, you would forgive me when I do not wish to show my pieces to a large crowd," he pleaded. "No one seems to know that a medal must be held by the rim; people finger the most beautiful raised lettering, the cleanest surface, and rub the most precious pieces between thumb and forefinger, as though this were a test suitable for objects of art. Without even considering that a large sheet of paper should be held with both hands, they seize with one hand an invaluable copper-plate engraving or an irreplaceable drawing, just as any foolish politician might take hold of a newspaper to indicate beforehand his opinion of world events by his crumpling of the pages. No one realizes that if only twenty persons should handle an object of art in this way, the twenty-first would not have much to look at."

"Have *I* not sometimes given you reason for worry, too?" Ottilie asked. "Have *I* perhaps occasionally harmed your treasures without realizing it?"

"Never," the Architect replied. "Never! That would be impossible for you! You do the right thing instinctively."

"In any case," said Ottilie, "it might not be a bad idea, if in a future edition of the Laws of Etiquette—after the chapters, entitled 'Rules on How To Behave When Eating and Drinking in Good Society'—a very detailed chapter should be inserted on 'How To Behave in Private Art Collections and Museums.'"

"It would certainly encourage curators and private collectors to show their rarities more readily," the Architect agreed.

Ottilie had long since forgiven him; but when she saw him so deeply concerned about her reproof and heard him again and again reassure her how much he enjoyed letting people see his things, how he liked to do everything his friends wished—she knew that she had hurt his feelings and felt that she was in his debt. Therefore she could not flatly refuse something he asked of her after this talk; although she was not quite sure how she could conscientiously do what he wished.

This is what he had asked: he was hurt that, because of Luciane's jealousy, Ottilie had been excluded from the *tableaux vivants* and he had deeply regretted that Charlotte, because of her delicate condition, had been able only occasionally to attend this brilliant part of the entertainment. He did not wish to leave without having given additional proof of his gratitude by arranging (in honor of one of his friends and for the entertainment of the other) a performance, far more lovely than anything that had been done. Unknown to himself, he was probably moved by another secret impulse as well. It almost broke his heart to leave this house and this family, and it seemed impossible to him that a time should come when he would no longer see Ottilie's eyes, her calm and friendly look, which alone had sustained him during these last weeks.

The Christmas holidays were at hand, and it suddenly occurred to him that these "living pictures" had developed from the Nativity Groups, which pious folk made at this holy season to express their adoration of the Divine Mother and her Child, showing how these two were venerated in their apparent lowliness, first by shepherds and then by kings.

197

He had a perfectly clear vision of the execution of such a living picture: a handsome, lively baby boy would be found, and there would be no want of shepherds and shepherd-esses. But without Ottilie the whole picture was impossible. He had exalted her to the character of the Mother of God, and there was no question in his mind that should she refuse, the whole undertaking would come to nothing. Ottilie, half-embarrassed at his request, asked him to speak to Char-lotte, who was happy to give her permission. She also suc-ceeded in persuading Ottilie to lay aside her hesitation in assuming so sacred a character. The Architect worked day and night in order to make everything ready by Christmas Eve.

He literally worked day and night. His personal needs had always been few, and Ottilie's presence seemed to be food and drink to him. When he was working for her, he did not sleep; when he was in her presence, he felt neither hunger nor thirst. Consequently, everything was ready on the Holy Eve. He had managed to bring together a small orchestra of wind instruments, which played an overture to create the desired atmosphere. When the curtain rose, Charlotte was completely taken by surprise. She had seen the picture re-produced so often that she had hardly expected to be im-pressed by it now. But here reality seemed to give it a special quality. The stage was not merely dim but dark as night, yet every detail in the center could be seen clearly. It had been the artist's excellent idea that all light should radiate from the Child and he had achieved this by a clever trick of light-ing; the mechanism was hidden by the figures in the fore-ground who were in shadow, illuminated only by lights on the side. Happy girls and boys stood about, their ruddy faces sharply lit from below. There were angels, too, whose inner light paled beside that of the Divine Child; their ethereal bodies seemed solid and bereft of radiance in the presence of the Word made Flesh.

Fortunately, the baby had fallen asleep in a graceful position, so that nothing distracted the onlookers from their contemplation of the mother, who, with infinitely gentle grace, lifted a veil to reveal her hidden treasure. The picture seemed to have been caught just at this moment. Blinded by the radiance and overcome by awe, the surrounding group seemed to have just turned away their dazzled eyes; but their furtive gaze was directed toward the Child with expressions of wonder and joy. Rapture and adoration showed particularly clearly on the faces of some of the elderly figures.

Ottilie's whole appearance, her gesture, the expression of her face and eyes surpassed anything ever conveyed by a painter. Any connoisseur of art, seeing this spectacle, would have feared that some detail might change; and he would have doubted whether anything could ever give him such enjoyment again. Unfortunately, no one present was capable of grasping the complete effect. Only the Architect who, as a tall, slender shepherd, peered from the side over the heads of the kneeling figures, had, to some degree, an impression of the whole; and even he, standing where he was, was not afforded a complete view. And who could describe in words the expression on the face of the Queen of Heaven? Pure humility and a winning modesty at the great and underserved honor bestowed on her, as well as an immeasurable happiness, showed in her face, expressing not only her own emotion but also a profound understanding of the role that she enacted.

Charlotte was extremely happy to see this beautiful picture, and the Child in particular moved her deeply. Tears welled into her eyes, and she imagined herself most vividly in the near future holding so dear a babe in her own arms.

The curtain fell, partly in order to let the actors relax a little, partly to change the tableau. The artist had planned to transform this first scene of night and lowliness into one of day and glory; and to this end had prepared a dazzling flood of light from all sides, which was to be lit during the intermission. Ottilie, in her half-theatrical pose, had felt until now quite unembarrassed knowing that no other spectators, with the exception of Charlotte and a few members of the household, were present at this religious spectacle. She was, therefore, somewhat taken aback when, during the intermission, she heard that a stranger had arrived in the hall and had been kindly welcomed by Charlotte. No one could tell her who he was. She put the matter out of her mind, because she did not wish to make a disturbance. The candles and lamps burned brightly, and she was surrounded by a perfect blaze of light. The curtain rose, and the scene presented a startling spectacle: all was bright, and, instead of shadows, colors distributed with great skill, gave a soft and subdued effect. Looking out from under her long eyelashes, Ottilie saw the figure of a man sitting next to Charlotte. She did not recognize him but she thought the voice was that of her tutor at school. A strange emotion ran through her. How many things had happened since she last had heard the voice of her faithful teacher! Like a forked flash of lightning, a whole chain of her pleasures and unhappiness passed rapidly before her mind, together with the questions: Can you tell him everything and confess everything to him? And how little do you deserve to appear before him in the guise of this holy figure? How strange he must feel to see you in this costume? With incredible swiftness emotion and reflection struggled in her heart. Her eyes filled with tears, while she forced herself to remain motionless. With great relief she felt the baby move; and the Architect had to give the sign for the lowering of the curtain. If a painful feeling of being unable to hurry and welcome a dear friend had, during the last moments, been added to Ottilie's other emotions, she now felt even more embarrassed. Should she meet him in this unusual costume? Should she change it? She did not hestitate for long; she changed her dress, trying, at the same time, to get control of herself and to calm her emotion. But she regained her usual poise only when she went to welcome their guest, dressed as usual.

chapter 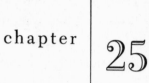 25

Since the Architect wished a pleasant time for his kind friends, the thought of their having such good company in the person of the deserving tutor was very agreeable to him, particularly as he himself had now really to think of leaving. But when he thought of his friends' special kindness to him, he could not help being a little distressed to see himself so quickly and (as he thought in his modesty) so well and even completely replaced. Formerly he had always hesitated; but now something urged him to leave, for he did not wish to see with his own eyes what he could not prevent from happening, after he had gone.

To the great relief of his low spirits, the ladies, at the very last moment, made him the present of a vest which he had seen both of them knitting over a long period; and he had secretly envied the fortunate unknown to whom it would one day belong. Such a gift is most enjoyed by a man who loves or admires the giver, because, as he remembers the never-tiring play of lovely fingers, he cannot help flattering himself that, at such long-lasting work, the heart as well cannot have remained entirely unsympathetic.

Now the two women were hostesses to a new young man for whom they had the kindest feelings and whom they wished to put at ease in their company while he stayed with them. All women have their own inner, unchangeable interests to which nothing in the world can make them disloyal; in their outward social relationships, however, they allow themselves, gladly and easily, to be influenced by the man with whom they are for the moment occupied; and in this way, by refusing as well as responding, by persisting and by yielding, they are actually in command, and no man in the civilized world dares to refuse them obedience.

While the Architect, following his own wishes and his inclination, had exercised and proved his talents for his friends' entertainment and their purposes; while occupation and conversation had been conducted in this spirit and to this end—the presence of the Tutor soon created an entirely different mode of life. His great gift was to talk well, and in conversation to discuss all sorts of human problems, particularly those concerning the education of young people. Accordingly, a rather distinct contrast to their previous way of life made itself felt, the more so, because the Tutor did not entirely approve of the interests which had for so long kept them occupied almost exclusively.

He did not once mention the *tableau vivant* he had seen when he arrived. But when, with great satisfaction, they showed him the church, the chapel and everything in it, he could not hold back his views. "As for me," he said, "all this imitating and mixing of the Sacred and the Sensuous does not please me at all. Nor do I like the consecration and decoration of places, set apart for the specific purpose of creating and sustaining a feeling of piety. No environment, not even the lowliest, should disturb in us that sense of the Divine which can be with us everywhere and can consecrate any place into a temple. I like to see a religious service conducted in the same hall where people usually take their meals, have their social gatherings or enjoy themselves with games and dancing. The highest and the best in man cannot be given form, and we should beware of giving it any form except that of noble action."

Charlotte, who already knew something about his general way of thinking and who was soon to probe it more thoroughly, at once assigned to him a task in his own field. She had her little gardeners, whom the Architect had just passed in review before his departure, march up to the great hall: they looked very attractive in their clean gray uniforms, with their rhythmic movements and their natural liveliness. The Tutor examined them after his fashion; and, by his many questions and his way of putting them, he soon found out something about the disposition and the aptitude of each child. At the same time he subtly instructed them and gave them a good many new suggestions; and all this in less than an hour.

"How do you manage it?" Charlotte asked, when the boys had marched off. "I listened very attentively. Only familiar things were mentioned, yet I would not know how to introduce these subjects into a discussion so systematically and in such a short time."

"Perhaps we should never reveal the tricks of our trade," the Tutor replied. "But I can tell you a simple principle that will help you to achieve these results and a great many more. Take up any topic, any subject, any idea; stick to it, make yourself thoroughly acquainted with it in every detail—and it will be easy for you to discover, as you talk with a group of children, how much of it they understand and what you may still have to develop and to impart. Their answers to your questions may be very unsatisfactory and may wander far from the subject; but if your questions in return bring the children's attention back to the subject, and if you do not allow yourself to be diverted from your own viewpoint, the children will eventually think, understand, and grasp, what you want them to learn and precisely in the way you want them to learn it. A teacher makes a most serious mistake when he allows himself to be drawn away from the subject by his pupils or if he is unable to keep steadily to the point he is discussing. Try this sometime; it will give you great pleasure."

"This sounds very sensible," Charlotte said. "I can see that the best method of teaching is the very opposite of the way we must behave in life. In society we are told never to stay too long on one subject; whereas in teaching the first commandment is to avoid any distraction."

"Variety without distraction would be the finest motto for both teaching and life, if only this highly commendable balance were so easy to keep," answered the Tutor. He was about to say more when Charlotte called him to look again at the boys, whose merry procession was just then moving across the castle courtyard. He expressed satisfaction that the children were kept in uniform. "Men should wear uniforms from early youth," he said; "they must accustom themselves to act in unison, to lose themselves among their fellowmen, to obey as a unit, and to work for the good of the whole. Moreover, any kind of uniform develops a martial spirit and a strictly disciplined deportment. Boys are, in any case, born soldiers; watch them playing war-like and competitive games, storming and scaling walls!"

"Then you will not blame me for *not* dressing all my girls alike," said Ottilie. "When I introduce them to you, I hope to delight you with a gay and colorful group."

"I quite approve of that," the Tutor replied. "Women should wear all sorts of dresses; and each should follow her own taste in her own style, so that she may discover what is really becoming and suitable to her. There is a still more important reason for all this: namely—that it is women's lot to be on their own and to act alone all their lives."

"That seems to me a paradox," Charlotte protested. "Surely we are almost never alone."

"Oh, but you are," the Tutor replied, "at least in respect to other women. Think of any woman—when she is in love, when a bride, wife, housewife or mother—she is always quite alone and wants to be alone. The same thing is true even of a vain woman. Each woman excludes all others. That is natural, for every woman is called upon to perform all the tasks which comprise the whole womankind. It is entirely different with men. A man needs another man; he would even create a second man for himself if no other existed. But a woman could go on living for ever and ever without even dreaming of creating a being like herself."

"If truth is formulated only in a peculiar manner, the oddest things will in the end seem true," Charlotte said. "Even though bearing in mind the most valuable of your remarks, we women, as women, will nevertheless stick together and work together with other women, in order not to give men too great an advantage over us. I hope you won't begrudge us the small malicious satisfaction we must feel, if, in the future, we should see that the gentlemen, too, are sometimes not getting along too well with one another."

The Tutor now closely examined the way in which Ottilie treated her little pupils, and expressed his definite approval. "You are quite right in educating these children for immediate usefulness," he said. "Cleanliness will make them enjoy keeping themselves clean, and much is gained if they are encouraged to do what they are doing with cheerfulness and self-confidence."

To his great satisfaction he found that nothing was done

for form's sake only, or for mere outward show; everything was rather done for spiritual profit and the indispensable needs. "The whole business of education could be summed up in such a few words, if only people had ears to hear!" he exclaimed.

"Wouldn't you like to try my ears?" Ottilie asked, friendly and interested.

"Yes, I would," he replied. "But you must not give away my secret. Boys should be taught to be servants, and girls to be mothers—and all would be right with the world."

"To be mothers?" asked Ottilie. "I suppose, women would readily agree to that, for they must always prepare themselves, if not to become mothers, at least to take care of children. But I suspect that our young men would think themselves too good to *serve*. You can easily see for yourself that every one of them considers himself much more capable of being a master."

"For that very reason we shall not say anything about this to them," the Tutor replied. "We begin by flattering ourselves with high hopes but life does not flatter us. How many people would voluntarily choose that which in the long run they are forced to do? But let us disregard these observations which do not really concern us here. I think you are very fortunate in being able to apply the right method with your pupils. When your youngest girls carry their dolls about and stitch together a few little rags for them; when the older sisters take care of the younger, and each member of the household serves and helps the others, the next step in life will not be so difficult; and such girls will find in their husbands' homes what they left in their parents'. But on a higher level of society the problem is very complicated. We have to consider much more highly developed, more delicate, refined, and differentiated social conditions. We teachers must, therefore, give our pupils an education designed for the world they live in. This sort of education is necessary and essential and it may be valuable if we do not go too far with it. For, while planning to extend the education of our pupils we may easily become too vague and lose sight of their specific spiritual requirements. This is the problem which educators are apt to miss, or may solve only inadequately. I am concerned about many of the things we teach our pupils at the boarding school, because experience tells me that these will very likely be of small use in their future lives. So much is at once discarded, so much forgotten, as soon as a girl finds herself in the position of housewife or mother! But since I have devoted myself to this work, I must cling to the modest hope that some day, together with a faithful companion who will assist me, I may succeed in fully developing in my pupils what they really need when they leave for their own sphere of activity and are independent. Perhaps I may then be able to say to myself, 'In this sense their education is completed.' Of course, another sort of education immediately follows, and another and another, almost every year of our lives, forced upon us, if not by ourselves, then by circumstance."

How true these remarks seemed to Ottilie! She had learned so much during the past year through her unforeseen passion, and how many trials awaited her when she looked into the imminent future!

The young man had deliberately mentioned an assistant— a wife—for, in all modesty, he could not keep himself from hinting vaguely at his intentions. Several circumstances and occurrences had encouraged him to move a little closer to his goal during this visit.

The headmistress of the school was already advanced in years and had for some time been looking about among the members of her staff, men as well as women, for someone to be her associate. She had finally offered this post to the Tutor, who merited her highest confidence. He would share the the management of the institution with her, work for it as if it were his own, and, after her death, as her heir, become its sole proprietor. The principal condition seemed to be that he find a congenial wife. A vision of Ottilie was always before him; he was somewhat hesitant, but there were certain favorable circumstances which made him hopeful. Luciane had left the school, and Ottilie would be free to come back. There had been some rumors concerning her relation to Eduard, but, as in similar cases, the whole matter was not taken too seriously; this incident might even contribute to Ottilie's return. Nothing, however, would have been decided and no definite step would have been taken if unexpected visitors had not once more brought the matter to a head. After all, the appearance of exceptional people in any circle is never without some consequence.

The Count and the Baroness were often consulted about the value of different schools, since everyone has to face the problem of his children's education; they had, therefore, decided to inspect this particular school which had such an excellent reputation—an inspection which they could now undertake together because of their changed circumstances. But the Baroness had still another purpose in mind. During her last visit with Charlotte they had discussed Eduard and Ottilie in detail. She had insisted repeatedly that Ottilie should be sent away, and had tried to encourage Charlotte, who still feared Eduard's threats. They had also talked of ways and means, and, when the school was mentioned, and the Baroness learned of the Tutor's attachment for Ottilie, she was all the more determined to visit the place.

She and the Count arrived at the school, met the Tutor, inspected the establishment and mentioned Ottilie. The

Count was always glad to speak of her, since he had learned to know her better during their recent visit. Ottilie had approached him and had even been attracted by him, for she thought she found in his interesting conversation something which had until now been entirely unknown to her. When she was with Eduard the world was forgotten, while in the presence of the Count, the world seemed desirable for the first time. Any attraction is reciprocal. The Count became very fond of Ottilie and liked to think of her as a daughter. Once again she stood in the way of the Baroness, and now even more so than at first. Who knows what the Baroness would have plotted against the girl in times more violently passionate than our own. Now, she would be satisfied to find her a husband and so remove a danger to married women.

She urged the Tutor, therefore, unobstrusively but effectively, to arrange a little excursion to the castle where he should take steps to realize his plans and desires, which he had not kept secret from the Baroness.

With full approval of the headmistress, he started on his journey, his mind filled with the happiest expectations. He knew that Ottilie did not dislike him, and, although there was some disproportion in their social status, this would not count too much, considering the liberal views of the period. The Baroness had, moreover, given him to understand that Ottilie would always be without a fortune. To be related to a rich family is said to be no help to anyone; even persons of immense wealth have serious scruples against deducting any considerable sum from the inheritance of those who seem to have an indisputable right to it, because of a closer relationship. Strangely enough, a man rarely uses his great privilege to dispose of his property after his death, for the benefit of those who are actually closest to his heart; apparently out of respect for tradition he bequeaths it only to those who would become the heirs of his fortune in any case, even if he made no will.

While the Tutor was on his journey, he felt himself on a completely equal footing with Ottilie. The kind welcome at the castle also raised his hopes. It is true that he found Ottilie not quite so open with him as formerly; but she was also more mature, more cultivated, and perhaps more communicative in general than she had been when he knew her before. Like a close friend, he enjoyed confidence about many matters, particularly those that concerned his profession. But when he wished to approach the real purpose of his visit, a certain shyness always held him back.

Charlotte once offered him an opportunity when she said to him, in Ottilie's presence, "Well, now that you have seen almost everything that is developing within my little realm, what do you think of Ottilie? You may speak frankly before her."

The Tutor replied with great understanding and quiet objectiveness that he had found Ottilie very much changed to her advantage; that she behaved with more ease, expressed herself more freely, and showed greater understanding of the ways of the world; all of which appeared in her actions more than in her words; but that he still believed that it might be very useful to her if she returned to the school for a short period, in order to learn, thoroughly and systematically, the lessons that the world was teaching her only in fragments, fragments more confusing than satisfying, and sometimes almost too late. He did not wish to go too much into detail, he said: Ottilie herself would remember that she had suddenly been taken out of a systematic course of instruction.

Ottilie would not deny this; but she could not reveal her feelings on hearing these words, for she was hardly able to explain them to herself. Nothing in the world seemed unsystematic to her when she thought of the man she loved; and she could not understand how—without him—anything could make sense at all.

Charlotte's reply to the suggestion was wise and kind. She said that both she and Ottilie had for a long time wished for Ottilie's return to school. But now the presence of such a dear friend and helper had become indispensable to her; she would not, however, later put any obstacle in Ottilie's way if it was then still her wish to go back to school long enough to finish the work she had begun and to complete any courses which she had not finished, when she left.

The Tutor received this suggestion with a very happy heart. Ottilie did not dare to object, but she shuddered at the mere thought of having to leave. Charlotte's only concern was to gain time. She hoped that when Eduard returned he would find himself a happy father and would become his old self again. She was convinced that all would be forgotten and that, in one way or another, something could be done for Ottilie as well.

After an important conversation which gives all participants much food for thought, a lull, resembling a general embarrassment, usually sets in. They walked up and down the salon. The Tutor leafed through some books and finally came upon the folio which was still lying where Luciane had left it. When he saw that it contained only pictures of monkeys, he clapped it shut at once. This little incident may have given rise to a conversation, traces of which we find in Ottilie's diary.

From Ottilie's Diary

It is incomprehensible that people can have the heart to draw hideous monkeys with so much care. We already lower ourselves when we look at monkeys simply as animals; but

212

we become really vicious when we yield to the temptation to try and discover people we know behind these animal masks.

It is a sign of perversity when people delight in looking at caricatures and grotesques. I am grateful to my Tutor that I was never tortured with the study of natural history: I always had an uneasy feeling about worms and beetles.

Today he confessed that he felt the same. We should not know anything of nature but what is alive and actually around us, he said. With the trees in our gardens, whether in flower, in leaf or in fruit, with any bush we pass, any blade of grass we step on, we have a true relationship; they are all our true fellow-creatures. The birds, hopping up and down on our branches and singing among our leaves belong to us; they have spoken to us since our childhood and we have learned to understand their language. Is it not true that any strange creature, torn from its natural habitat, makes a certain frightening impression on us which can only be dulled by habit? Indeed, a colorful and noisy background is needed for us to put up with monkeys, parrots and blackamoors.

When I have been seized sometimes by a mood of curiosity about such exotic things, I have envied travelers who see all these marvels together with others in their natural everyday pattern of life. But the traveler, too, will become a different man. No one walks under palmtrees with impunity, and I am sure that one's outlook will change in a country where elephants and tigers are at home.

We admire only that naturalist who knows how to describe and depict for us the strangest and most unusual objects in their proper locality and environment. How I should like to hear only once Humboldt talk.

A cabinet of natural curiosities must look to us like an Egyptian burial place, where the various nature-gods and animal-gods stand about mummified. It is perhaps fitting for a priestly class to occupy itself with these matters in a twilight of mystery; but they should not be introduced into general education, especially since they may easily displace something more familiar and of greater value.

A teacher who can rouse in us enthusiasm for a single good deed, for a single good poem, accomplishes more than the teacher who crams our minds with the names and characteristics of series after series of inferior natural forms; for the only result of this cramming will be something we know in any case: that the human form is the only superior form, created in the image of God.

The individual may be free to occupy himself with whatever attracts him, pleases him, or seems useful to him; but the proper study of mankind is man.

chapter 26

VERY few people care to occupy themselves with the immediate past. Either we are forcibly bound to the present, or we lose ourselves in the remote past and try to recall and restore as much as possible of what is gone irrevocably. Even in great and wealthy families who owe so much to their ancestors, we generally find that everyone remembers his grandfather better than his father.

These thoughts arose in the Tutor's mind as he walked, on one of those lovely days when the departing winter pretends to be spring, through the extensive older part of the park, admiring the avenues of tall linden trees and the formal grounds, laid out by Eduard's father. Everything had, remarkably enough, turned out as the man who planted had intended; and now, when the time had come to appreciate and enjoy, no one ever talked of the formal grounds: they were very rarely looked at. All interest and expenditure had now been turned in another direction: into the open country and toward freer vistas. On his return, the Tutor commented on this fact, and Charlotte did not resent it. "While life is carrying us along with it," she said, "we imagine that we act from our own motives and choose what we do and what we enjoy; but, if we look more closely we

215

will find that we are actually compelled to carry out the ideas and tendencies of our time."

"That is true," the Tutor replied. "Who, after all, can resist the force of the tendencies of his period? Time moves on, and with it opinions, ideas, prejudices and fashions. If the early years of a young man fall in a period of transition, we can be sure that he will have nothing in common with his father. If the father lived in a period which tended toward acquiring a good deal, toward protecting this property, restricting and confining it, and in the sequestration from the world securing its full enjoyment—the son will be inclined to expand, to communicate, to extend and to open up what was closed."

"Whole periods resemble this father and son you have described," Charlotte agreed. "It is hardly possible for us to conceive of that remote period when every small town had to have its walls and moats; when the nobleman still built his manor in the middle of a swamp, and the smallest castles could be entered only by a drawbridge. Nowadays even larger towns pull down their walls; the moats of castles are filled in; towns are nothing more than large open places, and when we travel, we can see all this, and might almost believe that universal peace has been established and that the Golden Age is near at hand. No one nowadays feels comfortable in a garden which is not like open country; nothing must remind us of art and constraint; we wish to breathe with absolute freedom and feel unconfined. Do you really think that we could return from this condition into another, older one?"

"Why not?" the Tutor answered. "Every condition has its difficulties, the restricted as well as the unrestricted. The latter state presupposes abundance and leads to extravagance. Let us stick to your very striking example. As soon as want reappears, self-restriction is at once re-instituted. People who must make use of their land, begin to raise walls around their gardens in order to protect their produce. Gradually a new outlook develops. Considerations of usefulness once more gain the upper hand, and even the rich landowner finally comes to the conclusion that he too should make use of all his acres. Believe me, it is quite possible that your son will neglect all the new grounds you have laid out and will again retire behind the austere walls and under the tall linden trees of his grandfather."

It gave Charlotte a secret pleasure to hear the Tutor predict that her child would be a son, and so she forgave him his somewhat unkind prophecy concerning the future of her beloved and lovely park. She said very amiably: "Neither of us is yet old enough to have seen a recurrence of this opposition of one generation to another; but when I remember my early youth, and the complaints I heard from elderly people, and then think of the subsequent changes in city and country, I cannot contradict you. But should it not be possible to bring about an understanding between father and son, between parents and children? You have been kind enough to predict a son for me; is it necessary that he should oppose his father? Why should he destroy what his parents have built, instead of completing it, and, if he continues the work in the same spirit, even improving it?"

"There is, of course, a sensible remedy which people only too seldom apply," the Tutor replied. "A father should make his son a partner; he should let him help with the building and planting and allow him some of the harmless whims that he allows himself. One activity may be woven into another; but they cannot be merely pieced together. A young shoot can easily and willingly be grafted onto an old trunk to which a grown branch can no longer be joined."

The Tutor was glad, that just when he was obliged to

leave, he had been able to say quite accidentally, something agreeable to Charlotte, and so had confirmed her good opinion of him. He had already been away from home too long; but he had always hesitated to return, until the moment when he fully realized that he could not expect any decision concerning Ottilie before Charlotte had given birth to her child—an event which was imminent. He therefore submitted to circumstances and, still nursing his hopes and prospects, returned to the school.

Charlotte's hour drew near, and she kept more to her rooms. The women who had gathered around her were almost her only company. Ottilie looked after the household, but she could barely keep her mind on what she was doing. Although she had given up all hope for herself, she was anxious to do everything possible for Charlotte, for the child, and for Eduard, even if she could not imagine how this would be possible. Nothing could save her from utter despair but the daily performance of her duties.

A son was safely born to Charlotte, and all the women insisted that he was the very image of his father. Ottilie alone, when she went to wish Charlotte happiness and to welcome the child affectionately, did not think so. Even during the preliminaries to her daughter's marriage Charlotte had keenly felt the absence of her husband. Now the father was not to be present at the birth of his son; he would not choose the name which the child should bear.

The first of all the friends who came to wish Charlotte happiness was Mittler; he had posted messengers all over the neighborhood to bring him the news of the event at once. He arrived in an excellent mood and could barely, in Ottilie's presence, hide his triumph. But when he was alone with Charlotte, he expressed his satisfaction at the top of his voice, and was just the right man to remove all difficulties and brush away all momentary obstacles. The christening should not be delayed longer than was necessary. The old clergyman—already with one foot in the grave—would, with his blessings, bind the past to the future. The name of the child should be Otto: he could not possibly be given any other name than that of his father and of their friend.

It was the determined insistence of Mittler that brushed aside the hundreds of scruples: the opposition, hesitation, indecision; the "knowing better" and "having a better idea," the wavering and constant shifting of opinions; for on such occasions one scruple removed usually breeds more and more new ones; and when we try not to offend anyone, we are sure to hurt someone.

Mittler took care of all the letters announcing the birth, and of those to the godparents. He wished them to be written and sent off at once, for he was very eager to let the often ill-disposed and ill-judging world know of the happy event which was, in his opinion, so important for the family. And he was right, because the previous passionate vibrations had not escaped the attention of a public which is at all times convinced that whatever happens, happens only to provide them with food for gossip.

The ceremony of baptism was to be dignified but short and in private. Ottilie and Mittler were to hold the child as sponsors. The old clergyman, supported by the sexton, approached with slow steps. The prayer was said, and the child placed in Ottilie's arms; but when she looked down at it with affection, it opened its eyes. She was shocked; she seemed to look into her own eyes. The likeness would have startled anyone. Mittler, who was the next to hold the child was startled, too, when he saw in the child's features a striking resemblance to the Captain. He had never met with the like before.

The weakness of the old clergyman had prevented him from conducting the ceremony with more than the customary liturgy. Mittler, however, filled with the spirit of the occasion, remembered his former ministerial function; he had a curious tendency to imagine, on any occasion, how *he* would speak and what *he* would say. On this occasion he could control himself all the less, as he was surrounded by only a small group, all of whom were his friends. So he began, toward the end of the service, to put himself, with perfect ease, in the place of the clergyman and, in a spirited speech, to hold forth on his duties as godfather and his hopes for the child; and he dwelt all the longer on the subject when he thought he read approval in Charlotte's happy face.

The fact that the old clergyman longed to sit down escaped the vigorous orator who suspected still less that he was on the point of causing a serious accident. After having impressively described the relation of each person present to the child, thereby putting Ottilie's composure to a severe test, he turned to the aged man with the words: "And you, my venerable patriarch, you can now say with Simeon: Lord, now lettest thou thy servant depart in peace, for mine eyes have seen the savior of this house."

He was in full swing, and was winding up his speech very brilliantly, when he noticed that the old clergyman to whom he held up the child, first seemed to incline a little toward it, but then suddenly sank back. Barely prevented from falling, he was carried to an armchair; but, in spite of instant assistance given him, he was found to be dead.

To experience so immediately birth and death, coffin and cradle, not only to imagine them but to see these tremendous contrasts with their own eyes was a difficult trial for those present, particularly since they had been completely taken by surprise. Ottilie alone contemplated with a kind of envy the sleeping old man, whose sympathetic face still showed its expression of kindliness. The life of her soul had been destroyed; why should her body be kept alive?

Although the sad events of these days now frequently directed her thoughts toward the transitoriness of all things human, toward separation and loss, she was given the comfort of strange nightly visions which, by reassuring her that the man she loved was still alive, gave her own life security and new strength. When she lay down at night, and was still suspended between sleeping and waking, she seemed to be looking into a perfectly clear and softly lighted space. There she could see Eduard quite distinctly, not dressed as she had formerly seen him, but in military uniform, and each time in a new attitude and always perfectly natural and plausible: standing, walking, lying down, or riding. The figure, accurate to the smallest detail, moved easily before her eyes without any effort on her part, without her willing it, and without strain to her imagination. Sometimes she saw him surrounded by something in motion, something darker than the light background. But she could hardly recognize the shadowy figures which now seemed to her to be human, now like horses or like trees or mountains. Usually she fell asleep while the vision was still there, and, when she woke again in the morning, after a restful night, she felt refreshed and comforted, thoroughly convinced that Eduard was alive and that their close relationship was unbroken.

chapter | 27

Spring had come—later but also more quickly and delightfully than usual. In the garden Ottilie could now gather the fruits of her careful labor: everything was thriving and came to leaf and flower; everything that had been nursed in the greenhouses and hotbeds now burst forth at once in the open air; and all the care and work that still had to be done was not merely a labor of hope, as before, but produced enjoyable and immediate results.

Ottilie had to comfort the gardener for the many gaps among the potted plants, caused by Luciane's rash behavior, and for the destroyed symmetry of more than one tree top. She tried to console him by saying that all would soon be as it was before; but he was much too sensitive and had too severe a conception of his profession to be comforted easily by well-meant arguments. A gardener should not be distracted by any other interests, just as the quiet course which a plant follows to its lasting or passing perfection should not be interrupted. A plant is like a stubborn person from whom we can obtain anything if we handle him in the right manner. Quiet observation and consistency in doing precisely what must be done in any season and at every hour, are probably required of no one more than of a gardener.

All these qualities the good man possessed to a high degree, and for this reason Ottilie liked to work with him; but for some time past he had not been able to practice his true talent as he pleased. He was an expert at any kind of fruit and vegetable gardening—it is difficult to be successful in both—and was also capable of doing all that was required in an old-fashioned flowergarden; but, although he might have challenged Nature herself in his management of the orangery, the flower bulbs, the potted carnations and auriculas, he was unfamiliar with the new varieties of ornamental shrubs and the flowers now in fashion, and felt a kind of grumbling awe before the infinite field of botany, lately opened up, with all its humming foreign names. Everything his master and mistress had ordered last year he considered a useless expense and a waste, the more so, because he saw many expensive plants die out, and because he was not on particularly good terms with the plant-dealers who, he believed did not serve him with sufficient honesty.

After a number of his own experiments he had developed a sort of system in which Ottilie strongly encouraged him, since it was basically related to the return of Eduard, whose absence was, in this case as in many others, daily felt as a disadvantage.

While the plants were gradually developing more and more roots and were putting forth new shoots, Ottilie felt herself becoming increasingly attracted to the green-houses. It was now exactly a year since she had come here as a stranger, a person of no importance. How much she had gained for herself in that time! But, alas, how much had she also lost! She had never before been so rich and so poor.

These feelings of gain and of loss alternated in her heart from one moment to another, and even intersected deeply, so that her only resource was, to take up with interest, and almost with passion, the next thing that had to be done.

That she was inclined to take particular care of everything dear to Eduard was only natural; and it was also natural that she hoped he would soon return and personally and gratefully note the thoughtful services she had rendered her absent friend.

But she also set herself another task in his behalf. She primarily took charge of his child, whose exclusive nurse she could become quite easily, for it had been decided that a wet nurse would not be engaged but that the child should be brought up on milk and water. Since the little boy was supposed to be mostly out of doors in this beautiful season, Ottilie loved to take him out in her arms into the fresh air, and to carry the innocently sleeping little creature about among the flowers and blossoms which would one day smile in such a friendly way upon his childhood; among the young shrubs and plants which seemed destined, by their youth, to grow up with him. When she looked about her, she realized what a great and rich life this child could expect: very nearly everything, as far as the eye could see, would one day belong to him. How desirable, it would be, therefore, that he should also grow up under the eyes of his father and mother, confirming their restored and happy union!

Ottilie felt all this so deeply that she imagined it as a definite reality and completely left herself out of the picture. Under this unclouded sky, in this bright sunshine, it became suddenly quite clear to her that her own love ought to become entirely unselfish in order to perfect itself. There were even moments when she believed that she had already reached this height. She wished only the happiness of her friend; she believed herself capable of renouncing him, even of never seeing him again, if she could only know that he was happy. About one point, however, she was firm: she would never belong to another man.

They had taken care that the autumn would be as glorious as the spring. All the so-called estival plants, that do not cease flowering in autumn and even boldly challenge the frost—asters in particular—had been sown in great numbers and in a variety of colors, and planted now everywhere, would later form a starry heaven on earth.

From Ottilie's Diary

We like to record in our diaries any fine thought we have read, or anything striking we have heard. If we would also take the trouble to copy out unusual observations, original ideas, casual intelligent remarks from our friends' letters, we would become very rich. We keep letters and never read them again; one day we destroy them out of discretion, and in this way the most beautiful and direct breath of life vanishes irretrievably, for us and for others. I intend to make up in future for this negligence.

Once more the yearly fairy-tale repeats itself. We have now, thank Heaven, reached its most charming chapter. Violets and lilies-of-the-valley are, as it were, its headings and its vignettes. We are always pleasantly impressed when, opening the book of life, we again come upon these pages.

We are cross with the poor, particularly with children, who idle along the roads, begging. Why do we not notice that, as soon as there is something for them to do, they will start to work at once? Hardly has Nature displayed her bountiful riches when the children eagerly set up in business. Not one of them begs any longer. They hold out to you a bunch of flowers, picked before you have wakened from your sleep, and their pleading look is as sweet as the offered gift. No one ever looks miserable, when he feels that he has a right to ask something from us.

Why is a year sometimes so short and at other times so long; why does it seem so short as it passes and in our memory so long! This I feel about the past year, and nowhere so acutely than in the garden, where I see the transitory interfuse with the lasting. And yet—nothing is so ephemeral that it does not leave behind some trace and something of its own kind.

We can put up with the winter, too. We imagine that we are less confined when the trees stand before us so ghostly and so transparent. They are nothing and they hide nothing. But as soon as buds and blossoms appear, we become impatient to see the full foliage, the landscape shaping itself and the tree advancing upon us in its full form.

Anything perfect in its kind must transcend its kind; it must become something different, something incomparable. In some of its notes the nightingale is still a bird; but then it transcends its own kind and seems to intimate to all feathered creatures what singing really is.

Life without love, without the presence of the beloved, is only a bad *comédie à tiroir*. We pull out one drawer after another, push it quickly back and hastily try the next one. Whatever good or of importance may occur, has little connected meaning. Everywhere we have to begin all over again and everywhere we should like to end.

chapter 28

CHARLOTTE herself was well and very happy. She delighted in her healthy boy, whose physical development gave great promise, and occupied her eye, mind and heart every hour of the day. He formed for her a new link between herself, the world and the estate. Her old activity again stirred in her; she saw how much she had accomplished in the past year, and felt happy concerning everything she had done. Moved by a strange impulse, she walked up to the summer-house with Ottilie and the child; and when she laid her son down on the little table, as upon a domestic altar, and saw the two empty seats, she remembered past times, and new hopes rose in her heart, for herself and for Ottilie.

Young women perhaps look modestly at this or that young man, asking themselves secretly if they would like him for a husband; but the person who has a daughter, or is the guardian of a girl, surveys a wider circle. This was what Charlotte did at this moment, and a marriage between the Captain and Ottilie did not seem impossible to her when she thought how they had sat side by side, once before, in this little summer-house. It had not remained unknown to her that the prospect of an advantageous marriage for the Captain had come to nothing.

They climbed farther up the hill, Ottilie carrying the child. Charlotte was absorbed in all kinds of reflections. Even on dry land shipwrecks can occur—to recover from them as quickly as possible, and to restore a former condition is wise and praiseworthy, for life calculates only gain or loss. Who has not made plans, to be interrupted in them! How often one turns into a road, only to find it impassable and to lose it again! How often is our attention turned away from a goal we had eagerly in view, only because we wish to attain a higher one! A traveler may be extremely vexed when a wheel of his coach breaks on the journey; but this unpleasant accident may lead to his making the most charming acquaintances and to his forming connections which will influence his whole life. Fate grants our wishes, but only in its own way, in order to give us something more than our wishes.

These, and similar thoughts, occupied Charlotte while she walked up to the new building on the crest of the hill; and up here, all her thoughts proved right. The view was now much lovelier than they could have foreseen. Obstructions on all sides had been removed; all the important features of the landscape, all that Nature and Time had done for it, now appeared in clear relief to the eye; and the new groups of trees and shrubs planted to fill in several gaps and to connect the separate parts in an agreeable way, were beginning to show green.

The house itself was almost ready to be occupied; and the view—particularly from the upper rooms—offered great variety. The longer they looked about, the more beauty they discovered. What superb effects would the changing of the different hours of the day, and sun and moon, create here! To live in this house seemed highly desirable; and Charlotte's delight in building and creating was again quickly aroused when she discovered that all the rough work had been finished. A carpenter, a paper-hanger, a resourceful painter who could manage a few stencils and a little gilding, were all that was needed, and in a very short time the building was habitable. Kitchen and cellar were quickly stocked, for, being so far away from the castle, they had to be provided with all essentials. Now the two women and the child lived upon the hill, and from this new residence, as from a new center, they discovered unexpected walks. They also greatly enjoyed in this higher altitude the fresh air and the lovely weather.

Ottilie's favorite walk, which she sometimes took alone and at other times with the child, led her, along an easy footpath, down to the plane trees, and from there to the point where one of the boats was moored that people used to cross the water. She enjoyed rowing, but she never took the child because Charlotte would have been uneasy about it. Ottilie also never missed her daily visit to the gardener in the park; she always showed special interest in his care of the many cuttings which he had been nursing in the hothouse but which were now set out in the open.

During this lovely season, Charlotte was much pleased by the visit of an Englishman who had met Eduard abroad, and was now curious to see the beautiful park, about which he had heard so many enthusiastic reports. He brought a letter of introduction from the Count and introduced to them his traveling companion, a quiet and very likeable man. While he walked about the countryside in the company of Charlotte and Ottilie, or with gardeners and hunters, frequently with his friend, and now and then alone, it could be gathered from his comments that he was a great lover and connoisseur of such 'landscape gardens,' and that he himself must have laid out some of the same type. Although no longer young, he showed a warm interest in everything that makes life more beautiful or lends it distinction.

In his company the two women for the first time fully enjoyed everything about them. His trained eyes took in every effect freshly, and he was all the more delighted with the improvements, since he had never seen the place before and could hardly distinguish between the natural and the artificial.

It might even be said that through his comments the park became actually richer and more beautiful. He was able to anticipate the future effect of the new and growing groups of trees. Not one spot where he thought a beautiful effect might be better set off or a new beauty created, escaped his notice. Here, he would point out a spring which, if cleaned out, might become the ornamental center of a whole group of shrubs; there, a grotto that only needed to be cleared and widened to form an attractive place to sit and rest; they needed to cut down only a few trees in order to obtain from this point a prospect of magnificently towering rocks. He considered the owners of all this very fortunate indeed; there was still much left for them to develop, and he urged them not to do anything hurriedly but to keep alive for themselves, for years to come, the pleasure of creating and arranging.

Apart from the hours they all spent together, their visitor was hardly noticeable; for the greater part of the day he was occupied in catching the picturesque views of the park in his portable *camera obscura* and in making drawings from these, in order to bring home from his travels mementoes for himself and for others. He had done this for many years in all the remarkable places he had visited and had compiled a most pleasurable and interesting collection. He showed the ladies a large portfolio he had brought with him; and entertained them equally with the pictures and with his descriptions. There in their solitude, they enjoyed traveling so comfortably all over the world—seeing pass before their eyes shores and harbors, mountains, lakes and rivers, cities, castles and many other places which have a name in history.

Each of the two women had her special interest. Charlotte's was a more general one, in places which were historically remarkable; whereas Ottilie's attention was primarily arrested by the parts of the world of which Eduard had often spoken, where he had liked to stay, and to which he had frequently returned. For everyone, certain local features exist—far or near—which attract him according to his character, and which he considers particularly endearing and exciting, because of the first impression they have made on him, because of certain associations, or because of habit.

Ottilie, therefore, asked Lord . . . which one of all these places he had liked best; and where he would live, if he had the choice. He then showed her more than one lovely part of the world, and told her kindly, in his slow peculiarly accentuated French, what had happened to him here or there, to make him love and admire that locality.

But he answered her question as to where he usually lived, and where he best liked to return, very frankly, although in a way which was rather unexpected for his listeners.

"I am now quite accustomed to feel at home everywhere; and I think that nothing is more convenient than to let others build and plant and keep house for me. I have no longing to return to my own estates, partly from political reasons, but mainly, because my son, for whom I really planned and arranged everything—and to whom I hoped to transfer all, and with whom I hoped to enjoy everything for still a little while—has no interest in the property, but has gone to India like many others—where he thinks he can make better use of his life; but perhaps will only waste it.

"It is true that we make much too elaborate preparations for life. Instead of beginning at once to live happily, in moderate conditions, we forever expand, and thereby make our lives more and more uncomfortable. Who now enjoys my house, my park, my gardens? Not I, not even my family: but strangers, curious visitors, or restless travelers.

"Even with considerable means, we are always only half at home and particularly so in the country, where we miss many things we have become used to in the city. The book we are most anxious to read is not at hand; and just what we needed most has been forgotten. We always settle down in order to leave again; and if we do not leave of our own free will, or from a purposeless whim, we are forced by circumstances, passions, accidental events, necessity, or whatnot."

Lord . . . did not suspect how deeply the two women were touched by these general reflections. How often do we all run a risk, when we make such casual statements, even in the presence of persons whose circumstances are well known to us! Charlotte was quite used to such occasional thoughtless words, which wounded, even when they came from kindly-feeling and well-meaning people; but she knew the world so well that it did not shock her particularly when someone forced her—thoughtlessly and carelessly—to direct her attention to this or that unpleasant facet of life. Ottilie, however, who was still in her half-conscious youth, who felt more than she saw, and who was allowed, even bound, to turn her eyes away from what she neither should nor wished to know—Ottilie was thrown into the most anguished state of mind by these careless words, for they tore a graceful veil rudely from her eyes; and it seemed to her as if everything which had been done all this time for this house and this home, for garden and park, and for all the environs, was actually in vain, because he to whom it all belonged did not enjoy it; because he, too, like their present guest, had been driven out by those dearest and closest to him, to wander about all over the world; and was, moreover, driven into the most dangerous situation. She was accustomed to listen and keep silent; but on this occasion she found herself in a most difficult position, which only became more so when the foreign visitor continued, in his cheerful circumspect manner: "I believe I am now on the right road, since I consider myself at all times as a traveler who renounces much in order to enjoy much. I am now used to constant change; it has even become necessary to me, in the same way as we are always waiting, at the opera, for a new stage-setting, since there have already been so many. I know what to expect from the best inns, and what from the worst; they may be as good or as bad as they come, but, at least, I can always expect something new. And in the long run everything comes to much the same thing—whether we depend upon a necessary habit or entirely upon the caprice of chance. Now I need no longer to worry that something cannot be found or is lost, that the room in which I am used to living is uninhabitable because of repairs, that my favorite cup is broken and that for a long time nothing will taste good from another cup. I am spared all this, and, should the house start to burn over my head, my servants would quickly pack my things, we would drive out of the inn yard, leave the town, and look for another lodging. When I consider these advantages and reckon up my expenses at the end of the year, I find that I have not spent more money than it would have cost me to live at home.

While he went on with his description, Ottilie saw only Eduard before her: marching along rough roads, in discomfort and hardship, encamped in open fields, exposed to danger and misery. Homeless and friendless in this hazardous life of constant change, he would have become used to throwing everything away, in order to have nothing to lose. Fortunately the friends separated for a short time, and Ottilie had an opportunity to be alone and to cry her heart out. Never had her silent suffering overwhelmed her more desperately than in this sudden realization which she tried to make even clearer to herself, as we do when we torture ourselves in a situation by which we are already tortured.

Eduard's present condition seemed to her so miserable and pitiful that she decided to do everything in her power to bring about his reunion with Charlotte; to hide her own pain and love, in some quiet place, and to deceive them by any kind of activity.

Lord . . .'s companion, a sensible and quiet man, but a keen observer, had meanwhile noticed the blunder his friend had made in the conversation, and had drawn his attention to the similarity of the circumstances. Lord . . . had not known any particulars about the situation in this family, but his friend—who, on his travels was, in fact, in nothing more interested than in strange occurrences, caused by natural or accidental relationships, by the conflict between the lawful and the uncontrollable, between feeling and reason, between passion and prejudice—had some time previously (and especially while staying here at the castle) informed himself of everything that had happened, and of the present state of affairs.

Lord . . . was sorry, but he did not feel embarrassed. "We should always have to hold our tongues in society if we wished nothing of this sort to occur; for not only meaningful remarks but also the most trivial pronouncements may upset the feelings of those present," he said. "We shall set things right this evening and avoid all general talk. Do tell us some of the many pleasant and remarkable ancedotes, with which you have, on your travels, enriched your portfolio as well as your memory."

But even with the best intentions the two strangers did not succeed in amusing their friends with an apparently harmless entertainment. For after Lord . . .'s companion had told various strange, remarkable, gay, moving or terrifying stories, which arrested their attention and frequently held them in suspense, he thought of concluding with an unusual though less exciting incident. He did not suspect how deeply it would affect one of his listeners.

The Amazing Young Neighbors
Novella

"Two young persons of good family, living near one another, grew up together in the pleasant expectation of one day becoming husband and wife; and the parents of both looked forward with happiness to their future marriage. But it soon became quite evident that their plan would probably come to nothing, because a strange antipathy between the two young people, who were both of excellent character, manifested itself very distinctly. Perhaps they were too much alike. The minds of both were directed toward their respective interests; they were determined in their desires and firm in their resolves; each was loved and admired by his or her playfellows; but they were always antagonists when together. Each was constructive alone but destructive

235

in the other's company; wherever they met, they were not competitors for one goal but fighters with only one purpose in mind. They were both, on the whole, good-natured and amiable, and hostile or even malicious only in their relations to each other.

"This curious attitude revealed itself early in their childhood games; it increased with their years. Once, when the boys played at war and divided into battling factions, the girl, defiant and courageous, placed herself at the head of one of the armies and fought against the other with such vehemence and spirit, that the other side would have been disgracefully put to flight, if her own personal enemy had not held out bravely, finally disarmed his opponent, and taken her prisoner. But even then she defended herself so furiously that, in order to save his eyes without doing her any harm, he had to snatch off his silk scarf and tie the hands of his antagonist behind her back.

"This she never forgave him. Indeed, as time went on, she made so many secret attempts and plans to do him harm that his parents, and her own, who had been watching these strange passions for a long time, came to an agreement and decided to separate the two hostile children and to give up their own precious hopes.

"The boy soon distinguished himself in his new circumstances. Any instruction had splendid results. Following the wishes of those who were interested in him, and his own inclination, he decided to become a professional soldier. He was loved and respected everywhere. His excellent character always made him work for the benefit and well-being of others; and deep in his heart, he was very happy, if scarcely conscious of the fact, that he was rid of the one and only adversary whom nature had destined for him.

"The girl, on the other hand, suddenly reached a very

different stage. Her age, her growing maturity, and a certain instinct made her avoid the wild boys' games in which she had formerly participated. She seemed, however, to miss something; nothing around her was worth exciting her hatred; and she had not yet found anyone worthy of her affection.

"A young man, older than her former neighbor and enemy, of rank, fortune, and distinction, well liked in society and fascinating to women, now turned all his affection toward her. It was the first time that a friend, a lover, a suitor, had wooed her seriously. The preference he gave her before so many others who were older, more educated, more brilliant, and of higher station than herself, gratified her exceedingly. His continual attention, without insistence, his loyal aid in various unpleasant circumstances, his quiet and patient courtship—concerning which he had informed her parents, as she herself was indeed still very young—all this made her think favorably of him; and habit, as well as the fact that their relationship was now taken for granted by everyone, contributed to this feeling. She was so often called his fiancée that at last she herself believed she was; and neither she nor anyone else thought that a test might be necessary before she exchanged rings with the man who for such a long time had been considered her betrothed.

"The quiet course which their friendship had been following, was not quickened by the final, formal engagement. Both partners allowed matters to go on as before; they were happy to be together and planned to enjoy to the end this fine season which should be the spring of their future and more serious life.

"Meanwhile the neighbors' son had completed his studies with distinction. He had climbed to a well-deserved rung in his career and now came home on leave to visit his family.

He saw his lovely neighbor again and found himself in a perfectly natural though rather peculiar situation. For some time her heart had known only the kindly feelings of domestic happiness which befit a future bride; she was in harmony with everything around her; she believed herself to be happy, and in a certain sense she was happy. Now, for the first time in years she was again confronted with something: she could not hate it, for she was no longer capable of hatred. Her childish animosity, which had actually been only a vague recognition of an inner value, now expressed itself in a happy surprise, an amiable admission, and a half-willing, half-reluctant attraction. And all this was mutual. Their long separation gave them occasion for prolonged talks. Both had matured, even their childish and absurd behavior of years before now amused them when they exchanged memories, and it seemed as if the least they could do was to make up for that teasing hatred by a mutual friendliness and consideration—it was as if these vehement misunderstandings of earlier days now required implicit understanding as compensation.

"On the youth's side, everything remained within reasonable and desirable limits. His profession, his circumstances, and his ambition occupied him so completely that he accepted the friendly behavior of the betrothed young girl quite naturally, as a gratifying gift, without assuming that it had any consequences for himself, or begrudging the fiancé his bride; he was, by the way, on very good terms with him.

"But with her it was quite different. She felt as though she had wakened from a dream. The struggle with her young neighbor had been her first passion; and that struggle had been, after all, nothing but a violent, almost innate affection in the form of opposition. When she now tried to remember, it seemed to her that she had always loved him. She smiled when she thought of her hostile pursuit with weapons in her hands; she recalled her most pleasurable sensation when he had disarmed her; she imagined having felt bliss when he bound her; and all her schemes to harm and to annoy him, now seemed to her to have been only an innocent means of attracting his attention. She loathed their separation; she bewailed the sleep into which she had fallen; she cursed the languid dreamy habit which had made her accept such an unremarkable man as her fiancé; she was changed—changed, in a double sense, to the past and for the future, as one might say.

"If anyone could have looked into her heart and entered into her feelings, he would not have blamed her; but she kept everything a secret. Her fiancé could not be favorably compared to the neighbor when they were seen side by side. Although no one could deny a certain feeling of trust to the one, the other inspired complete confidence; if one liked to meet the first, everyone wished the second as a friend: and if one had imagined occasions that demanded energy and resolution, one might have had a slight doubt concerning the fiancé, while the neighbor's son inspired a feeling of complete security. For these fine shades of character, women possess an inborn and particular instinct, and they have reason as well as opportunity to train this gift.

"The more the girl indulged in her secret emotions, the less people found an opportunity to say anything in favor of her fiancé or to remind her what her circumstances and her duty seemed to advise and require. Her loving heart continued to indulge its partiality. On one side, she was indissolubly bound by social standards, by her family, her fiancé, and her own pledge; the ambitious young man, on the other, made no secret whatever concerning his own plans and prospects and behaved toward her like a faithful but not even particularly affectionate brother. When at last he spoke of his imminent departure, her former childish spirit seemed to be roused in all its malice and violence, angry and ready to function now even more effectively and perversely. She decided to die, in order to punish the youth she had once hated and now so passionately loved, for his indifference; and, as she could not possess him, at least to be forever united with his memory and his remorse. He was never to rid himself of her dead image, nor ever to cease reproaching himself that he had not recognized, not fathomed nor treasured her feelings.

"This strange madness did not leave her for one moment. She kept it hidden under many disguises; and, although people may have thought her queer, no one was perspicacious or wise enough to discover the actual root of her queerness.

"Meanwhile, friends, relatives, and acquaintances had exhausted themselves in arranging all sorts of festivities. Hardly a day passed without their organizing something new and unexpected. There was almost no beautiful site in the neighborhood which was not decorated and arranged for the reception of many merry guests. Our young visitor, too, wishing to do his best before he left, invited the young couple with a small family group for an excursion by boat. They boarded a handsome prettily decorated yacht, one of those elegant boats with a dining saloon and a few cabins which transfer the conveniences of the land to the water.

"They glided along the river to the sound of music; during the hot hours of the day the company assembled in the cabins below deck and amused themselves with games of skill and chance. Their young host, who could never remain inactive, had taken charge of the wheel, in order to relieve

240

the old master of the vessel, who had fallen asleep at his side. Just at this moment the wary young man needed all his presence of mind, since the boat was nearing a place where two islands narrowed the channel and where their shallow gravelly banks stretching out, first on one side and then on the other, made navigation dangerous. The cautious and sharpsighted helmsman was almost tempted to waken the captain; but he thought he could manage by himself; and took his course toward the narrows. Just then his lovely enemy appeared on deck, a wreath of flowers in her hair. She took off the wreath and flung it to her friend at the wheel. 'Take this as a memento,' she called out.

" 'Don't disturb me!' he exclaimed, catching the wreath, 'I need all my strength and attention.'

" 'I shall not disturb you any longer,' she cried. 'You will never see me again.' With these words she ran toward the bow of the boat and jumped into the water. Several voices shouted 'Save her, save her—she is drowning!' The young man found himself in a most terrible situation. The old skipper woke up and tried to take the wheel at the young man's command; but it was too late; the boat ran aground, and the young man, throwing off his heavier clothes, plunged into the river and swam toward his lovely enemy.

"Water is a friendly element for a person who is familiar with it and knows how to deal with it. The stream carried him easily, and the skilful swimmer mastered it. Soon he had caught up with the girl, who had been carried away by the current; he clutched her and was successful in lifting and carrying her. Both were now swept away by the force of the stream, until the islands and shoals were far behind them and the river was again broad and quiet. Only now did the young man survey matters clearly; after the first immediate danger he had acted quite mechanically and without con-

241

scious thought. He raised his head high and swam with all his energy toward a shallow bushy place where the land projected conveniently into the river, and he could carry his lovely prize onto dry land. There seemed to be not a breath of life in her. He was desperate, but, looking about, he discovered a path running through the underbrush. He took up his precious burden and soon caught sight of a solitary house, and found kind people, a young married couple. The emergency needed no long explanation. What he asked for was instantly brought. Soon a bright fire was blazing, and woolen blankets were spread on a couch; furs, pelts, and other warm coverings were quickly accumulated. Their wish to save a human being overcame any other consideration. Nothing was neglected which might call life back to the beautiful, half-rigid, naked body. They succeeded in reviving her. She opened her eyes, saw her friend, and flung her arms around him. She held him for a long time; and then, tears gushed from her eyes and completed her recovery. "Are you going to leave me now, that I have found you?" she cried.

"'Never!' he exclaimed; 'Never!' But he hardly knew what he said or did. 'But be careful now!' he added. 'Think of yourself, for your sake and mine.'

"She suddenly became conscious of herself and only now noticed the state she was in. But she could not feel ashamed in the presence of the man she loved, the man who had saved her life. She let him go to attend to himself: his clothes were still wet and dripping.

"The other young couple consulted with one another; the husband offered the young man, and the wife the young girl their complete wedding outfit, which had not yet been stored away, and would dress them from top to toe, inside and out. In a short time the two adventurers were not only dressed but charmingly so. They looked very handsome and were transfixed with amazement when they saw each other again; they rushed into one another's arms with passion, still half-smiling at their quaint disguise. The power of youth and the animating spirit of love completely revived them in a few moments, and only music was missing to invite them to dance.

"The sudden transition from water to firm ground, from death to life, from the circle of their families into a wilderness, from despair to delight, from indifference to passion and affection—all this at once—was almost too much for the head to grasp: it would burst or become confused. The heart had to do its best to make such a shock bearable. Since the young couple were entirely lost one in the other, some time passed before they could think of the apprehension and anxiety of those left behind. They began to feel some alarm at the thought of how they would face their families. 'Shall we run away? Shall we hide?' the young man asked. 'We shall stay together,' the girl said, clinging to him.

"The farmer, who had heard from them that their boat had gone aground, hurried to the river without asking further questions. There he saw the yacht coming downstream; with great efforts those on board had freed it and were now uncertainly sailing along, taking their chance and hoping to find their lost friends. The farmer tried to attract the attention of the people on board by shouting and signaling to them; he ran to a point where a convenient landing could be made and continued to shout and beckon until the boat headed in to shore; and what a sight it was when they landed! The parents of the two young people managed to land first; the fiancé was almost beside himself. They had hardly heard that their children were safe when the couple themselves appeared in their quaint costumes. No one recognized them until they had come quite close. 'Who is that?' the mothers exclaimed.

" 'What is that?' the fathers cried. The rescued pair knelt down before them.

" 'Your children,' they cried. 'We are engaged!' 'Forgive us!' said the young girl.

" 'Give us your blessing!' asked the young man.

" 'Give us your blessing!' both implored, while all the others stood speechless with amazement.

" 'Your blessing!' was heard for the third time, and who could have the heart to refuse it?"

chapter 29

THE narrator paused or, rather, he had just finished his story, when he noticed that Charlotte was deeply moved. She got up and left the room with an apology. She knew the story. The incident had actually occurred between the Captain and a girl in his neighborhood, not exactly as the Englishman had told it, yet still not essentially different. Only a few details had been altered and embellished, as can happen wtih that sort of tale after it has passed through the mouths of many and finally through the imaginative mind of a man of intelligence and taste. The usual result is that everything and nothing is left as it was.

At the request of the two guests Ottilie followed Charlotte; and it was now Lord . . .'s turn to remark that perhaps a second blunder had been made and that his friend had recounted something well known to the family or even connected with them. "We must be careful not to make any more embarrassing mistakes," he added. "In return for all the kindness and hospitality we have enjoyed, we have, apparently, not been very fortunate in our talk. We had better try to take our leave in a tactful manner."

"I must confess that there is something special which keeps me here," his friend answered, "and for that reason I should be very sorry to leave this house without learning more about it. Yesterday, when we walked through the park with your *camera obscura*, you, sir, were much too busy looking for a place from which you could catch picturesque views to notice anything else that was going on. You turned off the main path in order to reach a less frequented spot by the lake which would offer you a charming vista. Ottilie, who accompanied us, hesitated to follow you and asked if she might go there by boat. I joined her and watched with delight the skill of my lovely captain. I assured her that never, since I had been in Switzerland, where very charming girls sometimes take the place of ferrymen, had I been rocked so agreeably on the water; but I could not resist asking her why she had refused to walk on that bypath. I thought I had noticed, in her shrinking away, a really painful uneasiness. 'If you will not laugh at me, I will give you an explanation,' she answered, without the slightest resentment. 'Although even I find the fact a little mysterious, I have never walked on that path without being overcome by a peculiar chill which I have never felt anywhere else and which I cannot explain to myself. I rather avoid, therefore, exposing myself to that sensation, especially since immediately afterward I feel a pain in the left side of my head—a pain from which I suffer at other times, too.' We went ashore; Ottilie spoke with you; and meanwhile I examined the place she had pointed out to me from a distance. I was very surprised to discover unquestionable traces of coal. I am convinced that, by digging a little more, a considerable bed of coal might be found below the surface. I am sorry, sir; I see you smile and I know very well that you listen so patiently to my enthusiastic pursuit of these things in which you have no faith at all, only because you are a wise man and my friend; but it is impossible for me to leave this place without having tried my pendulum experiment with this girl."

Every time the matter came up, Lord . . . never failed to repeat his arguments against this experiment—arguments to which his friend, in turn, always listened patiently and modestly, while persisting in his own opinion and desires. He pointed out that one should not discredit such experiments because not everyone was successful with them; on the contrary, one should test their results even more carefully and exactly; perhaps, many new relations and affinities among inorganic substances and among organic substances, as well as between organic and inorganic, might be discovered—all of them at present unknown to us.

He had already spread out his apparatus, consisting of gold rings, marcasites, and other metallic substances, which he always carried with him in a neat little box; and he now lowered pieces of metal, suspended on threads, over other pieces lying beneath them. "I do not resent the mischievous delight I can see on your face, sir, at the fact that nothing will now move for me. But this performance is really only a pretext. If the ladies should return, I want them to become curious about what we are up to."

The ladies did return. Charlotte understood what was going on at once. "I have heard a great deal about these matters," she said, "but I have never seen any results. As you have everything so nicely assembled, let me try to see if it works for me."

She held the thread in her hand: and, because she took the matter very seriously, she held it steadily and calmly; but not the slighest oscillation could be seen. Then Ottilie was asked to try. She held the pendulum even more quietly and innocently over the metals which lay beneath. But immediately the suspended piece of metal was swept away as if in a distinct swift rotation, turning first to one side and then to another with each change in the position of the tray beneath, now in circles, now in ellipses; or it swung in straight lines, as effectively as the experimenter could expect, and even beyond his expectations. Lord . . . himself was taken aback; but his friend, in his delight and eagerness, could not stop and asked Ottilie again and again to repeat and vary the experiment. The girl was obliging enough to agree, but at last she asked him to let her go, because her headache had again appeared. He was amazed as well as delighted at this and assured her enthusiastically that he could completely cure her of this trouble if she would entrust herself to his treatment. The two women hesitated for a moment, but Charlotte, who quickly grasped what sort of treatment was meant, declined his well-meant offer, for she was unwilling to permit in her domestic sphere, experiments about which she had always felt a strong apprehension.

The guests departed; and, although they had been the cause of some strange experiences, they left in the mutual hope of a meeting somewhere in the future. Charlotte now used the pleasant days to return the last of her neighbors' calls—quite a difficult task, since everyone in the surrounding country (some out of genuine interest, some only as a matter of form) had frequently called on her to inquire about her health. At home, the sight of the little boy gave her new life; and he was certainly worth her love and care. Everyone thought him an unusual child, even a prodigy. His looks, his size, his fine proportions, his strength, his health— all were delights to the eye; but the most astonishing fact was his double resemblance, which became more and more striking. In form and features the child resembled the Captain more and more; and from day to day it became more difficult to distinguish between his eyes and Ottilie's.

Because of this strange affinity, and perhaps still more because of a woman's sweet feeling of tender affection for the child of a beloved man—even though it should be the child of another woman—Ottilie was like a mother to the growing little creature or rather like a second mother. When Charlotte was absent, Ottilie stayed at home with the child and its nurse. Nanni had resentfully deserted her for some time past and had returned to her parents; she was jealous of the little boy to whom her mistress seemed to give all her affection. Ottilie continued to carry the child into the open air and gradually extended her walks with him. She always took his nursing-bottle with her in order to feed him, if necessary. But she rarely forgot to take a book along, and in this way—the child in her arm and reading as she walked—she made a very graceful *Penserosa*.

chapter | 30

THE main objective of the campaign had been attained, and Eduard was honorably discharged with medals and other marks of honor. He immediately returned to his small farm, where he found detailed news concerning his family waiting for him—the family which, during his absence and without their knowing it, he had kept under close observation. His quiet refuge looked very pleasant to him; many repairs and improvements had been made while he was away, according to his directions, so that the convenient arrangements in the house itself compensated for all that it lacked in size and area.

Eduard, grown accustomed to more definite decisions in a livelier sort of existence, now made up his mind to realize immediately the plans he had had sufficient time to think about. First of all he invited his old friend the Major (who had been promoted from Captain) to come and see him. Their reunion was a great joy for both. Early friendships have, like blood relationships, the distinct advantage that mistakes and misunderstandings of any kind are never fundamentally harmful to them; the old relationship is always quickly re-established.

After a cordial welcome, Eduard inquired about the situation of his friend and heard how perfectly Fortune had favored the latter's wishes. In jesting familiarity, he asked if there was not, perhaps, some happy alliance in the offing; but his friend denied this.

"I cannot, and I must not, be secretive with you," Eduard went on. "I must tell you at once of the state of my own feelings and of my intentions. You know of my love for Ottilie; and you have known for a long time that it was this passion which drove me into the campaign. I do not deny that I wished to rid myself of a life which, without her, had no longer any meaning for me; but at the same time I must confess that I could not bring myself to feel utterly hopeless. Happiness with her seemed so beautiful, so desirable, that I found it impossible to resign my hope entirely. So many happy omens had strengthened my belief, my illusion, that Ottilie might one day be mine. A glass, engraved with our initials and flung into the air when the cornerstone was laid, did not break; someone caught it, and it is again in my possession. After I had endured so many miserable hours in this lonely place, I said to myself: I shall put myself in the place of this glass which shall be a symbol either for the possibility or the impossibility of our future union. I shall go in quest of death—not like a madman but like a man who still hopes to survive. Ottilie shall be the prize I fight for; it will be *she* whom I hope to win and conquer—in line of battle, in every entrenchment, in every besieged fortress. I shall perform miracles with the wish to be spared myself, with the thought of winning Ottilie, not of losing her. These emotions have guided me; they have helped me through all dangers; but now I feel like a man who has reached his goal, like a man who has overcome every obstacle, whose way is now plain before him. Ottilie is mine; anything that still lies between this thought and its realization I can only regard as unimportant."

"With a few strokes you eliminate everything I could and should interpose, and yet I must repeat my objections," the Major replied, "I leave it to you to recall to your memory the great value of your relationship with your wife—and you owe it to her and to yourself, not to close your eyes to it. But at the sheer thought that a son has been given to you, I must at once declare that you and Charlotte belong to one another forever; that, for the sake of this little creature, it is your duty to live united, so that, united, you can take care of his education and build a happy future for him."

"It is nothing but the conceit of parents to imagine that their presence is so necessary to their children," Eduard objected. "Anything that lives finds food and assistance; and if a son, after his father's early death, does not have such a carefree and favored youth, he may just for that reason gain a quicker training for the world, for he will early recognize that he must get on with other people, a fact which we all have to learn, sooner or later. But in our case all this is quite irrelevant; we are sufficiently well-off to provide for several children, and it is neither our duty nor to his benefit to accumulate so much property on one single individual."

When the Major began to allude to Charlotte's value as a person and to Eduard's long-standing relationship with her, the latter quickly interrupted him. "We have been very foolish, as I now see all too clearly. He who tries to realize, in his middle years, the desires and hopes of his early youth, always deceives himself, for each decade of a man's life has its own happines, its own hopes and its own chances. Not with impunity does a man, driven by his circumstances or by his delusions, try to capture something that lies before or behind him! Charlotte and I have acted foolishly; should this folly last for a whole lifetime? Should we refuse to ourselves, because of some scruple, what the morals of our time do not forbid? In how many situations do not men retract their intentions and their actions, and why should it not be done in this case, where everything is at stake, not just one particular, not this or that condition of life but life's whole complexity!"

The Major did not fail to point out, with much emphasis and skill, what Eduard owed to his wife, to their families, to the world, and to his estates; but he did not succeed in making the slightest impression.

"All those considerations have passed before my mind, dear friend," Eduard said, "in the tumult of battle, when the earth shook from the continuous roar of cannonades, when the bullets whizzed and whistled, and my comrades fell to right and left, when my horse was hit and my cap riddled; these thoughts have haunted me by the still campfire, at night, under the starry vault of heaven. At such moments everyone with whom I was connected appeared before my soul; I have thought of them and deeply felt for them; I have weighed everything and drawn my conclusions; I have come to terms with myself—many many times and now for good and all.

"You, too,—why should I keep it from you—were then in my thoughts; you, too, belonged in my circle; for have we not belonged to one another for such a long time? If I have ever been in your debt, I am now in a position to pay you back with interest; if you ever owed me anything, you are now able to make a good return. I know that you love Charlotte, and she deserves this love. I know that she is not indifferent to you—and why should she not recognize your worth! Take her from my own hands! Bring Ottilie to me— and we shall be the happiest people on earth."

"Just because you wish to bribe me with such precious gifts, I must be all the more prudent and firm," the Major replied. "Your suggestion—for which in my heart I am grateful—does not make things easier but even more difficult.

The question now concerns not only you, but me as well; and not only the destiny but also the good name and the honor of two men is at stake—two men of, until now, irreproachable characters, who run the risk, by such strange action—to put it mildly—of appearing in the eyes of the world in an extremely curious light."

"The fact that we have been above reproach until now, gives us a right to let ourselves be criticized for once," Eduard retorted. "A man who has proved himself honorable for a whole lifetime, makes an action honorable which would appear ambiguous in others. So far as I am concerned, I feel justified, after the trials I have taken on myself, and the difficult and dangerous actions I have performed for others, to do something for myself. We shall leave Charlotte's case and yours in the hands of the future; but neither you nor anyone else will keep me from my resolution. If any hand should be offered me, I shall be ready and willing to do what is wanted; but if I am deserted or should meet any opposition, I shall be driven to a desperate action—come what may."

The Major thought it his duty to oppose Eduard's resolution as long as possible, and he now skillfully changed his tactics by apparently yielding to his friend and by discussing only the form and the legal proceedings which would have to be undertaken in order to bring about the separation and the new unions. In this connection numerous, unpleasant, difficult, and offensive matters came up which put Eduard into the worst of tempers.

"I now see quite clearly that the fulfillment of our wishes must be taken by storm not only from our enemies but also from our friends," he cried at last. "I shall keep my eye fixed upon what I want, what is indispensable to me, and I shall seize it and certainly soon and quickly. Relationships like ours are neither dissolved nor formed without the toppling of much that once stood firm, and the giving way of much that would like to continue. Such matters do not come to a final conclusion through a process of reasoning—all rights being equal for the reasoning mind; and it is always possible to place another weight on the rising scale. Therefore, my friend, make up your mind and act; for your sake and for mine disentangle, untie and bind again these knots. Do not allow yourself to be put off by any scruples; we have already given the world reason to talk about us; people will talk once more and then forget us, as they forget anything that has ceased to be new. They will forget us and let us do what we like without being interested any longer."

The Major was at his wit's end and had no other choice but to submit to Eduard's way of treating the whole matter as being conclusively settled; while the latter gaily discussed in detail every step of their procedure, he pictured the future in the most cheerful colors and even joked about it.

Once more serious and thoughtful Eduard went on: "To give way to the hope and expectation that everything will turn out well by itself, that chance will guide and favor us, would be an unpardonable self-deception. We cannot possibly save ourselves in this manner, nor restore peace for all all of us; and how should I be able to find any comfort—I, the innocent cause of all this? By my insistence I persuaded Charlotte to invite you to stay with us; and Ottilie, too, joined us in consequence of this first change. We no longer have any control of the outcome of it all; but we do have the power to counteract the harm we have done, and to direct the situation toward our happiness. Can you turn your eyes away from the beautiful and happy prospects I open up for us? Can you impose upon me, upon all of us a joyless resignation? Do you think this possible? *Is* it possible? If it is, and if we should decide to return to former conditions, would not many offensive, annoying and inconvenient things have to be suffered without any resulting good or happiness? Would the fortunate position which you hold make you happy if you were prevented from visiting me and from staying at my house? After all that has happened you must agree that this would be constantly embarrassing. With our ample fortune, Charlotte and I would only find ourselves in a melancholy situation. And if you, like other men of the world, should believe that years and separation will blunt such feelings, will erase deeply engraved impressions, those are the very years which no one wishes to spend in sorrow and resignation but rather in joy and happiness. And the final and most important argument is: even if *we*, owing to our external circumstances and our state of mind, could perhaps wait patiently—what will become of Ottilie? She would be compelled to leave our house, would be deprived of our protection, and would be harshly dealt with in a cold wicked world! Describe to me any situation in which Ottilie—without me, without us—could be happy; then you will have offered me an argument, stronger than any other, which I am willing to consider, even if I should not accept it."

This problem was not easy to solve; at least his friend could not think of a satisfactory solution. He could only impress on Eduard repeatedly how serious, how precarious, and, in many ways, how dangerous the whole undertaking was and that they should at least study with careful deliberation how to set about it. To this Eduard agreed, but on the condition that his friend should not leave him before they had arrived at an agreement about the whole matter, and not before the first steps had been taken.

chapter | 31

COMPLETE strangers or people who are entirely indifferent to each other usually open their hearts liberally, when they are living together for some time—necessarily creating an atmosphere of intimacy. It was all the more to be expected, therefore, that our two friends, who were now living under the same roof again and saw each other daily, had no secrets left. They talked repeatedly about the earlier years of their friendship, and the Major did not conceal from Eduard the fact that Charlotte had intended Ottilie for him at the time when he had returned from his travels, and that she had hoped that Eduard would finally marry the lovely girl. Eduard was almost beside himself at this disclosure; and he now spoke without any reserve of the mutual affection between Charlotte and the Major, which, because it fitted in conveniently and favorably with his own wishes, he painted in glowing colors.

Although the Major could not totally deny this affection, he did not wish to admit it altogether. But Eduard became only the more insistent and determined. Everything was fixed in his mind, not as a possibility but as already settled. Everyone concerned had only to agree to something desired by all; a divorce could certainly be obtained; the new marriages would follow as soon as possible; and then Eduard planned to travel with Ottilie.

Among the pleasant things which imagination pictures, nothing is perhaps more charming than young lovers or young married couples who hope to enjoy their new, fresh relationship in a fresh, new world, and to test and confirm the stability of their bond in many changing circumstances. The Major and Charlotte, meanwhile, would have full power to arrange and initiate any matter concerning property, money and other worldly and desirable affairs—justly and fairly and for the satisfaction of all concerned. But the point which Eduard stressed most strongly, from which he seemed to promise himself the greatest advantage, was this: that—as the child would remain with its mother, the Major would be in a position to educate the boy, to guide him according to his judgment, and to develop his abilities. Then it would not be in vain that he had been baptized by the name "Otto"—the name of both friends.

Eduard had arranged everything so perfectly in his mind that he could not wait another day to carry out all his plans. On their way to the castle they came to a small town where he owned a house and where he planned to stay and wait for the Major's return. But he could not yet bring himself to stop there immediately and accompanied his friend a little farther. Both were on horseback and rode on together, engrossed in a serious conversation. Suddenly they saw, at a distance and for the first time, the new house on the hill, its red roof-tiles shining. Eduard was all at once overcome by an irresistible longing; he wished everything to be settled this very evening; he himself would remain hidden in a neighboring village; the Major would impress Charlotte with the urgency of the matter; he would take her by surprise and, by his unexpected proposal, force her to express her feelings without reserve. Eduard had identified his desires so completely with hers that he felt certain he was meeting her determined wishes halfway, and he hoped to receive her immediate consent because he himself could not think of any other solution.

A happy outcome joyfully appeared before his eyes, and, in order that he might know the result quickly, he asked that shots be fired, or—if it had grown dark—that rockets give the signal.

The Major rode over to the castle. He did not find Charlotte there and was told that she was living at present in the new building on the hill but that today she had gone to pay a visit in the neighborhood and would probably not return until late. He walked back to the inn where he had stabled his horse.

Eduard, driven by his uncontrollable impatience, had meanwhile left his hiding place and stolen into his park along lonely paths, known only to hunters and fishermen. He arrived there toward evening in the thicket close to the lake; he saw for the first time its clear mirror spread out in its entire length.

Ottilie had gone to the lake this afternoon for a walk. She carried the child and was reading as usual while she walked. In this way she arrived at the oak trees by the jetty. The little boy had fallen asleep, and she laid him down beside her and went on reading. Her book was one of those which attract and absorb a sensitive mind. She did not think of time and hour and quite forgot that the way back to the new house was a long one by land; she sat, lost in her book and in herself—so lovely to look at that the surrounding trees should have been animated beings endowed with eyes to admire her beauty. Just at this moment slanting rays of the setting sun shone on her, tinging her cheek and shoulder with gold.

Eduard, who had, until now, managed to avoid encountering anybody, and had found his park deserted, with no living soul in the entire surrounding countryside, ventured on and on. At last he broke through the bushes near the oaks and saw Ottilie and she saw him. He rushed to her and threw himself at her feet. After a long silence, in which they both tried to calm their emotions, he explained in a few words why and how he had come here. He told her that he had sent the Major to Charlotte and that their common destiny was perhaps being decided at this very moment; that he had never doubted her love and was sure that she had never doubted his; and that he asked her consent to their marriage. Ottilie hesitated. He implored her and was on the point of asserting his old rights and taking her in his arms, when she pointed to the child. Eduard looked at it and was startled. "Good Heavens!" he exclaimed, "if I had any reason to doubt my wife and my friend, these features would bear terrible evidence against them. Is he not the very image of the Major? I never saw such a likeness."

"Don't say that!" Ottilie replied. "Everyone says that he is like me."

"Is it possible?" Eduard said; and at this moment the child opened his eyes: two large, dark, searching eyes, deep and friendly. The little boy already looked out into the world quite intelligently, he seemed to know the two who stood before him. Eduard fell on his knees before the child and then knelt again before Ottilie. "Yes, it is you!" he cried. "The eyes are yours! Ah, but let me look only into *your* eyes. Let me throw a veil over the hour which gave this little creature his existence. Shall I shock you with the terrible thought of a husband and wife who, having become strangers, embrace each other, and by their sudden desire are capable of profaning the sacred bond! Yes! Since we have gone so far, since Charlotte and I must be separated, since you will be my wife—why should I not admit it? Why should I not speak out the cruel words: this child is the fruit of double adultery! It divides me from my wife, and my wife from me—this child that should have united us. Let it bear witness against me; let these wonderful eyes tell yours that, in the arms of another woman, I belonged to you. Feel it, feel it deeply, Ottilie, that I can atone for my fault, my crime, in your arms alone!"

"Listen!" he cried, and jumped to his feet, believing that he had heard a shot and that it was the expected signal of the Major. It was only a hunter's gun in the near-by hills. No other sound followed, and Eduard grew impatient.

Ottilie noticed only now that the sun had disappeared behind the mountains. Its last rays were reflected in the windows of the house on the hill. "Leave me, Eduard!" she said. "We have been separated for so long; we have suffered so long! Remember what we both owe to Charlotte. She is the one to decide our fate; do not let us forestall her decision. I shall be your wife if she permits it; if she does not, I must give you up. Since you believe that the decision is so near, let us wait. Go back to the village where the Major believes you to be. So much can happen that must be explained. Is it really likely that anything so rude as a gunshot will tell you the result of this talk? Perhaps he is looking for you this instant. He cannot have seen Charlotte—not that I know. He may have gone to meet her, because she left word where she was to be. There are all sorts of possibilities! Leave me! She must be at home now. She expects me and the child at the lodge."

Ottilie spoke in haste. She was trying to consider everything at once. She was happy to be with Eduard, but she felt that she must now send him away. "I beg you, I implore you, my love!" she cried, "go back and wait for the Major."

"I shall obey you," Eduard cried, with passion and desire, taking her in his arms. She held him, too, and pressed him most affectionately to her heart. Like a star falling out of the sky, hope flashed over their heads. They thought and believed that they belonged to each other. For the first time they kissed, fully aware of what they were doing; and they parted unwillingly and with aching hearts.

The sun had gone down; dusk gathered, and a damp mist was floating from the shores of the lake. Ottilie stood confused and agitated; she looked across to the house on the hill and thought she saw Charlotte's white dress on the terrace. It was a long walk around the lake; and she knew how impatiently Charlotte would be waiting for the child. She saw the plane trees just opposite; only a strip of water separated her from the path which led straight up to the lodge. Her mind, like her eyes, had already crossed to the farther shore. Her hesitation about crossing the lake with the child vanished before her urgency. She ran to the boat; she did not notice the throbbing of her heart, nor the unsteadiness of her feet, nor that her senses threatened to fail her.

She jumped into the boat, took the oar, and pushed off. She had to use all her strength and push again; the boat swayed and then began to glide out into the lake. The child was in her left arm, she held the book in her left hand, the oar in her right; suddenly she lost her balance and fell back into the boat. The oar slipped overboard and when she tried to steady herself, the child and the book slipped into the water. She caught hold of the child's clothes, but her awkward position prevented her from rising to a sitting position. She could not at first turn around and raise herself; but at last she succeeded. She pulled the child out of the water, but its eyes were closed; it had stopped breathing.

In a moment she regained her presence of mind, but her

anguish was all the greater. The boat drifted almost to the middle of the lake; the oar floated far away; she could not see anyone on the shore—and what good would it have done if she had seen someone? Cut off from everything, she floated along on the treacherous water.

She tried to find help in herself. She had often heard about the resuscitation of the drowned. On the evening of her birthday she had actually seen such a thing happen. She undressed the child and dried it with her muslin dress. She hastily tore open her bodice and for the first time pressed a living being to her naked breast; but, alas! it was no longer living. The cold limbs of the poor little creature chilled her to the core of her heart. Tears streamed from her eyes; for a moment the stiffened body appeared warm and alive. She persisted in her efforts; she wrapped the child in her shawl and thought she was providing a substitute for the remedies she could not obtain, cut off as she was, as she pressed it close to her, breathed upon it, and covered it with kisses and tears.

It was all in vain. The child lay still in her arms; the boat stood still upon the water. But even in this situation her steadfast spirit did not forsake her. Sinking down on her knees in the boat, she turned to Heaven, and lifted the dead child with both arms above her breast, white as marble, and cold as marble. She turned her face to the sky, asking for help where a tender heart hopes to find it in its fulness, when there is need all about and everything else has failed.

She did not turn to the stars in vain. One by one they began to appear. A gentle breeze rose and moved the boat toward the plane trees.

chapter | 32

Ottilie ran up to the lodge; she called the physician and handed the child to him. Trained as he was for
any eventuality, the doctor applied in the usual sequence
one method after another to the frail body. Ottilie assisted
him. She prepared and brought him the necessary items and
took care of everything, although she moved as if she were
in another world, for extreme unhappiness, like extreme
happiness, changes everything about us. Only when the
physician, after having tried every possible measure, silently shook his head and then, very gently, answered her
question as to whether there was any hope, with a "No!" did
Ottilie leave Charlotte's bedroom where all this had taken
place; she had hardly entered the living room, when, unable
to reach the sofa, she fell exhausted face downward on the
carpet.

Just then Charlotte's coach drove up. The physician asked
those standing about to keep back; he himself wished to
meet and prepare her; but she had already entered the
room. She found Ottilie lying on the floor; and a housemaid
rushed in, shrieking and weeping. The physician, too, came
in; and she now heard everything at once. But she could not
immediately give up all hope. The physician, experienced,

skilful, and always sensible, implored her not to go and see the child now; he himself left her, pretending to continue his efforts; and she sat down on the sofa. Ottilie still lay on the floor; but Charlotte raised her, lifting her to her knees, on which Ottilie's beautiful head sank down. The physician came and went several times; he seemed to be concerned with the child but actually attended the two women. It was soon midnight and the deadly silence deepened. Charlotte no longer had any illusion that her child would return to life; she asked to see it. It had been neatly wrapped in warm woolen blankets and laid in a wicker basket, which they placed at her side on the sofa. Only the little face was un-covered; it was calm and lovely.

The exciting news of the accident had soon spread to the village, and reached the inn. The Major went up to the lodge, along familiar paths. He walked around the house and eventually stopped a servant who was running to fetch something from an outbuilding. From him he heard more particulars, and asked him to call the physician outdoors. He soon came, much surprised at the sudden arrival of his former patron. He informed him of the present situation and agreed to prepare Charlotte for the Major's unexpected visit. Then he went into the house and began a conversation with Charlotte drawing her attention to other matters, lead-ing her from one topic to another, and at last mentioning her friend, of whose deep sympathy she could be certain, since they were so close in spirit and feeling. This enabled him to speak of the Major's actual presence. She heard that her friend was at the door, and that he knew all and wished to be allowed to enter.

He came in. Charlotte greeted him with a sad smile. She lifted the coverlet of green silk which hid her dead child; and in the dim light of a candle he saw—with something of a secret shudder—the stiffened image of himself. Charlotte pointed to a chair; and so they sat opposite each other, in silence, all through the night. Ottilie still lay quietly against Charlotte's knees; she breathed gently and appeared to sleep. Dawn broke; the candle had burned down; and the two friends seemed to awaken from a heavy dream.

Charlotte looked at the Major and said, calmly: "Tell me, my friend, what strange coincidence brought you here, to take part in this tragic scene?"

"This is not the time nor the place," the Major answered in the same low voice with which Charlotte had spoken, as though afraid to waken Ottilie, "for me to be reserved, or to broach my subject gently. The circumstances in which I find you are so grave that even the important matter which brought me here loses its importance beside it."

He then told her, quite calmly and simply, the purpose of his mission, in so far as Eduard was concerned; and the purpose of his coming, in so far as his own free will and his own interests were involved. He laid both propositions very tactfully but honestly before her. Charlotte listened quietly and seemed to be neither surprised nor offended.

When the Major had finished, she answered in such a low voice that he was forced to draw his chair nearer to her. "I have never before found myself in such a situation; but in a similar crisis I have always said to myself, 'How will it be tomorrow?' I realize very clearly that now the fate of several persons is in my hands. I do not doubt what *I* must do; that can be said very quickly. I agree to a divorce. I should have made this decision earlier; by my reluctance, my resistance, I have killed my child. There are certain things on which Destiny stubbornly insists. Reason and virtue, duty and all that is sacred to us oppose them in vain. Destiny wishes something to happen which to it seems right, but does not seem right to us; and in the end Destiny will be the victor, fight against it as we may.

"But what am I saying? Destiny actually seems to take up and carry out my own wish, my own intention, against which I acted so imprudently. Did I not in the past wish to bring together Ottilie and Eduard who are so well matched? Did I not myself arrange their meeting? Have you not, dear friend, been an accomplice in this scheme? And why was I unable to distinguish between a man's stubbornness and true love? Why did I accept his hand when—as a friend—I could have made him, and another wife, happy? And now look at this unfortunate sleeping girl. I tremble for the moment when she will wake to consciousness from her deathlike sleep. How can she live, how can she comfort herself, if she cannot hope through her love to give back to Eduard what she—a tool of the strangest whim of chance— deprived him of? And she will be able to give everything back to him with her deep affection, the passion of her love. If love can suffer all, love can do still more—it can restore all. There should be no consideration of me at this moment.

"Leave me here very quietly, my dear Major. Tell Eduard that I agree to the divorce; that I leave it to him, to you, and to Mittler to start the legal proceedings; that I am not worried about my own future situation and that I have no reason to be. I am willing to sign any papers I receive; the only thing one should not demand of me is to be consulted, to think about the matter, or to give any advice."

The Major rose. Charlotte gave him her hand above Ottilie's head. He pressed his lips upon this beloved hand and whispered, "And I—what may I hope for myself?"

"Forgive me if I do not give you an answer," Charlotte replied. "We have done nothing to bring about our unhappiness; but neither have we deserved to be happy together."

The Major left, feeling in his heart a great pity for Charlotte, but without really feeling pity for the poor dead child. Such a sacrifice seemed to him necessary for the happiness of them all. He pictured Ottilie with a child of her own in her arms, the most perfect compensation for the child of which she had deprived Eduard. He dreamed of having his own son on his knee, who would resemble him, and be more entitled to resemble him than the child who had died.

These hopes and fantasies passed through his mind while he went back to the inn. There he found Eduard, who had waited the whole night out of doors in vain for some signal to announce to him a successful outcome. He had already heard of the accident; but he, too, instead of feeling sorry for the poor little creature, looked at the incident, without, perhaps, quite admitting it to himself, as a providential act which had at one stroke removed all obstacles to his happiness. The Major quickly informed him of his wife's decision and could, therefore, easily persuade him to return to the village and from there to the small town where they would confer about the next steps to be taken.

After the Major had left her, Charlotte remained, deep in her own thoughts, but only for a few moments, for Ottilie suddenly lifted her head and looked at her friend with wide-open eyes. She raised her head from Charlotte's lap, rose from the floor; and stood upright before her.

"For the second time," the brave girl began, with her irresistible, graceful seriousness, "for the second time this same thing has happened to me. You once told me that people often experience in their lives the same thing in the same way, and always at important moments. I see now that what you said is true; and I must make a confession to you. A short time after my mother's death, when I was a small child, I pushed my footstool close to you; you were sitting on a sofa as you are now; my head rested on your knees; I was not asleep, I was not awake. I heard everything going on around me, particularly every word which was said; but still I was unable to move, to speak, to give a sign that I was conscious—even if I had wished to. You talked with a friend about me; you felt sorry that I had been left alone in the world, an orphan; you described my dependent position and you said how uncertain the future before me was, unless an especially lucky star ruled my fate. I understood well, perhaps too well, everything you seemed to hope for me and to expect from me. I set myself rules, according to my limited insight, and kept them for a long time, and in compliance with them arranged all my actions, during the whole time you loved me, took care of me, and received me into your house; and for some time afterward as well.

"But I have strayed from my course; I have broken my vows; I have even lost my feeling for them; and now, after a terrible disaster, you have again made clear to me my present situation, which is more miserable than the first. While resting on your lap in a half-stupor, I heard your gentle voice as from another world; and I learned from you how it is with me. I shudder at myself; but again, as I did before, I have marked out for myself, in my sleep, a new course.

"I am as determined as I was before; and what I have decided you must hear at once. I shall never be Eduard's wife! In a terrible fashion God has opened my eyes to the sin into which I have fallen. I will atone for it; and no one should think of keeping me from my intention. With this in mind, my dear, my best friend, you should make your own arrangements. Call the Major back; write him that no steps should be taken. How uneasy I felt when I was neither able to move nor to give a sign when he left! I tried to rise, to cry out: 'Do not let him go with such wicked hopes!'"

Charlotte understood Ottilie's condition; she felt deeply for her; but she hoped that time and her own encouraging words would prevail upon her. But when she said a few words which indicated a better future, a relief from her suffering, and some hope, Ottilie cried, "No!" vehemently. "Do not try to persuade me or to deceive me! The instant I hear of your agreement to a divorce, I shall atone for my sin and my crime in the same lake!"

chapter | 33

RELATIVES, friends, and members of the same household who live happily and peacefully together usually talk more than is necessary or desirable about what they are doing and what they should do; they repeatedly inform one another of their plans, undertakings, and occupations, and, without taking one another's advice directly, discuss the whole course of their lives, as it were, in perpetual conclave. Yet, in serious predicaments (just when it would seem that people particularly need the assistance and reassurance of others) everyone withdraws into himself and acts for himself; everyone hides from others his own particular ways and means; so that it is only the outcome, the realized aims, which again become common property.

After so many strange and unfortunate incidents, a serious calm had settled on the two women, which showed itself in tender mutual consideration. The child had been very quietly laid to rest in the chapel—the first victim of an ominous fate.

Charlotte returned to her everyday life so far as she was able; and here she found that it was Ottilie who first needed her help. She occupied herself chiefly with her but in such a way that Ottilie would not notice. She knew how deeply the girl loved Eduard. Gradually she pieced out for herself the scene preceding the accident and gathered every detail, partly from Ottilie herself, and partly from the Major's letters.

Ottilie, on her side, made life much easier for Charlotte. She was open and more inclined to talk, but she never touched on the present or on the recent past in her conversation. She had always listened attentively and observed carefully; she knew a good deal; and all this now came to the surface. She entertained and distracted Charlotte, who still hoped in her heart to see her married to Eduard, since both were so dear to her.

But Ottilie's train of thought was quite different. She had disclosed the secret of her life's course to her friend and now felt herself quite free from her former reserve and submissiveness. Her remorse and her resolution had also released her from the burden of her wrongdoing and her misfortune. She no longer needed to put any restraint on herself. Deep in her heart, she had forgiven herself, but only on the condition of a complete renunciation which would be binding forever.

In this way, some time passed, and Charlotte realized to what an extent the house, the park, the lake, and rocks and trees daily kept alive only melancholy associations for them. It was evident that a change of place was necessary; but it was not easy to decide in what manner this could be accomplished. Should the two women stay together? Eduard's previously expressed wish seemed to demand this: his declaration and his threat seemed to make it necessary; but it could not be denied that both women, with the best intention, with all their reasonableness and in spite of all their efforts, found themselves, in this life of close intimacy, in a painful situation. Their conversation tended to be evasive.

There were times when one preferred not fully to understand the other; and very often a word was misinterpreted, if not by the head, at least by the heart. They were afraid of hurting each other, and this very fear was particularly painful and hurt the quickest.

If a change of place was decided upon, and, at the same time a separation (at least for a while)—the old question again arose: Where should Ottilie go? There was still that family of rank and fortune which had made unsuccessful attempts to find a congenial and stimulating companion for their only daughter. The Baroness, during her last visit at the castle and lately in her letters, had urged Charlotte to send Ottilie there; and now Charlotte mentioned this subject once more. But Ottilie refused to go where she would meet what is commonly called 'the great world.'

"Dear aunt," she said, "let me tell you quite frankly something that it would be my duty, under other circumstances, to conceal. I do not want you to think of me as narrow-minded or stubborn. A person who has had an unusual misfortune, however innocent he may have been, is marked with a terrible stigma. His presence arouses in everyone who sees him and knows about him, something like horror. Everyone imagines seeing him carry his terrible destiny like a burden; everyone is curious and at the same time terrified. It is the same with a house, or a town, where something monstrous has occurred; people are forever frightened when they enter them. There the light of day seems to shine less brightly and the stars seem to have lost their brilliance. How extreme and yet perhaps excusable is the indiscreet behavior of others toward such unfortunate beings—their familiarity and clumsy kindness! Forgive me for speaking like this, but I have suffered indescribably for that poor girl, dragged from the refuge of her room by Luciane, who tried

273

to force her to take part in games and dancing—all with the best intentions. When the child, more and more frightened, finally escaped and fainted, and when I caught her in my arms while the guests, shocked and excited, crowded around the poor unfortunate creature with exaggerated curiosity, I did not think that the same fate would await me. But my feeling for her is still as deep and as fresh as it was then. Now I can turn this compassion toward myself, and I can be careful not to give occasion for similar scenes."

"But, my dear child, you will never be able to avoid being seen by other people," Charlotte answered. "We no longer have convents which once offered sanctuary for such feelings."

"Solitude does not constitute a sanctuary, dearest aunt," Ottilie replied. "The best sanctuary is one in which we can be active. Penances and self-denials will not save us at all from an ominous Destiny that is determined to persecute us. The world repels and frightens me only when I have nothing to do and when I am exposed to the stare of others. But when I can work with all my heart and do my duty unflaggingly, I shall be able to bear the eyes of anyone, because I need not shrink before the eye of God."

"If I am not much mistaken, you should like best to return to school," said Charlotte.

"Yes, I do not deny it," Ottilie answered. "I think it is a happy vocation to educate others in the normal, customary way, after one has, like myself, been educated in the most unusual manner. And do we not know from history that the men who withdrew into the desert because of great moral disasters were not entirely hidden and protected there, as they had hoped to be? They were called back into the world to lead the lost back to the right path. Who could have been better fitted for this task than those who were already initiated into the maze of life? They were called to give help to the unfortunate; and who could better perform this task than those who no longer had to fear any earthly harm?"

"You have chosen an unusual vocation," Charlotte said. "I shall not oppose you; you may do as you wish, although I hope it will be for a short time only."

"How grateful I am, that you will not grudge me this experiment and this experience," Ottilie said. "Unless I flatter myself too much, it should turn out well. I shall remember at the school the many tests I was put to, and how small and unimportant they were, compared to those I was put to later. I shall be so happy watching the difficulties of young growing natures; I shall smile at their childish griefs and, with a light hand, lead them out of their small errors. The fortunate person is not the right person to guide the unfortunate; it is human nature to demand always more of oneself and of others, the more one has received. Only those who are recovering from misfortune know how to foster, in themselves and in others, the feeling that even any moderate good should be enjoyed with delight."

Charlotte thought for a moment and then said, "I have only one objection to make to your plan, and it seems to me a very important one. I am thinking not of you but of another person. You know the feelings of the good and honest Tutor. On the road you have chosen, you will daily become dearer and more indispensable to him. As in his heart he already believes that he cannot live without you, he will be unable in future—after having become accustomed to your working with him—to carry on his work without your aid. You are going to give him your help in the beginning and in the end spoil everything for him."

"Fate has not treated me gently," Ottilie replied, "and whoever loves me, has probably nothing very much better to expect. Our friend is so good and sensible that I hope he will develop a feeling of friendship for me. He will see in me a dedicated person, who can perhaps atone for an enormous misfortune, to herself and to others, only by devoting herself to the Holy which is invisibly around us and is the one protection against the formidable powers which weigh upon us."

Charlotte listened to everything Ottilie said, and considered it quietly. Several times she had very tactfully sounded out Ottilie to discover if some move of hers toward Eduard might be conceivable; but the slightest mention of this, the faintest expression of hope, seemed to wound the young girl deeply; once, when she could not evade the subject, she expressed herself very clearly.

"If your resolution to renounce Eduard is so firm and unalterable," Charlotte retorted on this occasion, "you must be careful of the danger of seeing him again. When we are far from the person we love, and the deeper our affection is, the more we apparently succeed in controlling ourselves, because the whole force of our passion, formerly directed outward, is now turned inward; but how soon and how quickly do we discover our self-deception when the person we thought we could renounce stands suddenly before us and seems more indispensable to us than ever. You must now do what you think is most suitable in your case. Examine your heart; you may even change your present resolution; but do it of yourself, with a free, determined heart. Do not let yourself be drawn back into the former state of things, either by chance or by surprise, because this would destroy your inner harmony and be unbearable for you. As I have said: before you take this step, before you leave me and start a new life which may lead you no one knows where, think once more—can you really give Eduard up for good and all? But, if you are determined, let us make a pact. Promise me that you will never have anything to do with him—that you will not even speak to him if he should come to see you or force himself into your presence."

Ottilie did not hesitate for a moment. She gave Charlotte her word, which she had already given herself.

But Charlotte's mind was still haunted by Eduard's threat that he would leave Ottilie alone only so long as she did not leave Charlotte. Since that time circumstances had, of course, changed so much, and so much had happened that his threat, wrung from him in momentary anguish, might be no longer considered valid in the light of the succeeding events. Still, she did not want to risk anything or to undertake anything which, even in the remotest sense, might hurt him. She wished, therefore, that Mittler would search out Eduard's feelings and desires.

Since the death of the child, Mittler had visited Charlotte several times, although never for more than a few minutes. The accident, which, in his opinion, had made a reconciliation between her and her husband highly improbable, had made a strong impression on him; but, in his usual hopeful way, he was secretly very happy about Ottilie's resolution. He had great faith in the soothing effect of the passage of time and was still convinced that he would be able to prevent husband and wife from separating, for he took such passionate upsets merely as tests of married love and faithfulness.

Charlotte had, at the very beginning, informed the Major, by letter, of Ottilie's first declaration and had urgently asked him to persuade Eduard not to take any further steps. They should keep quiet and wait until the dear girl had recovered from her shock. She had let him know what she thought necessary about later events and decisions, but now

Mittler had the difficult task of preparing Eduard for a complete change in the state of things. Mittler, however, knowing well that people will rather resign themselves to an accomplished fact than agree to something which is about to happen, persuaded Charlotte that it would be best to send Ottilie to the school at once.

Preparations for the trip, therefore, were begun as soon as he had left. Ottilie packed her things; but Charlotte noticed that she took neither the pretty dressing case nor any of its contents with her. She did not remark on this and let the silent girl do as she liked. The day of departure came; Charlotte's coach would take Ottilie, on the first day, as far as a town well known to them, where Ottilie would spend the night; the next day she would drive on to the school. Nanni would accompany her and stay with her as her maid. The temperamental little girl had found her way back to Ottilie immediately after the child's death and was now as devoted to her as before; she even seemed to wish to make good her past neglect with amusing chatter and by devoting herself exclusively to her beloved mistress. She was now quite beside herself at the prospect of traveling with her and of seeing strange places, for she had never been away from her birthplace. She kept running from the castle to the village, to her parents and relatives, to tell them about her good fortune and to take leave of everyone. Unfortunately, she happened to go into a house where a family was afflicted with measles, and at once caught the infection. The journey could not be postponed. Ottilie insisted on leaving; she had once before traveled over the same road; she knew the people at the inn, where she would stop overnight; the coachman of the castle would drive her; there was nothing to worry about.

Charlotte made no objection. She, too, hurried away, in

her thoughts, from these surroundings; the one thing she wished to do before leaving was to arrange the rooms, in which Ottilie had lived in the castle, for Eduard, in just the same way that they had been arranged before the Captain's arrival. The hope of bringing back old happy times flares up constantly in us; and Charlotte had again a right, indeed a need, to hope.

chapter | 34

WHEN Mittler arrived to talk matters over with Eduard, he found him sitting alone in his room, his head leaning on his right hand, his arm propped on the table. He seemed to be suffering extremely. "Do your headaches bother you again?" Mittler asked.

"They do," Eduard answered, "and yet I cannot hate them, because they remind me of Ottilie. I am imagining that, leaning on her left arm, she perhaps also suffers, at this same moment, and perhaps more than I do; why should I not bear it as bravely as she does? These pains are good for me; I might almost say they are a godsend, because they bring her before me more vividly and clearly—her patience, along with her other virtues. Only when we suffer do we realize fully all the great qualities that are needed in order to bear suffering."

When Mittler found his friend so resigned, he no longer concealed his mission but told the story chronologically, bit by bit, in the same way that the idea had sprung up between the two women and had matured gradually into a definite plan. Eduard scarcely made any objection. From the little he said, it seemed as though he was willing to leave everything to them to decide. His momentary pain had apparently made him indifferent to everything.

But as soon as he was alone again, he got up and began to pace up and down the room. He no longer felt his pain; his whole attention turned toward outer events. During Mittler's speech the imagination of the lover had already taken new flights. He saw Ottilie, he saw her alone, or as good as alone, traveling a road well known to him; at an inn where he was familiar with every room. He thought; he deliberated; or, rather, he did neither think nor deliberate —he only wished; he willed. He had to see her, to speak to her. Why? To what purpose? And what would come of it? These were meaningless questions to him. He did not resist; he acted.

He took his valet into his confidence, and the man actually found out the day and the hour of Ottilie's departure. The morning dawned. Eduard lost no time and rode on horseback, and unaccompanied, to the place where Ottilie would spend the night. He arrived there much too early. The landlady of the inn was surprised and delighted to see him; she owed him gratitude. He had obtained a military decoration for her son, who had distinguished himself as a soldier. Eduard, the only witness of his particular action, had brought it to the attention of the commanding general and had also defeated the opposition of some envious people. For this reason the landlady could not do enough for Eduard. As quickly as possible, she cleared the best room, which was, however, also her wardrobe and storeroom; but he told her that a young lady would arrive and take that room, and asked her to provide a small bedroom at the end of the passage for him, furnished only with the most necessary things. The landlady thought all this very mysterious;

but she was only too glad to do her benefactor a favor; and Eduard showed himself very interested and helpful with all the arrangements. With what emotions he spent the long, long hours until evening! He looked around the room in which he would see Ottilie; it seemed to him a heavenly abode in spite of its strange domestic atmosphere. Many thoughts crossed his mind. Should he surprise her, or should he prepare her? At last, the latter view got the better of him; he sat down and wrote a letter which she would read as a welcome.

Eduard to Ottilie

"While you are reading this letter, my love, I am close to you. Do not be afraid; do not be shocked—you have nothing to fear from me. I shall not force myself on you. You will not see me before you give your permission.

"Think first of your situation, and of mine! I must thank you for not planning to take any decisive step; but the one you have taken is important enough. Do not take it! Here, at this crossroad, as it were, think carefully once more! Can you be mine? Will you be mine? Oh, it would be a blessing for us all, and for me an infinite joy!

"Let me see you again in happiness; let me ask you the sweet question with my own lips; and give me your answer yourself. Come to my heart, Ottilie, where you have sometimes rested and where you belong forever!"

While he was writing, he was suddenly overcome by the feeling that what he most longed for was quite close and would be here in almost no time. She will enter through this door; she will read this letter; she will actually stand before me—she, for whose appearance I have longed so many times. Will she be the same? Will there be a change in her face, in her heart? He still held the pen in his hand and was about to write down what he was thinking when the coach rolled into the yard. With flying pen, he added: "I hear you coming. For one moment only—Farewell!"

He folded the letter and addressed it; there was no time to seal it. Then he rushed into his room, from which he could later step into the passage; but the next moment he remembered that he had left his watch with his seal on the table.

She must not see these belongings first. He ran back and managed to carry them off. He already heard the voice of the landlady in the hall, coming to show the room to her new guest. He darted toward the door of his room, but it had slammed shut. The key had fallen out when he ran back for his watch and was lying inside; the lock had snapped, and he was locked out. With all his strength he pushed against the door, but it did not yield. Oh, how he wished that he could slip like a ghost through the cracks! In vain! He hid his face against the doorjamb. Ottilie came up and the landlady, seeing him, stepped back. To Ottilie he could not remain hidden for a moment. He turned round, and once more the two lovers faced each other in the strangest of circumstances. She looked at him calmly and seriously, without taking a step forward or back; but when he made a motion toward her, she withdrew a little toward the table. He, too, stepped back. "Ottilie!" he cried "let me break this awful silence! It is pure accident that you find me here now. There is a letter on the table which was written to prepare you! Read it, I implore you! Read it! And then decide what you must decide!"

She looked down at the letter and, after having thought for a second, took it up, opened it, and read it. Her face did not betray the slightest change while she read; gently she laid the letter down. Then she raised her hands, palms pressed together, and brought them back to her breast, at

283

the same time bending forward a little and looking into Eduard's anxious eyes with a look of such pleading that he was compelled to give up all he had asked and desired.

Her gesture almost broke his heart. Her look was too much for him. He was afraid that she would fall on her knees if he insisted. In desperation, he fled from the room and sent the landlady in to her.

He paced up and down the hall. Night had fallen, and not a sound came from the room. At last the mistress of the inn came out, locked the door, and took out the key. The good woman was moved and embarrassed; she did not know what to do. Finally before turning to go, she offered the key to Eduard, who refused it. She put down the lighted candle and went away.

Eduard, completely crushed by his grief, flung himself on the threshold of Ottilie's room, weeping. Rarely have lovers spent a more miserable night so close to each other.

Dawn broke; the coachman was impatient to drive on; the landlady unlocked the door to Ottilie's room and entered. Ottilie was still asleep, fully dressed; the woman went back and gave Eduard a sign to come in, smiling sympathetically. Both stood before the sleeping girl, but Eduard could not bear this sight. The landlady did not dare to waken the sleeper and sat down opposite her. At last Ottilie opened her beautiful eyes and rose to her feet. She refused to take breakfast. Now Eduard came in again, begging her over and over to speak but one word and tell him what she had decided; he swore that he would do anything she wished! But she remained silent. Once more he asked her, full of affection and passion, if she would marry him. Eyes downcast, she shook her lovely head in a gentle "No." He asked her if she still wished to go to the school. Again she shook her head, with indifference. But when he asked if she would allow him to bring her back to Charlotte, she nodded a confident "Yes." He hurried to the window to give orders to the coachman; but, with a lightning movement, she darted behind his back out of the room, ran downstairs and into the coach. The coachman drove toward the castle, and Eduard, on horseback, followed at some distance.

chapter | 35

CHARLOTTE was completely taken aback when she saw the coach drive up with Ottilie, and Eduard following—riding at full speed into the courtyard! She hurried down and stood in the door while Ottilie stepped out of the coach and came up to her with Eduard. Ottilie took the hands of husband and wife and pressed them together; then she fled to her room. Eduard embraced Charlotte and burst into tears. He was unable to give her any explanation but asked her to have patience with him and to look after Ottilie and help her. Charlotte quickly went to Ottilie's room. She shuddered when she entered; it had been completely cleared and looked as enormous as it was depressing. Everything had been removed, with the exception of the little dressing case, which stood in the middle of the room, as no one had known what to do with it. Ottilie lay on the floor, her arm and her head resting on the case. Charlotte tried to raise her and asked what had happened; but she received no answer.

She left Ottilie with her own maid, who had come with restoratives, and hurried back to Eduard. She found him in the salon, but could get no information from him either. He threw himself at her feet; she felt his tears upon her hands; then he fled to his room. She was about to follow when she met the valet, who told her as much as he knew. She pieced the rest together herself, and at once energetically set about doing what the moment required. Ottilie's room was rearranged in no time. Eduard had found his rooms—to the last piece of paper—in exactly the same condition in which he had left them.

The three were now together again and in some sort of mutual relationship; but Ottilie continued to be silent and Eduard could do nothing but implore his wife to have the patience which he himself seemed to be lacking. Charlotte sent messages to Mittler and to the Major. The first could not be found; the latter came at once. To him Eduard poured out his heart, making a clean breast of every smallest circumstance of the events in question; and in this way Charlotte learned what had actually happened—what had so unexpectedly changed the situation, and what had caused this general excitement.

She spoke to Eduard with affectionate understanding, asking him to leave the girl alone for the present. Eduard recognized his wife's great strength of character, her love and her wisdom; but he was still dominated by his passion. Charlotte tried to cheer him and promised that she would agree to a divorce. He had no confidence; he was so disturbed that hope and faith alternately forsook him. Gripped by a kind of insane dejection, he urged Charlotte to promise him that she would marry the Major. In order to calm and sustain him, Charlotte did what he demanded. She pledged herself to marry the Major whenever Ottilie would agree to marry Eduard—under the explicit condition, however, that, for the present, the two men would go together on a journey. It was necessary that the Major go abroad for business matters, commissioned by the Court, and Eduard promised to accompany him. Preparations were made and a temporary atmosphere of quiet settled on everyone, since something, at least, was being done.

All this time it was evident that Ottilie took hardly any food or drink and persisted in her silence. They tried to coax her, but this distressed her, and they gave it up; for are we not, in general, so weak that we do not like to worry people, even if it is for their own good? Charlotte thought of all sorts of tactics, but finally she struck upon the idea of sending for the Tutor, who had great influence with Ottilie. He had written very kindly, when she had not arrived as expected; but he had not yet received a reply.

Not wishing to surprise Ottilie, they discussed this plan in her presence. Apparently she did not agree; she seemed to deliberate. At last she had apparently come to a decision. She hurried to her room and, before evening, sent the following letter to her friends.

Ottilie to her friends

"Why should I express in so many words what you all know, my dearest friends? I have strayed from my course, and I shall not find it again. A hostile demon, who has gained power over me, seems to hinder me from without, even if I should have regained my inner peace. My intention to renounce Eduard, to leave him forever, was entirely pure. I had hoped not to meet him again. It turned out otherwise. He stood before me—even against his own will. I have perhaps taken and interpreted too literally my promise not to enter into any conversation with him. Following my conscience and my feeling at the moment, I was silent and did not speak to my friend; and now I have no words left. Quite by chance, and on a sudden impulse, I have taken upon myself a strict binding vow, which might perhaps be painful and embarrassing if taken after deliberation. Let me be faithful to it as long as my heart commands. Do not call upon anyone to mediate! Do not urge me to speak or to eat and drink more than I absolutely need! Help me through this time with your tolerance and your patience! I am young, and youth sometimes unexpectedly restores itself. Tolerate me in your presence; make me happy by your love; instruct me by your conversation, but leave my soul to me!"

The long-prepared departure of the two men was put off, since there was some delay about the Major's business abroad, and how welcome this was to Eduard! Filled with new hope by Ottilie's letter, reanimated by her comforting and promising words which justified his perserverance, he suddenly declared that he would not go at all! "How foolish it is," he cried, "to cast away rashly something indispensable which, though there may be some danger of losing it, might possibly be preserved. And what is the reason for this? Only to pretend that man is able to will and to choose. How often have I, possessed by such foolish deceit, torn myself away from my friends, hours or days earlier than necessary, because I wished under no circumstances to be forced to leave by the inevitable appointed date. But this time I shall stay! Why should I go away? Is she not already gone from me? I would not think of taking her hand or of pressing her to my heart; I cannot even think of doing this without a shudder. She has not moved *away* from me; she has raised herself *above* me."

And so he stayed on as he wished, and as he was compelled to do. But nothing could be compared to his delight in being with her. She, too, still felt the same; she, too, could not resist this blissful necessity. Now as ever they were attracted to one another by an indescribable, almost magic, power. They lived under one roof; but even when they did

not so much as think of each other, when they were occupied by other things, or were with other people, they
drew closer. When they found themselves in the same room,
it was not long before they stood or sat side by side. Only
when they were as close as possible did they find rest, and
complete rest! Their being near to each other was enough;
no look, no word, no gesture, no touch was necessary—just
being together. Then they were not two beings; they were
one person, in an unconscious and perfect happiness, at
peace with themselves and with the world. Yes, if one had
been detained by force at the farthest end of the house, the
other would gradually have moved, nearer and nearer, in
stinctively and without premeditation. Life was for them a
riddle whose solution they could find only together.

Ottilie was completely calm and poised and no longer
gave her friends any reason for anxiety. She rarely left the
others and only insisted on having her meals alone, with no
one but Nanni to wait upon her.

Much that ordinarily happens to a person repeats itself
more often than we think, because a person's nature is the
immediate determinant of this. Character, individuality, inclination, disposition, environment and habits form together a whole, in which every human being floats, as it
were, in an element, an atmosphere, in which alone he
feels comfortable and at ease. It is for this reason that, to
our surprise, we find human beings, about whose change-
ability we hear so many complaints, unchanged after many
years, and unchangeable after innumerable experiences
from within and without.

So in the daily life of our friends everything moved again
in the old groove. Ottilie showed her obliging disposition
as always in many little services, and everyone else acted in
his or her way. Accordingly, the domestic circle appeared

like a deceptive illustration of their former life, and it was perhaps excusable that they had the delusion that everything was as it had been.

In those autumn days, as long as the days of spring had been, they returned to the house from outdoors at about the same hour. The beauty of the fruits and flowers, peculiar to this season, made them believe that this was the autumn following that first spring; they had forgotten the intervening time. Now the flowers which had been planted in those earlier days were in bloom, and the blossoms they had seen then were now ripe fruit hanging on the trees.

The Major came and went; Mittler, too, called more often. They generally spent their evenings in the same way as before. Eduard usually read aloud; he read with more animation and more feeling; he read better, even more gaily— as one might say—than ever before. It was as though he wished to dispel Ottilie's apathy and unlock her silence through both cheerfulness and emotion. He took his seat as he used to do, so that she could look into his book; he was even restless and distracted when he was not certain that she followed his words with her eyes.

All the disagreeable and embarrassed feelings of the intervening period were blotted out. No one bore any grudges, and all bitterness had disappeared. The Major, with his violin, accompanied Charlotte, at the piano, and Eduard, with his flute, again joined Ottilie's sympathetic rendering of the piano part. Slowly Eduard's birthday drew near—the birthday they had not been able to celebrate together the year before. This time it would be celebrated in their quiet friendly circle without any public festivity. They had all, half-tacitly, half-explicitly, arrived at this agreement. But the nearer this particular day approached, the more the solemn side of Ottilie's character, which until now they had rather sensed than actually noticed, increased. In the garden she often seemed to examine all the flowers; by means of gestures she pointed out to the gardener that he should spare the many varieties of summer plants and flowers; and she stood for a long while in front of the asters, which were blooming this year in great profusion.

chapter | 36

THE most important thing the friends observed, however, was that Ottilie had, for the first time, unpacked the dressing case and had selected and cut out several pieces of material, enough to make a complete dress for herself. When, with Nanni's assistance, she tried to put the rest of the material back into the case, she was barely able to get it in; the space was crammed full, even after part of the material had been taken out. The younger girl could not take her eyes off all the pretty things, particularly since even the smallest accessories had not been forgotten, such as shoes, stockings, garters with embroidered devices, gloves and various other trifles. She begged Ottilie to give her one or two of these. Ottilie refused, but immediately opened a drawer of her chest and allowed the child to choose whatever she liked. Nanni hastily and clumsily grabbed something and at once ran off in raptures with her prize to show it to the others in the castle.

Ottilie succeeded at last in folding everything so carefully that it went back into the case; then she opened a secret compartment, set into the lid, where she kept little notes and letters from Eduard, together with pressed flowers, mementos of their walks together, a lock of his hair,

and other keepsakes. Now she added one more—the miniature of her father—and then locked the case and hung the
tiny key on a little gold chain round her neck, against her
heart.

Meanwhile her friends had been stirred by hopes. Charlotte was convinced that Ottilie would begin to speak again
on Eduard's birthday, because she had recently shown a
secret activity, a kind of happy inner contentment; and
sometimes a smile like that of a person who conceals something pleasant and enjoyable from those she loves, appeared
on her face. No one knew that she spent many an hour in
great exhaustion, controlling herself only by the power of
her will in the moments when she was with her friends.

Mittler had been a frequent visitor of late, and had stayed
for longer periods than usual. The strong-willed man knew
only too well that there is but one single moment when the
iron can be struck. He interpreted Ottilie's silence, as well
as her refusal to break it, in his favor. Until now not one
step had been taken in the matter of the divorce; he hoped
to settle the future of the good dear girl somehow to her advantage; therefore he listened, he yielded, he made suggestions, and behaved as diplomatically as could be expected
from him.

But he always allowed himself to get out of hand as soon
as he found an opportunity to argue about subjects to which
he attached great importance. He lived much in himself,
and whenever he was with others, his only relation to them
usually consisted in doing something for them. When he
was, therefore, among friends, and his tongue loosened, as
we have already often seen, his speech rolled on and on
without any consideration for them—wounding or healing,
useful or harmful, according to the circumstances.

On the night before Eduard's birthday, Charlotte and the

Major sat together waiting for Eduard who had gone riding. Mittler was pacing up and down the room. Ottilie had stayed in her own room; she had laid out her dress and everything she was going to wear on the following day and had given her maid several directions by means of signs—directions which Nanni understood perfectly, obeying her wordless orders very skilfully.

Mittler had just come upon one of his favorite topics. He liked to maintain that—in the education of children and in the government of people as well—nothing was more stupid and barbaric than prohibitive laws and decrees. "Man is active by nature," he said, "and if you know how to give orders, he will immediately do what you tell him, and do it in the way you wish him to do it. So far as I am concerned, I should prefer to tolerate around me faults and failings, as long as I cannot impose the opposite virtues, rather than get rid of the faults without knowing anything worthwhile to put in their place. A man really likes to do the right thing for a good purpose, if only he gets a chance; he does it in order to do something, and thinks about it afterward no more than he would think about the foolish pranks he plays out of idleness and boredom.

"How often it annoys me to have to listen when the Ten Commandments are repeated over and over again in Sunday school! The Fifth is, at least, a fairly tolerable and reasonable rule: Thou shalt honor thy father and thy mother. If children take this to heart, they can practice it all day long. But look at the Sixth—what can be said for it? Thou shalt not kill. As though anyone would have the slightest desire to kill another! Men sometimes hate; they quarrel; they lose their temper, and for these and a few other reasons it may happen that one person occasionally kills another. But is it not a barbaric method to forbid children to kill or murder? If one would say: Be careful of another person's life; remove anything that could harm him; rescue him at the risk of your own life; if you hurt him, remember that you hurt yourself—these are the Commandments which should be taught in educated and rational nations; but in our Catechism they are only casually dragged in toward the end. 'What is meant by . . .'?

"But now we come to the Seventh, which is utterly disgusting! What? Should we rouse the curiosity of precocious children and induce them to pry into dangerous mysteries and excite their imagination with strange images and conceptions which tell them clearly and exactly what we wish to keep from them? It would be much better if that sort of thing were arbitrarily punished by some secret tribunal instead of being rattled off in church in front of the congregation."

At this moment Ottilie entered the room. "Thou shalt not commit adultery," Mittler went on. "How rude, how indecent! Would it not sound quite different if it read: You shall highly respect the bond of marriage; wherever you see a husband and a wife who love each other, you shall rejoice and be as glad of their happiness as you would be of a bright sunny day; if clouds should appear in their relationship, you shall try to dispel them; you shall try to calm these two, to appease them, to point out to them their good qualities, and unselfishly promote their happiness, by making them feel that any obligation, and most particularly this obligation which joins husband and wife indissolubly, is the source of the greatest happiness."

Charlotte was terribly embarrassed, particularly because she was convinced that Mittler was completely unaware of what he had said, and where he was saying it; but, before she was able to interrupt him, she saw Ottilie leave the room, with a face that had lost all its color.

"I hope you spare us the Eighth Commandment," Charlotte said with a forced smile.

"All the rest," Mittler answered, "if I can only save the one on which all the others are founded."

At this point, Nanni, with a scream of terror, rushed into the room. "She is dying! My mistress is dying! Come! Come!"

When Ottilie had reached her room with the utmost effort, the festive dress which she was to wear the next day was spread out over several chairs with all its accessories; and Nanni, who was walking up and down, passing everything admiringly in review, cried happily; "Look, dearest mistress! Look! It is a wedding gown, worthy of you!"

Ottilie, hearing these words, sank upon the sofa. Nanni saw her grow pale and faint; she ran to call Charlotte, who came at once. The doctor hurried to help; he thought it was merely exhaustion. He ordered some strong broth, but Ottilie refused it with an expression of disgust and almost went into convulsions when they raised the cup to her lips. The physician, made suddenly suspicious by the symptoms, asked what Ottilie had eaten today. The maid hesitated; he repeated his question; the girl then confessed that Ottilie had eaten nothing.

Nanni seemed to the doctor to be more nervous than was justifiable. He took her into the next room, and Charlotte followed; the girl threw herself on her knees and confessed that Ottilie had eaten almost nothing for a long time. At her urgent request Nanni herself had eaten the meals brought to her mistress and had said nothing about this, because of Ottilie's imploring, even threatening gestures; and also, she naïvely added, because everything had tasted so good.

The Major and Mittler now joined them and found Charlotte energetically helping the physician. The pale girl, beautiful as an angel, sat, apparently conscious, in one corner of the sofa. They begged her to lie down; she refused but made a sign that her dressing case should be brought to her. Then she put her feet upon it, and settled herself in a half-reclining comfortable position. She evidently wished to say good-bye; and her gestures showed her affection for the friends who surrounded her—her love, her gratitude, her apologies, and a warm farewell.

Eduard, as he dismounted, heard what had happened; he rushed into Ottilie's room, threw himself down by her side, grasped her hand, and wept. Here he remained for a long time. At last he exclaimed, "Shall I never hear your voice again? Will you not return to life for me with a single word? Very well! I shall follow you, where we shall speak with other tongues!"

She pressed his hand; she gave him a long look full of life and full of love. Then, after drawing a deep breath, and moving her lovely lips soundlessly for a moment, she cried out, with a slight effort, "Promise me to live!" and then at once sank back.

"I promise!" he cried, in answer; but he only called after her; she had already passed away.

After a night of sorrow, the task of arranging the burial of the loved remains fell to Charlotte. The Major and Mittler assisted her. Eduard's condition was pitiful. When he had roused himself out of his despair and had collected his thoughts in some degree, he insisted that Ottilie should not be removed from the castle; that she should be attended, nursed and treated as though she were alive—for she was not dead, she could not be dead. They did as he wished, or, at least, they did not do what he forbade. He did not ask to see her.

Another alarm and another worry kept the friends occupied. Nanni, who had been sharply scolded by the physician, forced, by threats, to confess and then crushed with reproaches, had disappeared. After a long search she was found; she seemed to be out of her mind. Her parents took her home. The gentlest treatment did not seem to have any effect, and she had to be locked in because she threatened to run away again.

Step by step they succeeded in rescuing Eduard from complete despondency, but unfortunately for him; for now he thought clearly and saw the plain truth that he had forever lost the happiness of his life. They found the courage to suggest that Ottilie, if placed in the chapel, would still remain among the living and have a quiet and peaceful home. It was difficult to obtain his consent, and he finally gave it only under the condition that she should be carried there in an open coffin; that in the vault, she should lie under a coffin-lid of glass and a perpetually burning lamp be placed there. After all this had been arranged, he apparently resigned himself to everything.

They clothed the graceful body in the festive dress which she had made for herself; a wreath of asters was laid round her head; they shone sadly like mournful stars. For the decoration of the bier, the church, and the chapel, all the gardens were stripped of their treasures. They lay wasted, as though winter had already effaced the beauty of their flowerbeds. In the early hours of the morning Ottilie was carried out of the castle in an open coffin, and the rising sun once more flushed her lovely face. The mourners crowded around the pallbearers; no one wanted to go ahead, no one to follow; everyone wished to be close to her and enjoy her presence for the last time. Boys and men and women—not one was unmoved. The girls were disconsolate; they felt more deeply than the rest what they had lost.

Nanni was not there. They had kept her away or, rather,

they had kept secret from her the day and hour of the funeral. She was closely guarded in her parents' house in a small room facing the garden. But when she heard the bells tolling she knew at once what they meant; and when the woman who was in charge of her left to see the funeral procession, Nanni escaped through the window onto the gallery, and, finding all the doors locked, climbed up into the open loft above.

Just then the procession passed through the village along the road strewn with evergreens. Nanni had a clear view of her mistress below her; she could see her more distinctly, more perfectly than those who followed the bier. Ethereal, as though carried on a cloud or a wave, she seemed to beckon to her maid, who, confused, dizzy and swaying, plunged down into the street.

With a horrified scream the crowd scattered. The crush and tumult forced the pallbearers to set the bier down. The child actually lay very close to it and seemed to have broken all her limbs. By accident or as a precaution they leaned her against the bier; with her last spark of life she seemed to be trying to reach her beloved mistress. But hardly had her limp body touched Ottilie's dress and her limp fingers Ottilie's folded hands, when the girl jumped up, raised her arms and looked up to heaven. Then she flung herself on her knees before the coffin, looking at her mistress with rapt devotion.

Finally she rose to her feet and cried with ecstatic joy: "Yes, she has forgiven me! What no one else could forgive me, what I could not forgive myself, God forgave through her look, her gesture, her lips. Now she again lies still and peaceful; but you all have seen how she raised herself, blessed me with her unfolded hands and looked kindly at me! You all have heard it—you are my witnesses that she

300

said to me 'You are forgiven'! I am no longer a murderess; she has forgiven me; God has forgiven me; and no one can hold anything against me any longer."

All crowded around her; all were amazed; they listened and looked at her and at the dead girl, and no one knew what to do next. "Now carry her to her rest!" Nanni cried. "She has done and suffered her share and cannot live among us any longer." The bier was again taken up and the procession moved on, with Nanni following directly behind—and so they arrived at the church and the chapel.

There now stood Ottilie's coffin, with the child's coffin at her head, and the little dressing-case at her feet—all enclosed in a shrine of massive oak. A woman had been engaged to watch, for a time, by the body which lay so beautifully under the glass lid. But Nanni would not allow anyone to assume this office. She wished to stay without a companion and take good care of the lamp, which had been lit for the first time. She asked for this favor so eagerly and persistently that they let her have her way, in order to prevent a quite possible aggravation of her disturbed condition.

But she did not remain alone for long; for, as soon as night fell and the suspended lamp began to spread its light, the door opened, and the Architect entered the chapel, whose devoutly decorated walls seemed to him more ancient and more ominous in the subdued illumination than he would ever have believed.

Nanni was seated at one side of the coffin. She recognized him immediately; but she only pointed wordlessly to her dead mistress. And so he stood on the other side, in the strength and gracefulness of his youth, motionless, absorbed in his thoughts, his folded hands wrung in pity, his head and eyes bent toward his lifeless friend.

Once before he had stood in this way in the *tableau vivant* of '*Belisarius*'. Quite involuntarily, he now assumed the same posture—how natural also on this occasion! Now as then, something of invaluable excellence had been thrown from its height; and if, in the first case, valor, wisdom, power, rank and wealth of one man were mourned as being irrevocably lost—if qualities, indispensable to a nation and to a sovereign at decisive moments had not been valued but even rejected—in this case, many quite different hidden virtues, called forth by Nature only a short time ago from the depth of her riches, had been quickly destroyed by her indifferent hand: rare virtues with a peaceful influence which the needy world must ever welcome and mourn with profound sadness.

The young man and the girl were silent for a long time; but when she saw tears welling up in his eyes, and noticed that he seemed to be overwhelmed by his grief, she comforted him with so much sincerity, with such kindness and assurance that, amazed at the fluency of her words, he was able to control himself; in his mind's eye he saw his lovely friend living and working in another world. His tears stopped; his grief grew less sharp; he knelt down, bade Ottilie a last farewell and then left Nanni, after a warm pressure of her hand. He rode away the same night, without having seen any other person.

Unknown to Nanni, the physician had remained in the church all night; when he came to see her in the morning, he found her cheerful and perfectly calm. He had been prepared to hear wild flights of fantasy; he thought she would tell him of conversations during the night with Ottilie or of other hallucinations; but she was normal, quiet and completely in her right mind. She remembered earlier days perfectly, and everything that had happened in the smallest detail; and in nothing she said did she stray from the ordinary course of reality, except for the incident at the funeral, of which she spoke happily and repeatedly—how Ottilie had raised herself, how she had blessed her, and forgiven her, thereby giving her peace forever.

Ottilie's continuing beautiful state, which more resembled sleep than death, attracted many persons. All the people of the village and of the neighborhood wished to see her once more, and everyone enjoyed hearing the unbelievable story from Nanni's own lips—some treated it with scorn, some with doubt, but others with a strong inclination to believe her.

Any need that is not really satisfied turns man necessarily toward faith. Nanni, her limbs shattered before the eyes of the crowd, had been healed after she had touched the saintly body; why should not others as well be granted this blessing? At first, loving mothers brought their children who were afflicted with some ailment, and believed that they saw a sudden improvement. The people's confidence increased, and finally no one was too old or too weak to come to this place for comfort and relief. The crowds grew, and it became necessary to lock the chapel and—except during the hours of service—the church as well.

Eduard did not have the courage to look at his departed friend again. He lived automatically—he seemed to have no tears left and to be beyond suffering. His interest in conversation, his appetite for food and drink declined with every day's passing. His only restorative seemed to be in drinking wine from the glass, which, after all, had prophesied falsely. He still liked to look at the interlaced initials, and at these moments the serious-serene expression of his eyes seemed to indicate that even now he had not given up all hope of a reunion with Ottilie. But just as the smallest circumstance seems a good omen to the fortunate, whose happiness is increased by any chance event, the most trifling incidents frequently combine to crush and hurt the unfortunate. One day, as Eduard raised the beloved glass to his lips, he put it down, horrified; it was the same glass and yet not the same; he missed a tiny marking. He questioned his valet, who was forced to confess that the original glass had been broken not long before, and that he had substituted another from the same set, which dated back to Eduard's youth. Eduard could not be angry; his fate had been sealed by the fact; how could he be shaken by the symbol? But still he felt deeply depressed. From now on he disliked drinking anything; and he seemed purposely to abstain from food and from conversation.

But now and then he was gripped by a great restlessness. At these times he expressed a wish to eat and to drink and he began to talk again. "Alas!" he once said to the Major who seldom left him, "how unhappy I am that all my efforts are never anything more than imitations or spurious attempts! What to her has been sheer bliss becomes to me pain; and yet, for the sake of that bliss, I am compelled to accept this pain. I must follow her, follow her on this road; but my nature as well as my promise deters me. It is a terrible task to imitate the inimitable. I feel only too deeply, dear friend, that genius is required for everything, even for martyrdom."

What shall we say of the efforts of his wife, his friend, and the physician, who alternately tried to do their best in this hopeless case? At last Eduard was found dead. Mittler was the first to make this tragic discovery. He called the physician and—with his usual presence of mind—examined closely the circumstances of the death. Charlotte rushed to him; she could not repress a suspicion of suicide and accused herself and the others of inexcusable carelessness. But the physician—on natural grounds—and Mittler—on moral grounds—soon convinced her that the contrary was true. It was quite obvious that Eduard had been surprised by his end. In a quiet moment he had taken from a small box and from his wallet every memento he had of Ottilie, and everything which up to now he had carefully hidden; he had spread it all out before him: a lock of her hair, flowers picked in some happy hour, all the little notes she had written him, from the very first one which his wife had handed to him accidentally and with so much intuitive instinct. All this he would not have wished to expose intentionally to a chance discovery. And now this heart, too, which only a short time before had been stirred to infinite emotions, had found the rest which can never be disturbed. And because he fell asleep while thinking of the saintly girl, one might well call him blessed. Charlotte gave him his place by Ottilie's side and ordered that no one else should ever be buried in this vault. On this condition she made ample endowments to the church and the school—to the clergyman and the school teacher.

Thus the lovers rest side by side. Peace hovers over their burial place; gay and kindred images of angels look down on them from the vaulting; and what a happy moment it will be when, one day, they will waken together once more.